Critical acclaim for Jane Adams

The Greenway

'A haunting debut.' Minette Walters

'*The Greenway* lingered in my mind for days. It takes the psychological suspense novel into new realms of mystery.' Val McDermid, *Manchester Evening News*

'Adams's narrative has a simplicity that is misleading. The story is compellingly told and rich with psychological insight.' *The Independent*

'An assured first novel, with a strong cast and a plot which twists and turns without a glitch.' *Yorkshire Evening Press*

Cast the First Stone

'Adams's debut last year hinted at a promising crime-writing talent. *Cast the First Stone* amply confirms that view.' Marcel Berlins, *The Times*

JANE ADAMS

Jane Adams was born in Leicester, where she still lives. She has a degree in sociology, and has held a variety of jobs, including lead vocalist in a folk rock band. She enjoys pen and ink drawing, two martial arts (Aikido and Tae Kwon Do) and her ambition is to travel the length of the Silk Road by motorbike. She is married with two children.

Cast the First Stone is Jane Adams's second novel, following her hugely successful and highly acclaimed debut *The Greenway*, which also features Mike Croft and John Tynan. *The Greenway* was nominated for the Crime Writers' Association John Creasey Award for best first crime novel of 1995 and the Authors' Club Best First Novel Award.

Macmillan will be publishing Jane Adams's third novel, *Bird*, in September 1997.

By the same author

The Greenway

Cast the
First Stone

Jane Adams

PAN BOOKS

First published 1996 by Macmillan

This edition published 1997 by Pan Books
an imprint of Macmillan Publishers Ltd
25 Eccleston Place, London SW1W 9NF
and Basingstoke

Associated companies throughout the world

ISBN 0 330 34919 8

9 8 7 6 5 4 3 2 1

A CIP catalogue record for this book is available from
the British Library

Phototypeset by Intype London Ltd
Printed by Mackays of Chatham PLC, Chatham, Kent

For Rachel, without whom Mike Croft might still be nameless.

And for Kay and Penny and the SCRIBO 'criminals'. Thanks.

Prologue

The boy in the red sweatshirt looked warily at the man who'd bought him chips and coffee. He probably shouldn't have accepted them, but the man had seemed OK. He had that ID card and everything, with his photo and an official-looking logo. Anyway, Ryan had felt half starved and his money ran out yesterday. He'd not done too well at begging for cash. Kept moving on, running scared every time he saw a policeman.

'Like I told you,' the man was saying, 'we've got this small hostel. It's not much, but it's clean and warm and there's a phone. You can call home, talk to your mum and dad, set their minds at rest.'

Ryan shook his head, tore his gaze from the man and looked across the crowded station café. The rush and flow of people, crossing and recrossing the platform, all with places to go, people to meet. Somewhere to belong.

'They don't want me back,' he said, his voice full of longing.

'You don't know that. Phone them from the hostel. Have a hot bath and we'll talk it all through.'

Ryan looked at him again, curious and still wary, half fearful, half desperate for any sort of lifeline. After five days of running and near enough going without food and sleep, he knew that he was no streetwise kid, able to fight his way through. He was just a kid. Tired, pissed off with the world and now, having eaten enough food to remind his body of how hungry he really was, Ryan was ready to give in.

But he wasn't going home. He couldn't face that. Not his mam's tears and his dad's bullying. But he desperately wanted to go somewhere.

'OK,' he said. 'I'll give it a go. But no way I'm going back home.'

The man nodded reassuringly, reached out and thumped Ryan gently on the shoulder. 'Good lad,' he said. 'Promise me, though, you'll make that call, eh? And I promise you, Ryan, no one's going to make you go back.'

Ryan was scared. He tried to recall the route they had taken to get here, but his mind baulked at the number of twists and turns that had brought him from the main city centre, through little streets and finally to a block of flats where they'd picked up this other man.

Then they'd driven here. To this little terraced place at the back of some large buildings that Ryan thought must be warehouses. The street was so quiet after the bustle of the city centre and there were no lights in the windows of the houses. Just the odd pinprick here and there showing through closed curtains and the yellow glow of the sodium lights deepening the twilight.

It wasn't anything the men had said or done that had made him afraid. They had chatted to him about his family, about the match last Saturday. About the things he might have expected them to talk about. But all the same, Ryan was scared.

They'd hardly mentioned the hostel since he'd got into the car. Told him nothing about the other kids that might be there and, when he'd asked, just said he'd find out soon enough. Mostly, they'd talked between themselves, the two men. Sharing the kind of half-conversation that adults do when they know each other well and talk becomes a kind of shorthand.

He should have run away earlier, he told himself vaguely, trying to get the thoughts to sort themselves out in his head. But they wouldn't stay still long enough for him to make any sense.

Increasingly frantic, he had stared ahead, looking for traffic lights or give-way signs or anything that might give him a chance. There had been nothing.

And then they'd stopped here, in this deserted street.

Ryan knew instinctively that he couldn't escape now. That no one would hear him if he tried to scream. That he was on his own.

The two men were laughing about something. Unfastening seat belts. Unlocking doors.

Ryan reached out casually for the handle and released the catch. Got out as slowly as he could bear. Then, the moment his feet touched solid ground, he began to run.

He got all of twenty feet before they caught him, brought him to the ground with a crash that knocked the air from his lungs.

Ryan wriggled sideways. Desperation freeing one leg,

he kicked out, made contact of some kind that loosened the man's hold. He filled his bruised lungs with air and tried to scream.

But it was no good.

There was no hostel. No lifeline. No help. Nothing.

Ryan never even made a sound.

Chapter One

Sunday afternoon

The house stood at the end of the cul-de-sac. It turned partly outwards from the main group, facing instead the little path that led to the playground.

The cul-de-sac was a quiet place, a dead end reached after several turns along equally obscure, equally quiet residential roads. There was little incidental traffic. The occasional stranger would get lost and be turned back by the obvious absence of a through road and the slightly anxious, slightly suspicious stares of the local populace, but that was all.

The residents were not an unfriendly bunch; just, perhaps, a little territorial, a mite over-protective. And, in the main, it was not a place that people came upon by accident. Those who came to the close generally had some business there. Those who came to live either committed to the general sense of belonging, or they left with a noticeable rapidity. Those who stayed tended to . . . well . . . stay.

It seems to be the rule of such communities – loosely strung, but none the less with a strong sense of bond – that one house should act almost as a transit camp. A point of temporary refuge for those who tried – and failed – to make whatever was the required grade.

Portland Close was no exception and this tall, three-storey house, facing somewhat sulkily a half-turn away from the rest and looking towards the wider world, was the one designated here as such a passing zone.

It had seen three families come and go in as many years. Nice people, but whose place was evidently else-where and whose departure was marked by no visible regret on either side.

Then this last family had come.

Ellie Masouk was never quite certain how it had happened. Events seemed to shape themselves suddenly and irrevocably. She never knew who had cast the first stone. In fact she'd barely become aware of the minor infractions upon community coherence before it seemed that Portland Close and its inhabitants had fallen upon madness.

And now this man, this police officer, was asking her calmly what seemed to be going on.

'And how long have you lived here, Mrs Masouk?' he asked, his voice calm and efficient.

Indifferent, Ellie thought.

'Three years,' she said. 'Well, two and a half, really, I suppose.'

She bit her lip nervously, noting the slight impatience indicated in the tightening of his mouth as he amended her reply.

'So you know the people round here quite well, then?'

Ellie frowned and hesitated. Did she? 'Well, some of them. I guess I know some of them quite well.'

He was looking at her, pen raised a little pointedly above the statement sheet, waiting to see if she changed this reply as well. In the end, he wrote nothing, laid his pen down on the clipboard and asked her, 'Did you see what these neighbours of yours were doing today?'

The change of tack caught Ellie off balance. She opened her mouth to respond, then closed it again, uncertain of the kind of answer he wanted. She sighed deeply and leaned back in the chair, suddenly feeling exhausted and wishing they would go away.

The WPC, who'd said little up until now, smiled across at her. 'How much longer do you have to go?'

Ellie was startled, then she smiled back, tried to relax a little under the other woman's seemingly friendly scrutiny.

'About three more weeks. That's if he waits that long.'

'He?'

The colour rose in Ellie's pale cheeks and her eyes, blue like washed-out delphiniums, lit for the first time since these unwanted strangers had come into her tiny, tidy little house.

'I had a few problems,' she explained. 'Had to have a late scan and they told us then it was a boy.'

'Bet your husband's pleased.' The male officer spoke up again, his hand gesturing towards the photograph of Ellie and Rezah's wedding. It took pride of place on the wall next to a large baby portrait of Farouzi.

'Yes,' she acknowledged, 'he is pleased. He's pleased that there's nothing wrong with our baby. I don't think it matters to him whether we have a boy or another little girl.'

She'd answered him with maybe a little more sharpness than was necessary, but the inference had been so clear. She was an English woman, married to an 'Asian' man – Middle Eastern, if you were going to be really fussy about it – and such men wanted sons.

Ellie found herself deeply resenting this officious little man with his pen and clipboard. She turned back to the WPC and answered the question her male colleague had put.

'Some of the people round here I know quite well. But we're very private, really. We get on well with everyone, you know, pass the time of day and that . . .'

'But you saw what happened here today.'

The man had spoken once again, making a flat statement of his words.

Ellie gave him a long, cold look and turned once more to his female colleague. 'I saw something, yes. I saw people in the street. Shouting. People in that house. The Pearsons.' She gestured behind her in the direction of the big house. 'I heard them shouting too. Then someone threw a brick and I heard a window breaking.'

'And then?'

Ellie shook her head and looked away. 'I don't know any more than that. Not really. It all went crazy out there. Things being thrown and people yelling. I was in the garden with my little girl when it started and we came straight away inside. I didn't see any more after that.'

The WPC looked, smiling, at the little girl curled up asleep on the sofa next to her mother.

'It must have been frightening for you, Mrs Masouk. For you and for your little girl.'

Ellie nodded. It had been frightening. The Pearsons' house was only a garden and a little footpath away from hers. She could see the front of it from where she'd been standing. Seen the bricks being thrown and the milk bottles being hurled out at the attackers. Ellie had been frightened enough to abandon her half-hung washing, grab Farouzi and run back into the house as fast as her swollen body would let her.

'But it was you who phoned the police?'

'You know it was,' she said defensively. 'It wasn't just me, though.' She looked at the woman officer, suddenly frightened by the implications. 'The man on the phone said he'd had another call just before I made mine. So I wasn't the only one.'

The WPC smiled encouragingly, calmly assessing the degree of Ellie's fear. 'No, Mrs Masouk, you weren't the only one.' She smiled again and said, brightly, 'You must be getting tired of all this, living as close as you do. I mean, this is the third call-out to Portland Close we've had this week. It's getting to be quite a habit.'

The male officer snorted somewhat rudely. 'Nice neighbours you seem to have round here.'

'They are,' said Ellie, startled into the reply. She bit her lip, painfully aware of their scrutiny. Of what they must be thinking. 'I mean. I don't understand it. We've been here three years, never had a moment's problem.' She looked helplessly at the two officers and finished lamely, 'They're nice people, really. Just ordinary, nice people . . . you know.'

The PC got to his feet, preparing to leave, evidently unwilling to waste any more of his precious time.

'Maybe you should tell that to the Pearsons,' he commented. 'We can see ourselves out.'

Ryan could see little from the window.

He had tried to open it. Prying at it with his fingertips, his short nails, even the buckle from his belt, but it had been screwed tight shut.

He thought about breaking the glass. The panes were far too small for him to crawl through, but maybe if he could break a couple he could smash his way through that bit of the frame as well.

But he was scared. How much noise would it make? Were the two men still downstairs? What if he broke the window and just shouted?

Despairingly, Ryan gazed out at the view of flat roofs and windowless walls.

No one to hear. There would be no one out there to hear.

Miserably, he sat down on the bed and looked around the tiny little room, trying to gain some inspiration, but there was nothing much to help him. Wooden floors covered in old lino. Walls coated in peeling paper, dampened roses and lattice trellis.

The door, the window. The narrow bed with a single blanket.

The room stank of damp and old age and now of piss where he'd been forced to relieve himself in the corner.

Ryan began to shake. He pulled the blanket round his shoulders and wrapped it tight.

He began to cry. Softly at first, as though ashamed, as though afraid he might be overheard. Then less quietly as despair took hold and pure, physical fear trembled through his body.

Chapter Two

Sunday evening

The food was good, the wine mellow and the company wonderful.

Mike leaned back contentedly in his chair and accepted another glass, admiring the deep redness of it through a moistly alcoholic haze.

Maria's flat at Oaklands was small. Kitchen, living room, bedroom and a cramped bathroom with a particularly uncomfortable corner bath – Mike usually used the shower. Maria's place had become a second home to him.

Few of the psychiatric staff lived on site at Oaklands, but Maria found it convenient and liked the fact that the two-centuries-old manor house, converted into a long-term treatment centre, was located in the middle of nowhere. The tiny flat was packed to the gills with books, curious, overly heavy pieces of antique furniture and all of the random bits and pieces that Maria couldn't bear to throw away.

Mike, whose own flat, rented part furnished and really never more to him than a place to eat and sleep, loved the eclectic fabrication that was Maria's home. There was little room for entertaining, though, and, with John Tynan taking up a third portion of the dining table, little space for manoeuvre around the cramped living room.

He rocked back, tilting the chair on to two legs and holding the wine glass so that it focused and distorted the red shaded glow from the small lamp perched precariously on the oak mantel shelf.

Pity the fire was gas and not real, he thought. Pity, too, that he would have to leave so early in the morning to get to the office on time.

'More wine, John?' Maria asked the older man.

He shook his head. 'No, thank you. I have to drive home.'

'You could stay over. There're always spare rooms laid on in case we need extra night staff.'

John smiled at her. 'Thank you, my dear, but I want to make an early start in the morning.'

Mike snorted. 'Not the only one. Still, at least they let me alone for the weekend.'

'Aahh, poor thing,' said Maria, her voice lightly mocking. 'A policeman's lot.'

Mike grimaced. 'This particular policeman could do without the lot that's been dumped in his lap just now.'

'I don't envy you this one, I have to admit.' John nodded thoughtfully. 'Sounds like a real can of worms.'

'You mean that Fletcher business? Do you think the appeal will get anywhere?'

Mike frowned. The last thing he wanted, he told himself, was to talk about this tonight. The Fletcher case had been a messy business the first time around. Mike had not been on the investigating team that had got the first conviction, and now it was coming up for appeal and there was all this mire of new evidence to sift through.

When the dossier had landed on his desk last thing on Friday he had spared it only the briefest of glances, but he had seen enough to know that he didn't like the feel. And then there were all the departmental toes he would have to tread on. Mike didn't even want to think about the consequences should he turn up something – anything – that made the original case suspect.

'I don't know,' he said, returning to the question Maria had asked him. 'I don't doubt that Fletcher was guilty – there were enough testimonies against him. Adults abused as kids; kids still under his care in the last home he'd been in charge of who'd been too scared to make complaints before. They all came out of the woodwork.' He tipped himself forward once more and deposited his glass back on the table with a slightly exaggerated thump.

'Twenty years of it. And at least two suicides to his credit. God alone knows what else.'

'So, what's new? Surely the appeal won't get Fletcher off the hook?'

Mike smiled grimly and shook his head. 'No. Fletcher's stuck inside for the term he was sentenced to. What's being called into question is the extent of his guilt. We always knew he wasn't operating alone but there was never enough evidence to convict the others he accused.'

'And now there is? From what I remember about the original case, Fletcher named some real class acts.'

Mike shrugged. 'So I understand.' He grinned broadly. 'I haven't read the full report yet.'

'First job for tomorrow morning, eh?'

'Unfortunately, yes.'

'So that fat set of folders squeezed into the plastic carrier bag isn't work after all?' Maria asked him, a wry smile playing at the corners of her mouth, the lamplight warm on her black skin.

Mike took a moment, just to admire the effect, before acknowledging it sheepishly. 'I don't have to look at it tonight. It's just, well, I thought, if I got a spare moment or two. If you were working . . .'

Maria laughed out loud. 'Well, as it happens I do have work to do. So you've just got no excuse, Detective Inspector Croft, not to be fully briefed by tomorrow morning.'

'I don't have to spend long on it,' he protested. 'Just half an hour or so to get an overview.' He sighed, ruefully. 'There's practically a cabinet full of the stuff back at Divisional. What's in the bag's just a CPS briefing.'

'So it'll spend one hell of a time saying one hell of a nothing.' John snorted contemptuously.'

Mike grinned at him.

'Well,' John went on. 'I'll give you a hand with the dishes, my dear, and then I'll be on my way. Let you two professionals get yourselves ready for your working week.'

He rose a little stiffly, easing the crunches from his back, and regarded the two of them fondly. Retired from the problems of the CPS I may be, but I won't have either of you thinking that I've been put out to grass. This ex-DI has a heavy week ahead of him.'

It was well past midnight. Maria had taken herself off to bed almost an hour before, but Mike had found himself drawn into the complexities and ramifications of a case he very much did not want to make his own.

It made disturbing reading. Nothing in the report shook his original belief in Fletcher's guilt. The man had been abusing the children in his care for the best part of two decades. His own admission and the overwhelming evidence of almost two dozen testimonies left no room for doubt on that score.

It was the rest of it. The harassment of both defence and prosecution witnesses; the mysterious fires in the offices of the lawyer preparing Fletcher's defence. The dead ends that seemed to have plagued the more controversial elements of the investigation. That was what bothered Mike.

It was hard to say what it was that didn't add up, but there was definitely something. Then, this latest piece in the puzzle. The alleged journal of a local JP, a man by the name Simon Blake, placed, if its contents could have been proved genuine, not just the JP himself but at least three other local high-ups in the frame along with Fletcher.

The original journal had been destroyed in the fire that had devastated the offices of the defence lawyer. Blake himself, Mike remembered, had died of a heart attack quite some time ago. There'd been a front-page obit in one of the local papers, harping on about his charity work and his military career. Quite a local celebrity, Blake had been.

Mike liked this less and less. Fletcher, who had seemed determined to take someone – anyone – else down with him, had pulled one local MP and at least two members of the legal profession into the mud after him.

Some of the mud had stuck; the concrete evidence hadn't. Fletcher had gone to court and from there to prison, alone. His alleged connections to a high-level, high-powered ring of child pornographers remained unproven. Those who had finally found the courage to speak out against Fletcher were either unwilling or unable to expand their statements to catch others in the testimonial net.

Fletcher was guilty, there was no real doubt about that. So what more was there to know?

Mike rubbed his eyes and stretched, then set the half-read report aside. Maria's living room was dimly lit, he'd left only the two little table lamps on. They glowed softly under red shades, casting odd, malignant shadows across the heavy bookshelves and the soft, rich fabric of the curtains.

This man who'd produced the possibly damning journal, who'd claimed, also, that much of the evidence against Fletcher had been fabricated. What should Mike make of him? What credence could he give to a man who had himself been accused of indecency?

Mike sighed, suddenly very weary. Well, it would wait until morning.

'Aren't you ever coming to bed?'

He smiled and looked towards the doorway. Maria stood, leaning against the door jamb, an old towelling robe thrown loosely around her shoulders. Head held slightly to one side, she regarded him with sleepy interest.

'I'm coming now,' he told her.

Drowsily, she nodded approval, turned and went back into the bedroom. 'And make sure you leave that bloody carrier bag behind.' Then, as though the thought had just occurred to her, 'Why the hell don't you get yourself a nice respectable briefcase or something?'

Mike reached out to switch off the lamps and grinned into the darkness. Sod the lot of it tonight, he thought. He'd think about it afresh when he'd had some sleep. The thoughts of settling into bed beside Maria and of black hands tipped by red painted nails were enough to drive just about everything from his mind.

Even lost evidence and possibly explosive journals consigned to the arsonist's flames. Even men like a certain Eric Pearson who claimed he had made a copy.

Ryan awoke to the sound of voices and footsteps on the stairs.

Outside, it was dark. In the room, too. Shadows gathered in the corners, thick as pitch, but it was the sudden light, forcing its way into his eyes as someone flicked the switch, that brought the real terror.

Ryan screamed, recoiling in horror from the men who entered the room. He skittered back from them, his feet kicking out and propelling him across the bed, becoming tangled in the blanket he had wrapped about himself.

He shouted again, calling in vain for help. There were four of them now and their faces were masked and hidden but he knew that two were the men who had brought him here.

They were going to kill him.

He was going to die.

'Helpmesomeonehelpme!' The words scrambled over themselves in panic.

One of the men laughed. There was no malevolence in his laughter. It was as though he didn't register the terror in the boy's voice. As though it was all a part of some outrageous game.

Ryan looked from face to face. Micky Mouse and Goofy, Snow White and the Wicked Witch stared back at him. Ducking and bobbing in front of his terrified eyes as though in some macabre carnival parade.

Then Snow White grabbed him by the ankle. A large ring on the man's hand scratched at Ryan's skin. Someone else had his arm. Fingers digging hard enough to bruise. They were pulling at his clothes. Tugging his red sweatshirt over his head and ripping his shirt.

He kicked and squirmed beneath their grip, but their hands seemed everywhere, until, suddenly, they released him. Backing off and looking down at him as though a break had been called in the game play.

Ryan lay naked and whimpering on the mattress. He curled on his side and looked up at the four men, blinking in the light, wondering, against all hope, if the sudden lack of action meant they would let him go now.

Then they laid hold of him again.

Chapter Three

Monday morning

Ellie went out the back way. The street was quiet, but in the last few days she had become scared of going out the front way into the close, and, even more, of coming back that way and never being sure what she'd find going on in the street.

Awkwardly, she steered the buggy out of the back gate and through the narrow gap in the fence that let her on to the footpath leading to the shops. A slight movement at one of the big house windows caught her eye. She looked up, sharply, as the sudden brightness of a camera flash lit the window.

Ellie stared. Mr Pearson, complete with camera, stared back at her.

'Doing a lot of that, they are, love.'

Ellie jumped again, then felt a friendly hand on her arm.

'Sorry, dear! I didn't mean to scare you.'

'Oh! Dora!' Ellie's heart was pounding. She lifted a hand as though to quiet it and laughed, embarrassed.

'There, love. You off to the shops? Sure you're up to it? I could get a few bits for you if you like.'

Ellie smiled at her middle-aged neighbour. 'No, I'm fine, really I am. Thanks ever so much but I want the walk.'

Dora fell into step beside her. 'Here, let me push that. Hello, my darling. You got that beautiful dolly with you?' She laughed as Farouzi first offered the doll and then snatched her back again.

Ellie smiled, glad of something to lessen the tension. 'Rezah was late home last night.'

'Yes.' Ellie nodded. They've a lot of overtime.'

'If he's late tonight, come and sit with us for a while. No sense being lonely.'

Ellie smiled gratefully. 'Thanks, we might just do that.'

They made their slow way up the hill and it wasn't until the shops were in sight that either woman spoke again. 'What did you mean?' Ellie questioned. 'About the Pearsons taking pictures?'

Dora laughed a little breathlessly and relinquished her dominance of the pushchair now they were on the flat.

'Strange thing to do, if you ask me. That's what started it all, yesterday's lot, I mean.' She clucked her tongue as though describing some minor misdemeanour.

'Pearson senior was nosing out of the window yesterday, watching Lizzie's kids playing in the paddling pool. Well, you know how hot it was and you know Lizzie's kids, only little things, they are. She'd got them stripped off and running round on the lawn and that Pearson, he stood there in his window taking pictures of them. Started yelling at Lizzie like there was something wrong with a couple of little ones running about in their birthday suits.'

Ellie frowned. It seemed absurd. 'But why take photographs of them?'

'Evidence, Pearson said. Or so Lizzie told me.' She shrugged. 'Well, you know Liz. She's not about to stand for that sort of thing, so she goes round and hammers on Pearson's door. I wonder you didn't hear her.'

'Well I did, Farouzi had just woken up and I didn't take a lot of notice.'

'Yes. Well, Liz went out there, ranting and raving and carrying on about how dare he take snapshots of her kids and how dare he criticize the way she looks after them. I mean to say, love, look at the Pearson kids. Day after day and they never set foot out of that house. You ask me, that's what half the problem's about. They should have let their kids out to play with the rest of them. Then there'd have been a lot less bad feeling round here.'

Ellie nodded, was about to comment, but Dora was in full flow now. 'Anyhow, the way they went about things. The Pearsons, I mean, treating us like our kids aren't good enough to play with their kids. Well, that sort of attitude doesn't do anyone any good.' She frowned, seeming to have lost her thread.

'You were telling me about the photographs.'

'Oh, yes. You going in here, love?' They had reached the automatic doors of the main supermarket. Ellie nodded. Let's share a trolley, then, save you struggling. Well, Lizzie's shouting got a lot of us outside, wanting to know what all the fuss was about. There was Pearson yelling from the window and Lizzie pounding on his door, shouting at him that she wanted the camera film, and then Mary from across the way, she pipes up that it's not the first time. It seems Pearson was taking pictures of her girls. Just walking by, they were. And she wasn't the only one. Regular habit he's making of it.'

'But why, Dora, and, I mean, when has all this been happening? I haven't heard about anything.'

Dora gave her a sympathetic but slightly pitying glance. 'No, love, but you've not been here very much, what with being in hospital that week or two and then having to rest up so much. But it's been happening, all the same,' she asserted, as though Ellie had expressed some doubt. 'Been photographing everyone that went past, he has. God alone knows what it must be costing him in film. Says it's for identification purposes. Identification! I ask you. Everyone knows who everyone is round our way.'

Ellie reached for a pack of tea bags and gave them to Farouzi, who shook them happily. 'And that's when the trouble started?'

Dora nodded. 'Nothing but trouble, they've been, ever since they came here. Don't know what the council was thinking of, sending them here.'

'Well, I guess they had to house them somewhere. Mrs Pearson said they had trouble in the last place they lived.'

'Yes, love, she told a lot of people that. You've got to give everyone their due. When they first moved here we all tried to be friendly. But they're a weird lot.' She wandered across the aisle and came back with tins of baked beans and tomatoes. 'I mean,' she said, as though it confirmed everything, 'they don't even send their kids to school. Can't be good, can it, keeping them cooped up like that?'

'Well,' Ellie said doubtfully, 'I guess quite a few people do teach their kids at home.'

'Maybe they do. But I'll bet they're not all like the Pearsons.'

Dora had a full head of steam going now and, Ellie knew, would need little stimulus to keep her going. She nodded again and made a noncommittal remark, allowing her mind to wander. She was feeling tired again and the heat, dissipated only a little by the shop's air conditioning, made her feel queasy.

She took the box of tea bags from Farouzi. The child had been chewing the corner and little bits of the plastic wrapper were beginning to come away. Absentmindedly, she checked Fara's mouth for fragments of the wrap.

Mr Pearson's behaviour had certainly been odd. But was it odd enough to justify people stoning his house? Breaking his windows?

She thought back to when the Pearsons had first moved in, only a few months before. Man, wife, half a dozen children. Not particularly well dressed – but then, who could easily afford to clothe six kids? – and the furniture they had brought with them, what there was of it, looked old and mismatched.

Ellie smiled slightly at the thought. You couldn't get much more patchwork than the bits and pieces she and

Rezah had moved in with; donations, mostly, from Rezah's family and stuff they'd bought second hand.

There had been nothing particularly strange in the Pearsons' lack of possessions. And they had seemed, at first sight, to be a lively lot. Kids running here, there and everywhere. Helping their parents to move the boxes. Getting in the way when they shifted the furniture.

There had been no hint of the trouble to follow. Even when the rumours started to spread that the Pearsons had been moved five times in the last three years, Ellie had still thought they could fit in on Portland Close.

And then, everything had started to go wrong.

Ellie just couldn't figure it out.

Dora noticed her slowing pace and took her arm. 'Come on, love,' she said. 'You got everything you need?'

'I think so.' She wasn't sure. She wasn't really sure she cared either.

Chapter Four

Monday morning

Eric Pearson crumpled the sheet of paper in his hand, then changed his mind and unfolded it carefully, smoothing out the creases and laying it as flat as he could on the table top.

He peered at the handwriting – blue ink, a neat, carefully joined and rounded hand. Then he sat back in his chair and gazed upwards towards the ceiling, re-reading the contents of the letter as though the words were set against the dulled white paint.

'My Dear Frank,' the letter began. My dear Frank. It was rare that Eric Pearson thought about his brother, but the discovery of this note, unsent and all but forgotten in the inside pocket of a coat he rarely wore, had brought the few memories he still allowed himself back with considerable force.

The letter was dated some three days after Eric and Johanna had left the only place they had ever called home.

It was filled with the sense of rage and deep injustice Eric had felt then. *Still* felt. At being abandoned by those he had called his family and his friends.

He picked it up, smoothed out more of the creases with his fingertips and began to read again.

My dear Frank,

    They have placed us in what they term
emergency accommodation. One room in which to
live and sleep and try to keep some sense of
belonging. One room for a man, his wife and five
little children. The two eldest and myself, we sleep
on mattresses on the floor in sleeping bags and
Johanna shares a single bed with little Paulie.

    There is so much noise here, Frank. Day and
night, people coming and going, every room in
this place crammed to breaking point with women
and children and their menfolk. Shouting and
banging and making noise.

    The children have nowhere to play. There's
just a tiny garden behind and a main road only
a step outside the front door.

    We don't deserve this, Frank. My wife, my
children, none of us deserve this. A sin has been
committed too great for me to comprehend as yet.
I would give or do or say anything just to come
back to you all. To turn back the clock and undo
what has been done.

    We have been placed on a list and have to wait
our turn for a suitable house but that may be many
weeks away and in the meantime we have to live
in this place. Muddle through as best we can.

Eighteen weeks they had waited, Eric remembered.
Eighteen weeks and three days of fighting their way
through a system already clogged by too much need.

Eighteen weeks and three days that had taken them from the overheated summer, in a room whose inadequate windows opened only on to the smoke of traffic and city dust, into the damp and chill of a despairing winter. Tempers had grown short, nerves set on edge by the slightest irritation. Even Johanna's seemingly infinite patience had been unable to hold out against the miasma of doubt and desolation that had settled in with the winter cold.

Then Danny had been born and they had been rehoused. Given the most basic of furnishings from the common store and been grateful out of all proportion for the charity. A grant had seen the new place carpeted, and a small stock of tokens provided the paint and mops and buckets to clean and decorate.

Compared with the home they had once had, the new place was as nothing. Small and cramped and barely adequate. But compared with the single room in the overcrowded hostel, it seemed like heaven.

Heaven, he remembered, had lasted for fifteen weeks and five days. Then, one day, Eric had come home and known that it was over.

It was the way his neighbours stared at him as he walked down the street. The way a mother hustled her children aside when he passed them on the pavement.

And then he'd known. Someone had recognized him. Someone had remembered. Someone knew who he was and what he'd been accused of. And once someone knew, it was only a matter of time before they all knew and the time of peace ended.

'Five times in three years, Frank,' Eric said softly, speaking to a brother he knew he might never see again. 'Five times in three years they've moved us on, like some damned itinerants with no rights.'

Abruptly he got to his feet and paced the length of the kitchen as though the room trapped him.

Five times the rumours had followed, then the suspicion, then the trouble. He'd learnt to look for it early since that first time.

At the first house, even the second, they had tried to fit in, tried to make a new life in a new community. But, of course, it hadn't worked. Eric could see now that it would never work. He and his kind, his family, they were outsiders. Always would be.

Eventually he had ceased even to try to belong. Had built walls about himself and his family. Shut them inside what little shelter he could still provide in such a hostile world and learnt to anticipate the trouble even before it showed signs of beginning.

He sighed heavily as he crumpled the letter in his hand once more and thrust it deep into his trouser pocket.

It would never end, Eric knew that now. Never end until he had been publicly vindicated. Until he had stood up in a court of law and shown the world that there were men, guilty men, far more worthy of hatred than Eric Pearson.

Chapter Five

Monday morning

Morning routine. Same as ever Mike checked the day book, accepted coffee, exchanged a joke with Symonds, duty sergeant for the first shift and still getting himself sorted with his electric razor in one hand and an unidentifiable hot sandwich in the other.

Mike listened to the morning briefing wishing the day had assigned him a more active role. He went to his desk carrying his bag of files and dumped it on the stained green carpet next to the waste bin as though hoping that was where the entire thing could end up.

Irritably, he rifled through his in-tray, grabbed a loose handful of report sheets and set to work, trying to rough out some sort of assessment of the Fletcher mess.

Eric stood in position by the living room window, sipping his second cup of tea of the day.

Johanna had persuaded him downstairs for breakfast. He'd eaten with a distracted air, listening vaguely to his children's chatter, to Johanna's replies, to the familiar sounds of the meal being prepared and eaten and argued over.

He had returned upstairs then, taking his tea and his camera, leaving Johanna and the children to clear away the remnants of breakfast and begin their morning lessons. Another duty he had once been so very conscious of, now left to Johanna. In his less self-indulgent moments Eric acknowledged that he left too much to Johanna these days. That he should do more to aid the running of their household and the daily welfare of his family.

But these moments passed quickly and came less and less frequently. Eric's was a mind under siege. A life imprisoned within a tall house, whose windows gazed out upon a world that he could no longer share.

Intensely, as though every nuance of movement mattered, Eric watched and photographed the local children leave their homes and set off for school, shepherded by their mothers and older sisters and brothers. Watched the postman following the curve of the close and delivering nothing to the Pearson house. Stared with rapt attention as Ellie Masouk, now back from her shopping, opened the door to take a package too large to fit through her letterbox. Listened with devotion as the milk float rattled its way down to the end of the close and delivered its daily crateload to his door.

He would have to go out soon, Eric knew. Get some money, do some shopping, leave the house eyeless and unguarded for at least an hour or so.

Eric Pearson sighed irritably and placed his empty mug on the windowsill, glancing briefly about the room as he did so.

Such a dreary room, the sun seeming to miss both windows, apart from the earliest shafts in the morning and the half-dead rays of late evening. Untidy, too, with the clutter of toys and books and papers not cleared away from one day's end to the next.

He frowned suddenly. He really ought to give Johanna more help. For all of two minutes Eric walked around the room picking toys from the floor and books from the chairs. Clearing the whole stack of unread papers from the table standing beside the back window.

Then, as though his purpose failed him, he let the entire bundle fall to the floor, leaving the mess so much worse than it had been. He stood still, his arms dropping to his sides and his eyes fixing once again upon the now empty street.

'Got a minute, Mike?' DI Miles stuck his round head round the door and followed it rapidly with his equally rotund body.

Mike looked up from his paper-strewn desk and grinned warily. 'Depends what you've got in mind.'

Miles came over, perched his large self on the desk and awarded Mike his broadest, most welcoming smile.

'Got an old dear down in the front office,' he said. 'Wants to talk to someone important, so we figured you'd do.'

'Oh?' Mike gave him a suspicious look. 'And what's her problem?'

'Says someone's stealing her garden, bit by bit. Trees gone last week and a whole stack of newly planted bulbs last night.'

He hopped off the desk and was across the office with surprising speed. 'Nutty as a friggin' fly biscuit,' he called back over his shoulder as he hopped it out of the door. 'But she's driving the duty sergeant round the bend.'

Mike got to his feet, half disbelieving, and followed him to the door.

'How come you can't deal with it?' he shouted at Miles's rapidly retreating back.

The big man laughed. 'It's a shit job, Mike. But someone's got to shovel it . . .'

A young WPC drifted by with her arms full of reports. She flashed a quick smile in Mike's direction. 'Hear they've got you dealing with old Mrs Delancey, guv.'

'Mrs who?'

'Old lady in the front office with the . . .'

'Disappearing garden . . . Regular, is she?'

'Set the clock by her, poor old soul. The council had to move her. She can't look after herself any more and she's no family. Had to put her in this sheltered housing place. In a little flat. And of course there's . . .'

'No garden. I get the picture. Someone phoned the home?'

'Yes, sir. Be about an hour, they said. Don't worry, guv, she's quite harmless.'

The young woman went off laughing and Mike mooched along to the front office. 'Harmless,' he muttered to himself. 'I'll just bet she is.'

Monday 3 p.m.

Eric had been away from the house for almost three hours. He hurried down the little path, anxious now that he had been gone too long. That something had happened.

Ellie Masouk came through the kissing gate towards him, pushing her child in its buggy. She looked up at the sound of Eric's footsteps, then glanced away swiftly as though afraid he might speak to her, engage her in conversation.

Her unease was written so clearly on her pale, blandly pretty face that Eric almost laughed aloud. He hurried by, feeling her unconscious withdrawal as he passed close to her. Her embarrassment.

She had no idea who he was, Eric realized. No idea that their paths had crossed before.

But he knew her. Who she'd been before she'd married Masouk. Who she was and what had happened to her.

Oh yes. Eric Pearson knew.

'It can't be easy,' the Superintendent sympathized, 'having to sift through this lot. Being expected to put the work of fellow officers under the glass.' He shook his head sadly. 'It makes for bad feeling, Mike.'

'It's not exactly my idea of fun, sir,' he said, realizing that his tone held more frost than was really warranted.

'No, no, of course not, Mike. Not a job anyone

35

would want, I know that. Anyway,' he continued, pushing himself to his feet again, 'just go through the motions. We'll soon have this thing all wrapped up.'

He turned to go. Mike called after him. 'It's not been explained to me, sir. Why assign me instead of someone from internal affairs?'

The Superintendent swivelled back to face him, a frown creasing his forehead. 'Internal affairs, Mike? This isn't a formal inquiry, probably never will be. Just a preliminary review of this so-called new evidence that might come up at the appeal.' He shook his head as though amazed that Mike could think it would go any further and crossed the room again, placed his hands, palms down, on Mike's desk and leant across.

'That's not going to be popular, Mike. This talk about internal affairs, it makes it sound as though you think we've something to hide.'

He smiled and backed off again. 'When DCS Charles requested you for the job I knew he'd chosen the right man. I won't lose any sleep about you covering this one, Mike, and I don't expect you'll have to either. It's a closed book, my friend. Just needs the i's dotting and the t's crossing and we can say goodbye to it once and for all.'

Dora couldn't wait to get home and tell her husband. It wasn't that she liked gossip. Not really. Just that this was too good to miss out on.

Just went to show, didn't it? These days the council didn't give a damn about who they housed and where.

Reaching her front door, Dora glanced across at the tall house. Its blank windows were unlit and gave little sign of life.

How could his wife stay with him, knowing he'd been accused of something like that?

Chapter Six

Monday evening

'Oh!' The first crash. The sound of glass shattering startled Ellie, sent her hands fluttering nervously to her throat.

She glanced anxiously at Farouzi, but the child slept on, her smooth, round-cheeked face and soft black curls illuminated gently by the warm pink glow of the night light.

Another crash. The sounds of shouting in the street. A woman screaming insults and someone laughing. The laughter mocking and abusive.

Ellie crept over to the window and peered out through the crack in the curtains. The swiftest of glances told her more than she wanted to know. Two boys from the next street – Ellie knew them by sight though not their names – were taking stones from her front garden. From the precious little rockery she had spent so long in building, planting with tiny alpines.

For a brief moment, her indignation got the better of her fear. She pulled the certain back further, half intending to open the window and yell her protest at the boys.

Even as reason reasserted itself one of the boys glanced upwards, attracted by the movement of the curtain across the dimly lit window.

He actually had the temerity to wave at her!

Horrified, Ellie stepped sharply away. Visions of some vague retribution, because she had seen their faces, filled her already overwrought mind.

If they broke the bedroom window would the flying glass reach Farouzi's cot?

Ellie knelt down beside the cot, releasing the catches that lowered the side. She letting it down as softly and slowly as she could, as though the little squeak of the nylon hoops moving against steel runners would be noticed above the rising tide of noise coming from the street.

'It's all right,' Ellie whispered, though her daughter slept on, as calm and beautiful and contented as she always was. 'It's all right,' she said again. Half the people in the street, they had kids themselves. No one would let them hurt Farouzi . . .

A sob rose bitterly in Ellie's throat as she thought of the Pearson house. Heard the breaking of the windows, the loud, and growing louder, pounding as someone began to beat upon something wooden. In her mind's eye, Ellie could see her friends, her neighbours, trying to break down the Pearsons' door.

There were children in the Pearson house. Children, like Farouzi.

Abruptly she reached out, gathered Farouzi, her blankets, her teddy, and, carrying them close, made for the bathroom where there was a lock on the door and only the tiniest of windows.

Ellie had reached the head of the stairs when someone began to hammer on the door.

Johanna Pearson crouched behind the shabby green moquette sofa, her arms circling the two smallest of her brood while broken glass fell in sharp-edged rain all around them.

She could hear her husband and the older ones in the room above. Eric had the water hose going. She heard the rush of water even above the sound of crashing glass and the jeers and shouts of those getting wet below. They had laid in a good supply of ammunition after the first window had been broken just over a week ago. Those boys. They'd said they had been playing football and the broken window had been accidental, but Eric had prepared the family anyway. Milk bottles thrown out at the yobs chucking stones seemed a fair exchange. And they had a good supply. Eric's early-morning forays, with Mark and Alexander to help him, had made certain of that.

Little Danny had begun to cry. Johanna shook him gently. 'It's all right, my darlings. We've got through this before. Nothing's going to happen to us.'

Through this before. Yes, many many times before. But, then, God had told her that life was never going to be easy. He'd simply lived up to his promise.

'Danny, Danny, it'll be all right,' she said again, straining her ears to hear what had caused the sudden lull of activity in the street.

Yes, it would all be right in the end. Let Eric just be able to prove that his new evidence was the truth. Let him present it in court and they would be vindicated. Yes, if they could just hold out against the flow of hatred and persecution for a little longer, everything would be fine.

There was silence now. Silence that in its own way was as menacing as the noise before.

'Yes.' She spoke her thoughts aloud to her bewildered children. 'That's what this is all about. They're trying to frighten us. Stop us from giving evidence.'

She scooped the still weeping Danny into her arms and, tentatively, emerged from their precarious cover.

Eric was downstairs now. Standing by what was left of the front door and shouting at the crowd. She couldn't hear his words clearly but could just make out the low, reassuring voice of the newly arrived policeman.

Johanna was not impressed. They were in it, of course. The police. Corrupt as Fletcher and the rest and out to protect the 'Named' against the 'Unnamed'. The likes of the Pearsons themselves.

Holding Danny closer and murmuring a prayer to give her strength, Johanna Pearson made her way across the room, feet crunching and slipping on the shattered glass, and went downstairs.

'Ellie! For God's sake, Ellie! Open the door. It's me, Dora.'

Dora!

Still clutching a by now wakeful and bewildered toddler, Ellie scrambled down the stairs, fumbling clumsily with the door catch in her haste to get it open.

She almost fell into Dora's arms.

'There, there, love.'

As in control as ever, Dora eased Farouzi from her mother's arms, pushed the door closed and coaxed Ellie through to the kitchen.

'Here, sweetheart.' She took one of Farouzi's favourite ginger fingers from her cardigan pocket and held it out. The child seized it eagerly. Dora made her say thank you before letting go. Then she reached out and took Ellie's hand.

'Harry thought I should come round. Looks like it's just as well I did. What are you doing, getting yourself in a state like this?'

'But, Dora. . . .' Ellie began to protest, then her face crumpled and she started to cry. 'I was so scared. I saw what was going on and I just got so scared.' She brushed flowing tears from her face and looked wetly at Dora, her mouth trembling. 'What's happening, Dora? Why are they doing this?'

Dora glanced away, momentarily embarrassed, uncertain how to answer. 'Blessed if I know, my love,' she said at last busying herself with the tea things. 'You just clean yourself up while I see to this kettle.'

'It's gone quiet out there,' Dora said a moment later as she filled the teapot. Nervously, Ellie followed her to the front door.

Outside two policemen emerged from their car and looked around them. Most of the kids Ellie had seen throwing stones had either scattered or stood around, innocently waiting for the next act.

The adult residents of Portland Close, similarly gathered, watched from their doorways.

Eric Pearson emerged from his battered house, baseball bat clasped firmly in his hands. He came to stand a little distance from his house, beneath the street lamp at the end of the close.

He looked terrifying. His entire body seemed to shake with rage. The glow from the streetlight showed blood on his face from a small cut above one eye and he hefted the baseball bat in both hands, shouting at the two police officers who stood, motionless, beside their car as though trying to decide on their next move.

'Just what are you going to do about this?' Pearson yelled at them. 'I demand you arrest them all.' He waved a hand, the gesture encompassing the entire population of the close. 'Arrest the whole bloody lot of them; they're all in it.'

He took a step forward and Ellie found herself taking an answering one back, into the hallway.

'But you won't, will you?' Pearson went on, his voice lower and more menacing. 'You won't, because you're in it too. The whole damn lot of you in it. Corrupt as hell.'

Ellie was close enough to hear both the younger PC speaking into his radio and the controller's reply.

'Oscar one zero to base. Responding to the disturbance in Portland Close. June, do you reckon we could have some back-up? It's like a bloody war zone down here.'

'Already on its way, Tony. We had reports of youths smashing windows. Any sign?'

The young officer laughed briefly. 'Well, they're not actually chucking things, control, but there's broken glass all over the shop and it looks as if half the street's turned out to watch.'

He paused and glanced over his shoulder at the sound of a car engine. Ellie followed his look and saw Rezah's old Cavalier pulling up.

'What's the ETA on the back-up, June?'

'Three to five, Tony. Oscar one zero, this is control out.'

The officer acknowledged, glancing sideways as Ellie ran from her doorway to greet the car. Rezah got out, looking about him in obvious confusion.

'Ellie, what's going on here?'

She shook her head. 'I don't know, Rezah, it's just been—' She broke off, waved a hand at the two policemen and the general confusion.

Further down the street Pearson was still ranting. Tony's colleague, head bent slightly as though to avoid the worst of the tirade, was nodding sympathetically and nudging the glass on the path with the toe of his shoe.

Neighbours crowded in the doorways, exchanging comments, glancing towards the Pearsons and the policeman and over at Tony himself. Kids, larking about on the corner, nudged each other, laughing or just staring, talking to their companions almost without moving their heads, as though afraid to miss any of the action.

The younger PC strode off, somewhat self-consciously, to join his colleague, picking his way carefully through the broken glass and curious stares.

Rezah and Ellie followed him and stood at the point where the footpath began to curve out of the close, waiting to see what he and his colleague were going to do.

'Take Farouzi and go inside.'

'No. I want to stay with you. Please, Rezah.'

Softly, Ellie touched his arm and he glanced down, noting the red rims of the pale blue eyes and the tear stains marking her pale cheeks. He softened a little and took Farouzi from her.

'She's too heavy for you to stand with. Here, pull the blanket down, her feet are cold. There, is that better, my princess?'

He kissed the top of Fara's curly head then turned his attention once more to the activity outside the Pearson house.

One of the older Pearson children had emerged from the house. The boy handed his father a camera.

'There's all the evidence you need!' Pearson declared triumphantly. 'Get that developed. It's all in there and there's more in the house.'

'Photographs?' Rezah was momentarily bewildered. 'He took photographs while all this was going on?'

Ellie shrugged. 'I don't know.'

'Oh, that's nothing.' Rezah looked over his shoulder at Dora who'd come up behind him.

'Takes photos of everyone. Probably got us all in his family album.' She raised her voice, deliberately, aiming her comments at Eric Pearson himself. 'I said, you've got us all in the family album, haven't you?'

Rezah gave her a puzzled look. 'I don't understand, Dora.'

The woman shrugged and tapped the side of her head with her finger.

'The man's one short of a dozen, if you ask me. Him and that camera of his. Takes pictures of everyone. Kids playing in the street – even Lizzie's two, and they were in their own garden. You can't go to the shops without him snapping a mugshot, can you, Ellie?'

She looked straight at Pearson and raised her voice again. 'Some folks are just perverted.'

Sighing irritably, Rezah shook his head. From the look of things, the police would be there for a good long time to come. He felt tired and had not eaten since lunchtime. He slipped an arm around Ellie's shoulders. 'Anything to eat?' he asked, knowing the answer already.

''Course there is.' She smiled. 'Dinner's been ready ages. It'll only take me a minute or two to reheat it.'

'Best thing,' Dora said, and patted Ellie on the arm. 'I'll get along inside as well now. See you in the morning.'

Rezah gave Pearson one last long look. He didn't like the sound of any of it. Maybe Ellie should go to his parents for a few days until things settled down again. She would be staying there anyway, for a week or two, after the baby came.

'Have *you* eaten yet?'

Ellie shook her head. 'I had something when I fed Farouzi, but I wanted to wait for you.'

He nodded. That would be nice, spend a little time together, try to relax. 'And you, my princess. Daddy's going to put you back to bed.'

He glanced over his shoulder once more. The police were clearing the street, coaxing people back inside their houses.

Pearson continued to rant and rave, though someone had by now removed his baseball bat. Only the camera was being waved at the few people still standing around in the street.

No doubt, Rezah thought, the police would be banging on doors half the night asking questions.

He sighed impatiently. It had been a long day. Now, it seemed, it was going to be an even longer night.

The man's hold on the telephone receiver tightened, his fingers whitening with the pressure as he listened to the voice.

'It needs removing, Jaques. Usual instructions. How you dispose of it is up to you.'

Jaques shook his head. 'No,' he said. 'No more. I told you last time that was it. I'll not do it.'

The man on the phone laughed softly.

'No is not a word you can afford to use, Jaques, you know that.' He paused, then added quietly, 'You'll do this little thing for us, Jaques. You know you will.'

The phone went dead. Jaques replaced the receiver and stood for a moment staring into the middle distance twisting the large ring on his right hand.

'Usual arrangements.' He knew what that meant. He would park his car in a pre-arranged spot. Leave the boot unlocked and take himself for a walk, a drink in the local pub, anything.

Twenty minutes later he would go back, lock the boot and drive away.

Five times before Jaques had been forced to play this charade. Five times before he'd promised himself that this would be the last.

'God Almighty!' Jaques swore. He couldn't go on this way.

His wife, calling him from the living room, cut through his thoughts.

'Just business, love,' he called back to her. God, he thought desperately, just business.

Chapter Seven

This was not the kind of morning he wanted to have.

Mike wasn't sure what kind of morning *would* have been preferable, but one where Eric Pearson's name figured large on the new developments list was not it.

He had driven to work through a chill, early morning haze, arriving just as the sun burned through. Things had been downhill all the way since then.

'OK,' Mike said, leaning back in his chair and assembling the facts. 'So, let's get this straight. About eight forty-five last night Pearson had a run-in with a couple of the local youths and ended up whacking one of them with a baseball bat.' He paused, frowning slightly. 'I take it as read, seeing as we don't have Pearson resident downstairs on an assault charge, that there was no major damage done.'

The young PC facing him across the desk shook his head. 'No, sir.' He grinned suddenly. 'Seems his aim wasn't too good, sir.'

Mike gave him a slightly frigid look. 'Quite,' he said. 'And by the time you arrived on the scene a mob had gathered and was smashing the Pearsons' windows.'

'That's about the size of it.' It was the other officer who spoke that time. An older man with the slightly weary air of one who has seen it all and now would like

49

to get the hell off home. Mike could sympathize with that. He sighed again.

'This is, what, the fourth call-out in two weeks?'

'Yes, sir, but there's also been a rash of minor complaints, folk calling into the front office or being given advice over the phone.' He shrugged. 'It's hard to say they have direct connection to the Pearson case, but, well, Portland Close. Fact is, sir, we hardly knew the place existed before the Pearsons moved there.'

Mike frowned. 'What kind of complaints?' he asked. 'And why weren't they followed up?'

'Because, for the most part, there wasn't a need.' The officer shuffled his feet, bored now and obviously willing his senior officer to let them get off duty. 'We had reports of nuisance calls, usual sort of thing. A couple of the victims wanted visits, but most were given advice, either here or over the phone, or they got in touch with BT.'

'We've been called to Portland before, though, sir,' Matthews, the younger officer, put in. Beside him, Pendon, the older one, sighed. What was the young idiot trying to prove? Too keen by half, he was.

'You mean, prior to this last two weeks?'

'Yes, sir. Domestics, mostly, neighbours complaining the Pearsons were taking pictures of their kids when they played in the street. Or that Eric Pearson made threats if they went on to his front.'

'The front door opens directly on to the path,' the other officer put in.

'Yeah, so of course the kids get close to the house. And I mean, sir, there's that bit of playground over at the back, but most of the mums won't let the little ones go there on their own and it doesn't give much space to play anyway.'

'I see.' Mike halted him in what looked about to become full flow. 'Listen, I know I've kept you both, best get off home.'

'Er, yes, sir.'

The younger officer looked a little disappointed. The older looked relieved.

They headed towards the office door.

'There was just one thing, sir,' Pendon remarked, hand ready upon the doorknob. 'Something Pearson kept saying, when we interviewed him. Well, it's in the report, sir. But he kept saying he reckoned this was all a set-up. Said we were trying to blacken his name, stop him giving evidence or something.'

'Evidence?' Mike prompted, guessing already what he was about to hear.

'Yes, sir. Kept going on about the Fletcher case. About how he was presenting new evidence or something and how we were all out to stop him.' The officer shrugged, grinned. 'Well, it's probably all bullshit, sir, but seeing as you're involved with the appeal, I thought I'd give it a mention.'

Mike nodded. 'Thank you,' he said, heavily. 'Now, get off home before you have your wife filing a missing persons.'

Pendon grinned again, opened the door and shepherded the younger PC outside.

Mike leaned back in his chair, tipping it back on two

legs, then, abruptly, set himself upright again and began skimming through the reports on his desk.

They said little more than the entries in the day book and what the attending officers had just told him.

Well, there would be no help for it. It was about time, perhaps, that he paid Mr Eric Pearson a visit.

Johanna swept broken glass and listened to the workmen hammering shutters across the empty windows.

Danny clung to her skirt, dogging her every footstep, his face reddened by tears and his voice whining with confused complaints.

Johanna tried to be patient, telling him, telling them all, that it would be fine. Setting their home in order as best she could.

Fragments of broken glass seemed to be everywhere, slivers of the stuff working their way into clothes and shoes. Into the pile of the carpet, the hems of curtains.

Damn! Johanna thought. It seemed still to be falling out of the air. Wherever she swept, more seemed ready to appear.

And Eric. Eric did nothing to be of help. Just stood in the doorway, watching her work or wandering from room to room, getting in the way. Wearing his anger like some thick, smothering cloak.

Passing through their bedroom, Danny still clinging to her, Johanna paused and knelt down beside the bed.

Beneath the bed was a dark green box file. Battered

and worn from the many moves it had made with them, its spring clip was broken and hung half attached.

Johanna lifted the lid and stared at the contents, raised the photocopied journal out of its protective box and set it on her knees.

This, Johanna thought. This was what it was all about. This stack of paper that contained such filth. Such cruelty.

Angrily, she thrust the journal back into the file and, with an impatient little shove, sent it skidding under the bed.

There were others named in there that society applauded. Others who wanted Eric silenced. Frightened away from telling what he knew.

Others who had tried to entrap Eric in their sordid, filthy conspiracy. Framed him when he'd threatened to expose them for what they were.

Anger giving new energy to her movements, Johanna got to her feet and strode from the room.

Well, they wouldn't succeed! She'd gone through hell so far to support Eric. No way could she have come this far, endured so much, that she could now bear to let them win.

Chapter Eight

Tuesday 4 p.m.

Traffic was unusually bad heading out of town. It seemed to Mike to be just about par for the rest of the day. The thought of finally meeting the infamous Eric Pearson was doing nothing for his patience as he waited in line for the lights to change and the idiot up ahead to remember how to shift gear.

He sighed heavily and adjusted position for the nth time. Next to him in the passenger seat Sergeant Price hummed quietly to himself, tapping, irritatingly, just out of time, against the window.

Mike found himself wishing for the stolid, calm presence of Bill Enfield, his usual sergeant who was presently on sick leave. Price, much younger than Bill and undoubtedly capable, enthusiastic, conscienscious – in fact all the things a sergeant should be – nevertheless had this knack of getting on Mike's nerves.

'Should have taken the area car, sir. High profile. Would've got us through a bit faster.'

Mike shrugged. 'Maybe,' he acknowledged, 'but I think that Portland Close has had enough high profile for now.'

Price awarded him a slightly supercilious, sideways grin. 'Oh, I don't know, sir, bit of excitement.'

Excitement! 'I think, perhaps, the mini-riot we were called to last night gave them all enough of that.'

Price grinned again. 'There'll be more,' he prophesied. 'You can be sure of that, sir. Got a taste for it now, they have.'

Mike grimaced and concentrated on the road ahead and on some fool in the wrong lane trying to make a right turn. He sighed again, trying to release some of the tension and wriggling his shoulders to get rid of the cramp that had settled there. He found himself, once more, wishing for Bill's calm presence instead of this cock-sure representative of local justice.

'I can't think of anyone in their right minds who would want a riot on their doorsteps,' he remarked calmly. 'But, no. No, I don't imagine we've heard the last of it.'

He flicked the indicator, changed down and made a left turn. The traffic here was suddenly lighter, the area changing from run-down, mid-town to light industrial and then residential.

'We're just about there, sir. Next left, then a couple of very quick right turns. It's a bit of a maze hereabouts.'

Mike nodded. It was a bit of a maze, all right. The twists and turns in the estate's main road, with its branch lines of sheltered cul-de-sacs, seemed designed both to slow any traffic and to completely lose the unwary. He found himself on Portland Close almost before he realized it.

'Down the bottom end, sir.'

'Yes, Sergeant. So I see.'

It would have been hard not to see. The tall house leant out slightly from the main group, its boarded windows giving it a derelict, abandoned look, quite at odds with the generally neat appearance of the rest of the Close.

Mike parked a few houses away. There were kids playing football and others riding bikes. Some stopped their game to look at him as he got out. A couple recognized the sergeant and shouted to each other. Curtains twitched. At other windows people stared out openly, their faces interested, slightly guarded.

Mike turned around, slowly taking in the entire prospect of Portland Close. The kids, the parents, the neat, ordinary, corporation-planned houses. Scraps of frontage separated most from the footpath, other doors, like the Pearsons', opened straight on to the street.

It was all deceptively normal. Deceptively calm.

'Ready, sir?' Sergeant Price was looking at him, eager to begin.

Mike nodded and the two men crossed the empty bit of roadway over to the Pearson house.

Slowly, Mike paced the length of the room. It was a long room, running front to back for the length of the house and, somewhat unusually perhaps for a main living room, was on the first floor.

There was little furniture. A rather battered-looking drop-leaf table stood beneath the back window, flanked on either side by two mis-matched chairs.

At the other end, again under the window, stood a low bookcase, crammed with books and papers. There were other shelves standing on either side of the window. Cheap, flatpack units, loaded down until they bowed under the weight of other books, piles of magazines and stacks of loose-leaf paper.

The carpet looked surprisingly new. Corded fibres, already tending to attract and trap the dirt, carried in by so many pairs of feet. The track from the uncarpeted stairs to the space in the centre of the room, occupied by two green sofas and three, chrome-framed chairs, was clearly visible.

The room had an unsettled look to it, as though the Pearsons were refugees on a short stopover rather than a large family trying to find some place to stay.

Eric Pearson had escorted the two men upstairs, though he had been very reluctant at first even to let them through the door. Mike figured it had been his rank that had convinced him.

Pearson stood, now, close to the entrance from the stairs, Johanna Pearson beside him. Mike was acutely aware that every aspect of his scrutiny of their living room was being just as avidly dissected by the Pearsons themselves.

The Pearson children – or four of them, anyway – sat, also watching him, in a tight row on one of the green sofas. Mike tried to ignore them all and continued his silent examination of the room.

It was the photographs, probably hundreds of them,

plastered all over the two long walls, that really got to him.

Hardly family snapshots, these. Pictures of children, of passers-by, talking to each other and clearly ignorant that they were being consigned to film. People getting out of cars, carrying their weekly shopping into the house. Neighbours, just going about their daily business. There seemed to be no aspect of life in Portland Close that Eric Pearson hadn't tracked. Much of it in close-sequence shots, as though taken on a motor drive.

There was an eerie, unsettling quality to the images, particularly to those shots that Mike guessed had been taken from the back window of the Pearsons' neighbours' gardens.

It was, if nothing else, a nasty, rather sordid, invasion of privacy.

The dim light from the two, low-wattage bulbs, suspended unshaded from the ceiling, somehow added to the strangeness of the tableau. That, and the stillness of everyone in the room. Even Price seemed to have caught the mood. He had stationed himself against the opposite wall, standing very still, only the odd, side-to-side movement of his head betraying that he too studied the photo images plastered chaotically over the living room wall.

Unreal, Mike repeated to himself. The whole scene, even with himself as participant, seemed somehow staged. Part of a performance. Or like one of those odd modern art events. Installations, or whatever they were called, that Maria was so fond of dragging him off to.

She would sure as hell appreciate this one.

Abruptly, Mike turned away from the pictures, uncomfortably aware that at least a modicum of his distaste showed clearly on his face.

'Aspirations towards photo-journalism, have you, Mr Pearson?'

Eric Pearson frowned at him. 'It's my way of keeping an eye on the situation,' he said, his voice sullen and suspicious.

Mike nodded thoughtfully.

Price butted in. 'And what situation might that be, Mr Pearson?' He didn't wait for Pearson to answer, instead turned back to the nearest photographs, tapped one with his finger. 'Here, for instance. Come over here, Mr Pearson, and tell me the story behind this one. Neighbours coming home with the shopping, it looks like to me.' He paused and bent to peer more closely at the images. 'My goodness, Mr Pearson, it seems they're in the act of restocking their freezer!'

Mike stifled the urge to smile. Pearson was clearly in no mood for Price's brand of humour.

Calmly, Mike repeated Price's initial question. 'And what situation might that be, Mr Pearson?'

Pearson glared at him, his shoulders rigid with hostility.

Mike took a step forward and said more gently. 'Just what happened here last night? Broken windows, half the street turning out to watch, from what I've heard.' He glanced over at the expectant faces of the children seated on the sofa. 'Bet you were frightened, eh? Not a very nice thing to have happened, is it?'

One of the older ones shook his head. Then, unexpectedly, his eyes lit with an odd excitement. He looked first at his father and then at the brother sitting next to him.

'Oh, we're used to it,' he said, his voice betraying almost a kind of pride. 'Paul and I, we took the garden hose upstairs and squirted them all out of the window.' He laughed as though telling Mike about some huge joke. 'You should have seen them running about, trying not to get wet.'

His younger brother started to laugh with him. 'We got them all wet. All soggy soaking wet,' he said, his voice rapt with pleasure. 'Running about like little ants.' He began to run his fingers about all over his older brother. 'Just like little ants.'

Mike glanced across at their parents. Johanna Pearson's face was totally impassive, unreadable in the dim, yellowish, light. Eric Pearson was smiling fondly at the two boys.

'As you see,' he said, 'my children have learnt to deal with a great many things.'

Mike looked at him more closely, not really understanding the almost gleeful satisfaction Pearson was displaying. The pleasure he seemed to be taking in the conflict.

'But why?' he asked. 'Why have they had to become used to these things, Mr Pearson? Mrs Pearson? Surely you would rather this wasn't happening? Surely you can't think that this is a good way for young children to have to live?'

Mike waited, knowing that his comments had been deliberately provocative.

Johanna Pearson looked directly at him for the first time. He held her gaze and took another step across the room. 'Maybe, Mrs Pearson, if you could tell me what went wrong – what's happening here – then we can find some way of sorting things out?'

She continued to gaze at him, her eyes cold and very tired. 'People often persecute those that they do not or cannot understand, Inspector. It is the way of things.'

Mike shook his head. 'It doesn't have to be.'

'Doesn't it?' The woman moved towards him, her gaze fixed and intent, mouth set in a firm, determined line. Dimly, Mike was aware of Price moving restlessly, unused to spending so much time in silence. Mike willed him not to speak.

'Doesn't it, Inspector?' Johanna Pearson said again. 'Then tell me how it's meant to be. Tell me why everywhere we've tried to live for the last four years has been like this. Persecuted, trapped like animals in a cage and with no help from anyone.'

'I'm here to help now.'

'Are you? Are you really, Detective Inspector Croft? Then you must be a very strange species of policeman. One of a kind, perhaps.'

Mike shook his head. 'I'm sorry, Mrs Pearson, but I don't know what you mean. I'm interested in getting to the —'

'You're interested in getting us off your hands, Inspector. Interested in discrediting my husband because

61

of one alleged mistake he's supposed to have made. Interested in passing the troublesome Pearson clan over to someone else. Make us someone else's problem.' She paused as though for breath and Mike felt Price move again. This time he willed him to speak, to break the spell this woman was weaving about them both, simply by the force of her pent-up anger.

'I don't think like that,' he said, gently. 'But this can't go on, you must see that. These same problems, time and time again. It isn't good for anyone; not you, not for those you're living near, not your children.' Especially not the children.

Johanna Pearson turned on him then with a verbal fury that felt almost physical.

'Not good for my children! Do you have any children, Inspector Croft? Do you pretend to know what's good for mine? I'll tell you what I want for my children. I want to see their father vindicated. See this systematic persecution stop and his reputation wiped clean. Let me tell you something, Inspector Croft. Very soon, very soon now the Fletcher appeal will take place and we'll be there when it does. And when we come to court with all the evidence people like you – those like you who are supposed to care, care about truth and justice and standing up for what is right – have tried to stop us presenting. Have tried to frighten us into denying we have. We'll be there, Inspector Croft, and if, in the meantime, my children have to suffer for what is right and just, then let it be so.'

'That's not the way I see it, Mrs Pearson,' Mike told

her, allowing a harder edge to creep into his voice. 'If the CPS believes you've got something new to present in court then you'll get your chance, the same as anyone else, to have your say. What I'm concerned with is the here and now. In what you have done to your neighbours and what your neighbours have done to you. And, yes, I'm concerned for your children and for all the other kids here on Portland Close who may get themselves caught up in the stone throwing and the name calling and the mindless, stupid violence that's going on here.'

Mike glanced sideways, as much to break visual contact with Johanna Pearson as to see what Price was doing. The sergeant was leaning against the photo-covered wall, arms folded across his chest, watching the exchange with interest. Mike half expected him to break into a paroxysm of ironic applause, just to put the cap on things. Seeing it that way brought an ironic twist of a smile to the corner of Mike's mouth. This situation was getting dafter by the minute. He was a policeman, here to make enquiries. Not someone with all the time in the world to hop on to some ill-defined moral soapbox and exchange insults with a one-woman heckling committee.

It seemed Johanna Pearson had no such qualms. No problem either with seeing her own concerns as part of a much bigger picture.

'Stupid violence, is it? Is it stupid violence to defend one's home? One's family? Is it so unreasonable to prepare one's children for what they may always have to face? They will always be outsiders, Inspector Croft, as we have always been. And it's the likes of you that will make certain it remains so. You and the corrupt police state you are a part of.'

She paused for the merest instant. Mike tried to cut in, but there was no space; she had taken her breath and moved on to her next tirade.

'Yes, those like you, who protect the corrupt and truly evil. Do you think we don't know who paid those vandals out there to do what they did? Do you think we don't know exactly who it is makes trouble for us wherever we go and will always do so until they're locked away where they belong?'

'These are serious allegations . . .' Mike managed, but his words didn't even seem to penetrate.

She was silent now, her face pale under the yellow light, features pinched with tension. She ran a hand through her short brown hair, ruffling it into spiky disarray and then, almost absently, reached out for her husband's hand.

'I think you'd better go now,' Eric Pearson said. 'I just want you to take these with you. It's evidence.'

Mike looked slightly puzzled. 'Evidence of what, Mr Pearson?' he asked.

Eric Pearson's expression was one of sheer exasperation. 'I took photographs, Inspector Croft. Pictures of those who attacked our house.' Impatiently, he tapped the covers of the two folders he was holding. 'There's all you need in there,' he said. 'You'll give me a receipt, of course.'

Mike looked at the two red folders, at Eric Pearson, at the children, silent now and still lined up on the old green sofa. The revulsion he felt was, he knew, completely irrational; completely unprofessional.

'Give them to my sergeant,' he said. Then he turned and walked swiftly down the stairs.

Sergeant Price joined him in the car a few minutes later, settling back in the seat with a deep, heartfelt sigh.

Mike had shifted gear and started off up the road before he spoke, still running the events through in his mind.

'Well,' he said, finally. 'And what did we learn from that little lot?'

Price was silent for a moment, then he grinned and looked at Mike.

'Not to argue with a lady, sir?' he suggested.

Chapter Nine

Tuesday afternoon

The drive out to Embury's place was always a pleasant one. Winding roads led out into the back of beyond and meeting a car coming the opposite way had real novelty value.

John Tynan was still a little puzzled as to why his old friend had called him, asking for help.

His relationship with the Reverend Embury went back a long way, to when Tynan was still on the force. It had diminished with time and with Embury's move to another parish, into the kind of casual remembrance at Christmas that many such relationships become. Until almost a year ago, when the friendship had been renewed, largely because of something Mike had been working on.

John turned off the road and on to the cart track that led to Embury's cottage. The track was deeply rutted by the passage of heavy farm vehicles and the ruts had dried in the summer sun, becoming permanent obstructions to anything with normal-sized tyres and that didn't happen to be four-wheel drive.

Resignedly, John pulled on to the verge and got out of the car. Poor old thing. He nursed it carefully from one MOT to the next, but it really wasn't up to the obstacles in Embury's cart track.

Embury had seen him coming and was waiting for him at the cottage door.

'John! Come in, come in.'

The front door opened straight on to the large kitchen. This had once been a foreman's cottage, the kitchen large enough to accommodate the seasonal labourers who would have lodged there. A young man sat at the long, scrubbed-pine table, the remains of a meal still in front of him and a large mug of tea in his hand.

'John, you've met Sam Pearson? No? Well, he's one of the two who're living here this year. Been farming out at Otbury, haven't you, Sam? Started here about a month ago.'

The young man smiled. He had a pleasant, open look to him, reddish hair and freckled skin and the kind of summer blue eyes that seem right with such colouring. He put the mug down and half rose, leaning across the table to shake John Tynan's hand.

'Glad to know you, Mr Tynan. The Rev'rend here's been telling me about you.'

John gave Embury an inquisitorial look. 'Reverend' was strictly a courtesy title these days. Embury had been retired for some years now, but old habits and local memories had a lot of staying power. John was willing to bet that his friend would go to his grave as Reverend Embury.

'And what's he been telling you?' John asked. 'Nothing too terrible, I hope?'

The young man smiled again and shook his head. He

could do with a haircut, John thought, though it would be a shame to lose that mane of red curls.

'Nothing but good things, Mr Tynan,' he said. 'Nothing but good.' He reached out for the large brown pot and a stripy mug. 'Sugar, is it, and milk as well? Best you put your own in, then. So you know it's right.'

John accepted the tea that Sam had poured for him and sat down opposite, guessing that whatever Embury had brought him out here for Sam was at the heart of it.

The young man suddenly seemed ill at ease, unsure of what to ask, so John sipped at his mug of scalding tea and watched Sam's large, rough-palmed hands as they pushed the dinner plate aside and shuffled the glass salt and pepper pots around in front of him, as he prepared to speak.

When he did, it was a while before he came to the point.

'The fact is, like, I wanted to ask a favour. No, I won't take it bad if you say no, Mr Tynan, you don't know me from Adam and don't have reason to care less. But the Rev'rend, he says you might be able to help, and, well, you might not want to help. Not those that don't deserve it. But they're family, and if I didn't least try and find them, well, I wouldn't be doing my duty, now, would I?'

He lifted his eyes from the cruet set at that point and looked Tynan straight in the eye, as though expecting instant help or refusal, and braced enough for both.

John frowned thoughtfully and shook his head.

'I'm sorry, Sam' he said. 'But I'm afraid you've lost me.'

The young man sighed and looked across at Embury for help. 'I'm sorry too,' he said. 'I never was too good at saying things. Doing things, yes. You give me something I can figure out with my hands and I can do it, but I never had much time to learn the right words.'

Embury smiled at him. 'You do all right, Sam' he said. 'We all have different ways of dealing with the world. Take John here, he was a fine policeman but I doubt he knows one end of a combine from the other.'

Sam looked uneasily at them, then nodded slowly.

'The fact is, Mr Tynan, I want to find my family. Well, not my family exactly, but my dad's family. They left where we all used to live about five year ago and we lost touch. Then my dad, well, he died about a year back and I didn't know how to find his brother. Let him know.'

He hesitated, as though very reluctant to even talk about his lost uncle.

'I didn't like him, see, but my dad, he left him some little things. Nothing valuable, but things that ought to go to a man's brother. That's where he wanted them to go.' He paused again, reached out abruptly and began playing once more with the cruet set.

'I only stayed on 'cause of my dad. I'd've left there long ago, but he never wanted to be no place else. Then when he died and I asked the Elders about giving his stuff to his brother. Well, they were all fire set agin me finding them. Said as how they'd disgraced the house and I should leave well alone.' He stopped again and frowned, as though struggling with a painful memory still very close to the surface.

John glanced over at Embury. Elders? What was the boy on about?

Embury shook his head slightly. Sam should tell his tale in his own way and in his own time. Tynan looked back at the young man and waited. Soon he began again.

'Then I left, see. When I'd met 'manda.' he lifted his head and flashed a swift, bright smile at Tynan. The effect was almost revelatory in the way it brightened Sam's plain features.

''manda's my girl, I met her last September down in Otley and when I left the house her dad gave me work on his place till I got meself sorted out here.'

'They're getting married next April,' Embury put in, the pride in his voice almost paternal. 'And Jack Arnott will be getting himself not just a son but one of the best stockmen anyone could wish for.'

Sam made a dismissive gesture. 'But the thing is, Mr Tynan, 'manda's a good girl and a good Christian, but she's not the same as us and I knew she wouldn't come and live at the house. Well, it just wouldn't be right for her. So I talked it over with the Elders and we agreed. It was time I went. And with my dad gone, there was nothing to hold me there, so off I went. And I got to thinking, then, since I'd left and the Elders weren't around to tell me things any more, that I'd better start to shift thinking for meself. So I think it through and I talk to 'manda's family and they think like I do. Eric Pearson was my dad's brother, after all, even if I didn't like the man. Even if he did give us all a bad name with what he done. So I decided. I'd ask the Rev'rend here how to go about looking for him and he said he'd talk to you.'

He looked up, hopefully, then got to his feet, clearly relieved to have got everything out into the open like this.

'Well, I'd best be going now. I'm late back to work. But it's been nice meeting you, Mr Tynan, and if you can tell the Rev'rend what you think I'd be more than grateful.'

He was gone, pacing rapidly across the room and out of the door, before John could say another word.

Embury was staring at him closely.

Eric Pearson, John thought to himself. Wasn't that the man . . .? Could it be the same one?

He saw Embury get up, go to the sink and fill the kettle once again.

'Now, tell,' Embury demanded, sitting back down at the table. 'What did my friend Sam say to you that brought such a gleam to your eye? I see a story there, John Tynan, and if I don't get it all I'll have to make one up myself and that will never do. Oh, dear me no, that wouldn't do at all.'

Tuesday night, late

Jaques imagined that the extra weight in the boot of the car slowed it somehow. He had driven out of the city and into the winding, darkened lanes beyond. It seemed that at each bend the load shifted, writhed, as though living. Something that fought to be free.

But, when finally he stopped, opened the boot and looked inside, there was nothing but an anonymous package, wrapped tight in black plastic.

It moved in his arms when he picked it up. Lay heavily across his shoulders as he staggered through the gate and across the field.

There were better places for this, Jaques knew that. But time was not with him. He was due at work on early call. He could hardly go through the entire shift with this thing in the boot. Awkwardly Jaques made his way to the far side of a clump of trees. Then he dumped his burden on the ground and left it where it lay.

Chapter Ten

Wednesday 11 a.m.

They had a late and leisurely breakfast, an unexpected bonus on a weekday morning, when Rezah would usually have left early for work. He would have to go soon, probably not be back until late, most of his work on the stores programme having to be done when the warehouse was not in full use.

There had been so many long days lately. So little time to sit down and really talk.

Rezah had Farouzi on his lap, feeding her tit-bits from his plate. She'd already devoured her own breakfast and investigated Ellie's, but Daddy's could always be counted on to be the most interesting.

Rezah smiled across at Ellie.

'You look a bit better this morning. Less tired.'

Ellie nodded. 'I feel it,' she said. 'It's been nice to wake up naturally, for once, and not have to dash about.'

Rezah smiled at her. He had a rather austere face, high cheekboned, thin-lipped, aloof. In looks, Ellie was the complete opposite, soft blond hair and a pretty, round face that showed every emotion with unnerving transparency.

'I was thinking,' Rezah continued. 'Maybe you should go to stay with my parents for a few days, until this trouble blows over.'

Ellie picked up the teapot and refilled her cup. Rezah drank coffee in the mornings. Black and strong and very sweet. Far too strong, she thought. She sipped her tea and then, slowly, shook her head.

'I'll be all right. It just shook me up a little bit and I've still got so many things I want to do before the baby arrives.'

He switched Fara to his other knee and reached out to touch Ellie's hair. 'Are you sure?' he said. 'You know they'd be more than glad to have you.'

'I know that.' She smiled at him. 'I just want to hang on here for a bit longer, just in case . . .'

'In case she calls?' Rezah's voice grew a little harsher. 'Ellie, Ellie, when are you going to realize that she just doesn't care? Your mother didn't even visit when Farouzi was born. When I phoned her to tell her the good news she hung up on me.' He paused, reached out again to gently caress his wife's neck and shoulder. She lowered her head, stroking her cheek against his hand. He could feel the wetness on it as the tears began to fall.

'Oh, Ellie. Don't let her hurt you any more. It isn't worth it.'

Farouzi wriggled off his lap and went to find her box of toy cars. Rezah got up and stood by his wife, stroking her hair and murmuring vague sympathies. He hated to see her hurting this much, but there was nothing he could do. Maternal disapproval was not a problem it was in his power to solve.

He watched his daughter sending her cars crashing one by one into the kitchen cupboard. Chattering to herself in her own odd mixture of English, baby talk and Arabic. He hugged Ellie closer to him.

'If she calls,' he said, 'then I'll drive you over there. I'll even stay outside in the car if she doesn't want me there and she can see you, see Farouzi, see the new baby. But, Ellie, you have to understand, I won't have her here. This is my house. Our home. It's not a place she will be welcome in.'

For a moment he thought she was going to argue with him, then he felt her nod slowly.

'I know, I can understand that. And I know I'm probably better off without her. But it's not right, Rezah, it isn't right.'

'I know, I know.' He sat down again, watching as Ellie groped for a tissue in the pocket of her dungarees. He was afraid the tears would start again and that he would have to leave for work, knowing that she was still upset. He searched around for something to distract her.

'What Dora said last night, about the Pearsons taking pictures?'

Ellie glanced up at him, her eyes red rimmed, but he could tell that she too was glad of the change of subject.

'I don't know why he does it,' she said, 'but he does. Takes them of everyone. He's a really weird man, Rezah. Gives me the creeps.'

'You should have told me this before,' he said. 'I don't like it, Ellie.' He paused for a moment, thinking. 'Have you had other trouble from him?'

'No. I've really not seen much of him. You can't avoid hearing him, though. He's always shouting at the kids, especially if they go on his front. I've talked to Mrs Pearson a couple of times, though.'

'Oh?'

'Hmm. She's hard to get away from. The sort that backs you into a corner and preaches.'

'Preaches?'

'Oh, I don't mean literally. It's just her way of talking, I suppose. Just stands there and criticizes everybody.' She smiled. 'I mean, everybody. The neighbours, the police, the town planners, the council. If she has a little black book, Rezah, then I think half the population's in it.'

Rezah frowned. The hours he worked meant that he was away a good deal and had little to do, directly, with his neighbours. What he had heard about Pearson, though, and the tail end of the strange and violent situation he had witnessed last night, that worried him.

'I should talk to him,' he said.

'Talk to him? But why? What happened last night . . .'

'What happened last night frightened you and Farouzi. I can't go to work this morning knowing that I've done nothing to protect you.' Ellie looked at him, uncomprehending. 'Talking to the Pearsons isn't going to change anything around here. They won't listen, Rezah. They don't listen to anybody. And it wasn't just the Pearsons last night. It was everybody.'

'I can't just let this go, Ellie, you must see that.'

Ellie wasn't sure that she saw anything. The Pearsons were, clearly, not people you could reason with and, after last night, they were going to be even more defensive.

She sighed. She could see that Rezah had made up his mind and wasn't going to be dissuaded.

'All right,' she said. 'Talk to him, if it'll make you feel better. But, Rezah, I don't even know what last night was all about.'

He shook his head rapidly and got to his feet. 'I don't care about that, I just worry about you both when I'm not here. You know that, don't you?'

Ellie watched him go, a worried frown creasing her brow. She felt, instinctively, that any interference on Rezah's part would only lead to more trouble. Farouzi had come back to the table, knelt on her father's chair and begun to run her cars in and out of the remnants of the morning's breakfast.

Sighing again and feeling the tiredness once more settling around her, Ellie began to stack the breakfast pots and carry them over to the sink.

The cul-de-sac seemed unusually quiet. Children had gone to school, workers to work. Rezah was aware, though, of the curious scrutiny of several pairs of eyes as he made his way round the corner and on to the Pearsons' front. Now that he was committed, Rezah was far from certain what it was he wanted to say to the man and, looking at the state of the house, some of the anger he had been feeling dissipated.

Whatever the man had done, did it really warrant this?

Every window in the house had been broken and was

now boarded up. Men had come during the night, their banging and hammering sounding for hours. The police had stayed on until the work was finished.

Looking, now, at the blank, unseeing windows, Rezah felt more than a pang of sympathy for those inside. Was in half a mind to turn away and leave his errand incomplete.

It must be so dark inside the house now. Not even a crack where the strong, summer sunlight could filter through. The Pearsons' children must feel like semi-prisoners inside their own home.

Resolutely, conscious of the twitching nets and watching eyes, Rezah stepped forward and knocked on the door.

'Yes? What do you want?'

The voice came from above him, accompanied by the crash and creak of an unwillingly opened window.

'Mr Pearson?' Rezah questioned.

'Yes. What do you want?'

'I am Rezah Masouk.'

'I know who you are. What is it that you want?'

Rezah frowned. The man's attitude was eroding a little of his sympathy.

He tried again. 'I just wanted to talk to you, Mr Pearson. My wife was very upset by what's been happening.'

Above him he could hear Eric Pearson laughing. It wasn't a pleasant sound. Rezah stepped back so that he could see the man's face at the crack in the window.

'Your wife was upset. *Your* wife! What about *my* wife? *My* children? What about them?'

'I had nothing to do with that, Mr Pearson. I am concerned—'

'So you say. You're in it with the rest of them.'

'Mr Pearson, I can assure you—'

'In it with the rest of them. You come here, saying you want to talk. That your wife was upset—'

'Mr Pearson, I came here with the best of—'

'I don't give a damn why you came here, Masouk. We don't need your so-called concern and we don't need you coming around here nosing into something that doesn't concern you.'

Rezah had lost all sympathy now. The man was downright unreasonable. 'Not concern me! You've taken photographs of my wife, made her feel afraid every—'

'Pictures of your wife, is it? Well, let me tell you, Masouk. I've got pictures of the whole damned lot of them. You worry about your family, Masouk. I'll defend mine any way I choose. Now get the hell off my front.'

Rezah was incensed. 'I am on a public footpath in a public street—'

'On my front. Get off or I'll call the police, tell them you've been harassing us again.'

'Harassing you! *Again*! You need not telephone the police, Mr Pearson. I will call them.'

Angrily, Rezah turned and strode back towards his house. The eyes were watching him again. Rezah was left with the uneasy feeling that Ellie had been right. He should have left things well alone.

Chapter Eleven

Wednesday midday

The switchboard put Tynan on hold and kept him there for quite some time, forcibly assaulting him with sweet muzak. He was on the verge of hanging up when he heard the phone begin to ring again and Maria's voice, very welcome and far more melodic, on the other end.

'Ah! I was just about to give up on you, damned tin tacky watch tunes. Hope this isn't a bad time.'

He heard her laughter. 'No, you've struck lucky, caught me between a patient and a meeting I don't want to go to.'

'Good. Well, I won't keep you.' He paused for a moment, not certain of how to phrase his next question. He settled for, 'Any chance of meeting me for lunch tomorrow?'

'Lunch? No, I'm sorry, John, booked solid all day. I doubt if I'm going to get any lunch.'

'Oh,' he said, disappointed but not surprised. 'Friday, then?'

'Friday . . . well, I could, but it would be a rush job. Evening would be better, be glad of an excuse to abscond. I could meet you over at your place if you like.' She paused. He could hear the smile in her voice as she said, 'Now come on, John. What's all this about?'

'Maybe I just like your company.'

'Maybe you do, but you're ringing in your John Tynan the policeman voice, so come on. What gives?'

Tynan laughed at her. 'All right, all right, I'll tell you. Do you know anything about a religious group called the Children of Solomon? They're based out this way, apparently, have been for years though I've got to admit today's the first I've ever heard of them.'

'Something on your old patch you don't know about? Well, that's a shock. Children of Solomon.' She paused again. John could see her in his mind's eye, leaning back in that clumsy old leather chair she kept in her office, eyes half closed, seeing what she could dredge up from the deep recesses of her memory.

'It rings a bell, John, but I can't quite place it. You got anything more than just the name to go on?'

Tynan frowned. 'Well, to be honest, my dear, not a lot. I believe it was founded by one Norman Luther. Couldn't tell you if that's his real name and it seems he died quite a time ago anyway. They own a farm out towards Otley, some kind of commune, it sounds like.'

'And what's your interest?' Maria asked him.

'A young man I met today who used to live there.'

'Well, that's all right, then. Had me worried for a moment, John, I'd begun to wonder if you'd caught religion.'

'At my age! I hope I've got more sense.'

'So, this young man . . .'

'He's got a problem. No, not one that needs your professional services, my dear. More of a personal thing.'

'Oh?'

'He's looking for his uncle. Seems the uncle left this religious group about five years ago. Some scandal, I guess, more from what he didn't tell me than what he did. But anyway, Sam Pearson's trying to find his Uncle Eric.'

He waited for a response, got none, so he carried on. 'Well, there's an Eric Pearson tied up in this Fletcher thing Mike's got himself lumbered with and I thought . . .'

'And you thought,' she was laughing now, a deep, throaty sound, warm and indulgent, 'you thought, John Tynan, that Eric Pearson wasn't such a common name and there's an outside chance it might be the same one Mike's looking at.'

'Well.' He laughed with her. 'You've got to admit, my dear, it is possible.'

'John Tynan, you're an old busybody who doesn't know when to retire – ' She broke off abruptly. Tynan could hear that someone had opened a door and spoken to her. 'Sorry, John, I'm going to have to go. I'll see what I can turn up for Friday night.'

'OK, my dear. And thank you.'

'Welcome, John. Try and get hold of Mike, will you? I don't think I'll have the chance from this end.'

Tynan smiled and nodded, forgetting that she couldn't see him. 'Certainly will, my dear. Look forward to seeing you.'

John put the phone down with a feeling of great satisfaction. Pity about tomorrow, though. He liked to get on with things once he'd sunk his teeth in.

Wednesday 5 p.m.

'So what do you make of it, sir? This little hobby of Pearson's, I mean.'

Mike shook his head.

'Peverted, if you ask me,' Price continued. 'I mean, you can understand the neighbours getting a bit arsy.'

'Provocative enough to smash all the man's windows, you think?'

Price laughed. 'Well, I grant you, that's taking it a bit far. But you know what they say, sir, mud sticks, and from what I know about Pearson there's a fair amount of the slimy stuff flying about.'

Mike glanced at him sharply. 'The case against Pearson never got to court,' he said. 'CPS threw it out. Lack of evidence.'

Price shrugged and shifted uncomfortably in his seat. 'Christ, but it's hot!' he complained. Then, 'They might have thrown it out, sir, but if you get round to looking at the records, it wasn't exactly lack of evidence; just lack of witnesses willing to testify.'

'Oh? The way I read it, three of the four kids involved withdrew their testimony and the fourth, well, his family moved back to the States or something.'

'California. Yes, sir. But what happened was the parents got together and decided putting their kids through some long-winded court process was just too much.'

'Couldn't they have used video evidence? There are precedents.'

'There are now, sir, but it's still unusual. You've got to remember, guv, it's five, nearly six years ago. Not long, maybe, but there still wasn't much allowance made at your average county sessions.'

He paused and shrugged. 'And the kids were very young. The shrink who was assessing them was all for backing off, giving them a chance to sort themselves out. After all, there was no real evidence Pearson did any more than take some rather dodgy photographs.'

'Photographs which magically disappeared, from what I remember.'

Price nodded. 'Yeah, that's right, guv, so it came down to what the kids said happened, and we know they had plenty of time to talk about it amongst themselves so we ended up with allegations of collusion. Leading questions, bad documentation by the first shrink who saw them. That sort of thing. It just got too damned messy. I think, to be honest, we were all relieved when the problem just upped and went away.'

'Yes, but it didn't just go away, did it? We're back with it again and this time it doesn't seem set to shift.' He smiled wryly. 'And now I've come along asking questions. Anyway, there's no evidence the attacks on Pearson have anything to do with that. More like what he's doing now than what happened then.'

'And how long is it going to be before someone does make the connection? It wouldn't take that much doing, guv. Especially not with Pearson shouting the odds about the Fletcher case.' He shrugged again, exasperated, and fell silent.

Mike got up and walked over to his office window, trying to force it open a few more inches.

'What I find so hard to understand is why. I mean, you'd think someone in Pearson's position – one close shave that nearly landed him in it up to his neck – you'd think he'd be content just to slip quietly into the background and rebuild his life. Not go around drawing attention to himself.'

Price grinned. 'Right exhibitionist, isn't he?' He shook his head. 'I know what you mean, though, guv. The guy lost everything, his home, his career, the whole shooting match. He was finished as a teacher. I doubt he'd find anywhere likely to take a chance on him again.'

'Hmm. No, it's not the sort of thing you'd put on your CV.'

'Seems the family've moved around quite a bit since then. Trouble wherever they've been,' Price added.

'So I've heard.'

'Belonged to some weird religious group. They kicked him out when all the trouble broke. Weird lot, they were. Own a big house and land out towards Otley. Turned it into some sort of organic farm.'

Mike glanced at him, interested. This was a part of the Pearson saga he was unfamiliar with. 'Not all religious groups are crazy,' he said. 'Some just want to live in their own way.'

Price gave him an indulgent smile. 'Guess you're right, guv. But they seemed like an odd lot to me.' He frowned, remembering. 'Had this great big oak door with a painted text above it. Something about kids.' He closed his eyes as though to see the memory more clearly. ' "Suffer little children." That was it. "Suffer little children." What the fuck's that supposed to mean? I mean, the sort of thing the Pearson woman was on about today about having her kids suffer for what's right . . . Well, that sounds weird enough to me.'

Mike smiled. 'Suffer as in suffrage or on sufferance, Sergeant. Not as in to make suffer.'

Price looked confused. 'Sir?'

'It's from the Bible.' Mike snorted in vague amusement and pushed himself away from the window.

'Well, I kind of figured that.' Price sounded vaguely hurt.

'Quite. The phrase is "Suffer the little children to come unto me. For theirs is the Kingdom of Heaven." ' He shrugged. 'Something like that, anyway.'

Price gave him a disbelieving look. 'Never took you for a religious type, guv.'

Mike laughed again. 'I'm not,' he said. 'Sunday school. Strange how these things stay with you.'

Yes, very strange, he thought. Memories of a crowded, dingy little room above the fish and chip shop. The faint sound of hymn singing from the Wesleyan chapel next door. Dust motes, circling in the narrow shaft of sunlight that burned its way through the uncurtained window and made promises of playtime, which the child Mike knew were never kept on a Sunday. And Miss Fuller. Wrinkled skin, dry as parchment, hair fixed tightly in a small bun stuck full of pins, reading 'First Bible

Stories' from a large, brown bound book wrapped in a tattered dust cover.

He'd not thought of her in years, and yet, there she was, so sharp and clear in his memory he could even taste the dust-dried air that filled the room.

'Never went myself,' Price said, jolting him back to the present. 'My mam and dad didn't have time for that sort of thing, thank God.'

Mike laughed, briefly.

He'd never sent Stephen, his own son, to Sunday school either. Mike's ex-wife had been a regular church-goer, all wrapped up in the social scene that went with it and happy that way. Stevie had often gone along with her, but not Mike. The Sundays he'd had free had been special times. Times he took his son and his wife – though as time went on just Stevie – as far away from the everyday world of work as possible.

But Stephen was gone now. All that promise, lost in a single moment.

Mike sighed heavily and dragged his thoughts away from the bad places in his memory. Places he really didn't like to go. Instead, he found the spaces in his thinking filled by the memory of the Pearson children, sitting side by side on a shabby green sofa and the tiny, determined shaft of sunlight, teeming with swirling motes of dust, that filtered through a gap in the boarded windows.

Chapter Twelve

Friday evening

Thursday had been a heavy day. Heavy with routine and uneventful in any way that really mattered.

The weather had been unbearably, turgidly, end-of-summer hot. Startling blue skies and hard-baked pavements. Unnatural stillness. The night, airless, despite the showers that broke in the early hours, breathlessly close, denying sleep to all but the most exhausted.

Friday had turned out to be no better.

Mike slid a hot finger inside his even hotter, sweatier collar, easing the damp fabric away from his neck.

He could feel the city grime working its way into his skin and the moist trickles running down his back and gathering, soggily, at his waistband. The air in the car tasted stale, as though he'd breathed it too many times.

His mind filled with thoughts of a shower and a cold beer, not necessarily in that order, and of an evening spent with Maria.

He'd taken to keeping spare clothes at John Tynan's place. A practice he was very glad of now. He could shower and change there and John, being John, would no doubt have something cooked and waiting for him and Maria when they got there.

It was a funny thing, Mike reflected. He'd never laid much store by family, his own parents both dead and the two brothers he'd half shared his childhood with living so far away. When he'd married, the idea of family had seemed an attractive one. He'd had visions of three or four kids, seaside holidays. A dog, maybe. All the usual clichéd adverts of modern family life.

It hadn't turned out that way, though. There'd only been Stevie followed by three, distressingly late miscarriages and then, as though the gods saw fit to rub it in, the road accident that had taken even his son away from him.

The open windows of the car let in a freshening breeze and Mike shivered unexpectedly. Glancing up and ahead, he noticed the clear blue of the summer evening was being encroached upon, rapidly, by gathering clouds.

So there was going to be a storm, was there? Lord knows, I'll be glad of it, he thought. Something to break the deadening tension of the overheated day. Moments later, fat raindrops splattered against the windscreen of the car. The clouds thickened visibly, blackening the sky, bringing sudden darkness and a vicious wind, sharp tanged with sea salt chilling the sweat on his chest and arms.

Mike shivered again and closed the window.

By the time he had turned down the narrow lane that led to John Tynan's the rain was driving hard against the windscreen, flooding the wipers.

He was profoundly grateful as the lights of Tynan's cottage came into view.

*

Johanna Pearson gazed out of her newly replaced living room window. Rain splashed heavily on to the narrow street, poured down and passed the already overloaded storm drains, flowing like a small and transient river under the kissing gate that led from the close.

Johanna laid her forehead against the window. She was alone in the room, the children and Eric having supper in the kitchen below.

When would this end? When would there be a time not haunted by the past? By the harsh accusations made against Eric? By other people's lies.

And they were lies. Eric had told her so many times. Lies told by those who resented his popularity with the children he had taught. Who could not bear for someone so different from themselves to have success in any measure.

Johanna Pearson sighed deeply.

She could hear Eric calling to her from the kitchen, urging her to come down and eat.

'I'm coming, Eric,' she called in response, and moved reluctantly away from the window.

All she wanted was to be left in peace to raise her brood quietly and happily away from all of this anger and controversy.

In her more honest moments, Johanna admitted how much she resented being cast out from the House of Solomon. Acknowledged that, in some small way, she blamed not just the Elders but also Eric for allowing such a thing to happen.

He called to her again and she heard him begin to climb the stairs.

'I'm coming,' she said, trying to keep the weariness from her voice.

'The rain's stopped,' Maria commented, peering out into the darkness at the rapidly clearing sky. She smiled at John Tynan and pushed her plate aside, accepted the offer of more coffee. They had talked over dinner, John telling them about Sam Pearson and his strange compulsion to find his uncle.

'Well, so it has,' John commented. 'Never last very long, these late summer storms. They've largely blown themselves out over the sea before they get this far inland.'

He frowned again, returning to his earlier topic.

'I did some reading,' he said. 'Local papers from about five years back. Seems that Eric Pearson faced an indecency charge before he left this religious group.'

'That's right,' Mike confirmed. 'It didn't survive long enough to get to court. The kids involved, well, it seems their parents decided not to let them testify.'

'Oh?' Maria asked. 'What went on?'

'Photographs,' he sighed. 'There were four children involved, all at the school Pearson taught at. It's one of those small, private places. Large fees and big houses. The kids – there were two seven-year-olds, a five-year-old and the other one I think was about eight. It was the older one who blew the whistle – said that Mr Pearson had been taking photographs of them and that he'd persuaded the younger ones to take their clothes off and pose naked.'

'There was more than that,' John put in.

Mike nodded. 'Yes, there were allegations that he touched the two seven-year-olds in a way that would certainly be viewed as indecent. But the problem was, the so-called evidence was procured a good while after the event and after close questioning from three very persistent teachers and a very inexperienced counsellor.'

'Hmm,' Maria said, 'common sort of problem, that. But the photographs . . .?'

'Disappeared. No trace, either at the school or Pearson's home. There were doubts that Pearson even owned a camera.'

'He could have borrowed one,' John said.

'He could. There's no way of knowing. Pearson stated his innocence from day one and continued to do so right up until the time the CPS decided to throw the case out on its ear.'

'And the Pearsons were still part of this sect – the Children of Solomon – at that time?' Maria asked him.

'Yes. But they left soon after. The council moved them into emergency housing when the Elders told Pearson he had to get out.'

'They turned the whole family out?' Maria was appalled.

John shook his head. 'No, from what Embury tells

me it wasn't like that. The Elders told Eric Pearson that he would have to go. Johanna Pearson said that if her husband was going to be excommunicated then that meant they should all go.' He grinned. 'I phoned Embury again today. Got him to ask Sam about it. Sam reckons they argued for days, then just upped and left one night and parked themselves at the local council offices. Well, you can imagine. Johanna was pregnant with their youngest and they'd already got the other five. Seems Johanna sat there, threatening to get straight on to the local press if the council didn't help them out.'

'And the Elders refused to have them back?' Maria asked. 'I mean, they'd be viewed as having made themselves deliberately homeless, just walking out like that. The council'd be bound to try and persuade them to go home.'

'Well, Sam reckons that the Elders were always willing to have Johanna and the kids return. Just not Eric Pearson.' John paused, thoughtfully. 'Embury says that Sam is very reluctant to talk about it. That he gets the impression Sam more than half believes the allegations made against Eric, but Embury can't get him to go into detail. Very close mouthed when he wants to be, I should think, our Sam.'

Just past dusk and after a fall of rain with a fast-clearing sky and a rather sickly half-moon dragging itself out into the open. Not the perfect time for rabbiting perhaps, but good enough.

Mal called the dogs close to heel. They wrapped about his footsteps, noses twitching, snuffling at the ground or raising their shaggy heads to catch some drifting scent.

Mal loved nights like this, though they happened less often now, since the twins had arrived and domesticity had taken its toll.

He carried the gun broken over his arm and moved softly, the dogs surprisingly quiet too, despite the pent-up excitement. He'd most like take rabbits back with him tonight, but the truth was, Mal enjoyed the space to himself as much as the thought of rabbit smothered in fresh herbs.

He climbed the bit of fencing at the field boundary and headed towards the copse on the other side. The ground was soft there, almost boggy, and beyond the trees was a slight rise and a bank with a sheltered dip behind. A good place for rabbits, and for the odd courting couple prepared to scramble the few hundred yards from the road.

Clicking his tongue to call the dogs back to him again, Mal strode across the rain-wet grass. He skirted the stand of trees and rounded on to the bank. Both he and the dogs moved more slowly now and the dogs kept close to him, noses down, hackles raised in anticipation.

It was late evening, but very far from being truly dark. Once away from the shadows of the trees the view across the dip was a good one and, Mal knew from experience, the warren large enough to mean that he would not have to wait long before tomorrow night's dinner presented itself.

Contentedly, Mal breathed in the damp, rain-chilled air and began to ease his way across the bank towards the flattened spot close to the old tree stump that was his favourite place for waiting.

'Was Sam born into the sect?'

'Yes. Yes, I believe so. He talked about never having lived anywhere else. And I got the distinct impression that the same went for his father. He didn't mention having a mother. I assumed she must be either dead or gone some other way.'

Again, Maria nodded, as though John's words confirmed her thinking.

'So what's going on in that head of yours?' Mike asked her. 'I've got to admit I can't figure out the set-up. I mean, I looked through the old files. Our lot took the place apart looking for the photographs. They say the cult members neither interfered nor helped. They made absolutely no resistance and asked no questions. One of the Elders called them all together, told them what was going to happen and said they were to just let it happen, and that's what they did. They accepted it as though it were an everyday thing to have big-footed plods digging up their flowerbeds.'

He frowned, as though puzzled by something.

'My sergeant, Price, tells me that they had to go back a couple of weeks later. Return some papers or something, and the whole place, well, Price reckons you'd not have known anyone had been there. Everything replanted. Everything immaculate.'

'Bloody tourists!' Mal muttered angrily. He was convinced that tourists and incomers were responsible for most of the ills he saw around him.

I mean, he thought angrily, what local would go dumping their bloody rubbish in a spot like this?

He unclipped his torch from his belt and shone it on the offending pile of black dustbin bags. A couple of them were already torn open and the fetid contents dragged across the grass. Foxes, probably, Mal thought.

He turned the torch beam back across the field towards the road, the light picking chewed-up turf and the tracks of several vehicles at the field edge.

Travellers, then, he thought, remembering vaguely some report he'd heard about police moving a group on a few days before.

'Time they learnt to take their fucking rubbish with them. Leaving their bloody mess.'

The dogs were nosing about in the pile. Irritably, Mal called them to him. The mood of the evening was spoiled now and his hunt, too, no doubt, if there'd been folk tramping about all over.

He kicked petulantly at the nearest bag, then stepped back, momentarily startled at the resistance, the weight of it against his foot.

He shone his torch at the heavy bag, then bent down

for a closer look, enlarging a small hole already torn in its side.

'Makes me downright suspicious,' Mike said. 'I mean, you hear such stories. Mind control. People cut off from their families, virtually held prisoner—'

'And all that's true,' Maria interrupted him, 'of some of the more extreme religious groups. You can't pin that kind of label on here, though.'

'So? Tell me.'

'I did some digging after John's phone call,' Maria said. 'There are three houses run by the Children. One here, which we know about. One in Scotland somewhere and another just outside York. They're farmers, groups of families that joined together about fifty years ago, formed the first community and expanded when their population did. They don't proselytize and they seem capable of becoming both part of the local scene and of standing outside it. This group out at Otley trade with the local farmers and are part of the combine collective.'

'The what?' Mike asked.

John grinned. 'They share the more expensive machinery. Smallholders who can't stump up the capital. They've been doing it for a while round here.'

'Ah!' Mike nodded. 'And what do they actually believe, these so-called Children?'

'Hoped you wouldn't ask that. They don't exactly advertise that part of it.'

'Embury says they believe their founder to have been the Lord's prophet, or something,' John put in.

Maria nodded. 'Though exactly what he prophesied is a bit vague.' She frowned, then reached over and investigated the contents of the coffee pot.

'I'll make you some more in a minute, my dear.'

'Thank you, John. It seems he predicted some kind of world crisis. Not the end of the world, exactly, but a great turmoil.'

'And for that they called him a prophet?'

She laughed. 'No, not exactly. He advocated gathering like-minded people, forming self-sufficient communities and protecting their children, sheltering them from what was going to happen on the outside.'

'So he wasn't into modern living,' Mike stated. Then frowned, suddenly. 'No, that doesn't fit. Pearson worked outside the community and I remember seeing photographs in the old report, some pretty high-tec stuff. Price said we had to call our computer buffs in to check things out.'

'I never said they did away with high-tec,' Maria objected. 'Just that they gathered together to protect themselves from the bad things.'

She smiled and added, 'In fact, Norman Luther advocated taking the best of the old and the best of the new. Of gathering together the knowledge of the past and of the present, from wherever it originated, and preserving it.'

'Sounds like an academic Noah's Ark.' Tynan joked.

Maria laughed. 'I think this Norman Luther was

quite a man in his own way. The community thrived, they were self sufficient within ten years and thinking of setting up a second house in twelve.'

Mike was frowning slightly. 'Sounds like a grand-scale return to "The Good Life",' he said. 'Weird, all the same. But you'd view them as fairly harmless?'

'Well,' Maria said cautiously, 'in Norman Luther we're not looking at some Jim Jones or David Koresh, if that's what you mean.'

'If it wasn't for their acceptance of modernity, they'd sound a bit like the whatchamacallits, the Mennonites and all that lot.'

Maria nodded thoughtfully. 'I'd guess something close to that,' she said. Then, 'Tell me, John. This Sam of yours, did he say if he'd ever gone back, visited his old home?'

'I asked Embury about that. It seems that when Sam left, well, that was it. His name was struck off the register – quite literally, from what I can gather. Sam's dead to them now. If he fails outside, he can never go back home to stay.'

It took Mal fifteen minutes of hard running to get to a phone. In his panic he'd run straight to the nearest visible road. It was a good mile following the bend in the road-way back to where he'd left his car. Mal had realized this almost as soon as his feet had hit tarmac. He'd turned the other way instead, to where he could see the lights of the closest farmhouse, yellow in the distance.

He clutched his shotgun, the weapon still broken over his arm. Cartridges loaded.

Swearing to himself, he ejected them, slipped them into an empty pocket and snapped the weapon closed, flinging it over his shoulder on its leather strap even as he picked up pace once more, the dogs loping beside him.

Mike stared out into the blackness beyond the window. The storm had passed but night seemed to have followed early.

How would it feel, he wondered, for someone like Sam to leave everything he had ever known, and, for all Mike knew, maybe believe he risked damnation as a result?

What would it feel like for Pearson?

Sam, from all accounts, was a practical man, intent on sorting out his life in a methodical if slightly plodding way.

But Pearson? Pearson had left the house to study to be a teacher, presumably, with the blessing of the Elders. But he had come back. To be forced to leave, be rejected by his own people, must have been a double blow for someone as intense and uncompromising as Pearson.

He glanced at Maria and then at John, getting up to make more coffee.

What would it feel like suddenly not to belong? To lose family, religion, livelihood all in one fell swoop?

Was it any wonder Eric Pearson took a bitter view of life? Was it any excuse?

'Penny for them?' Maria said.

Mike smiled at her. 'Not worth it. Mind wandering, that's all.'

She smiled back at him and reached across the table for his hand.

Out in Tynan's hall, the telephone began to ring.

Chapter Thirteen

Saturday 2 a.m.

By the time Mike arrived, the scene had been cordoned off and a narrow walkway, flanked by red and white tape, guided him to the place where the body had been found.

The police surgeon was already there, together with the SOCO. A young woman in white overalls was recording the scene on video. A stills camera hung from a strap across her body.

The entire area was illuminated by dragon lights. Two of them, strung up on makeshift supports. Their brilliance cast everything and everyone into stark relief, giving people and objects twice their own number of shadows. Colours were washed out almost to monochrome.

Price was already there. He saw Mike and came over, his face pale in the brilliant light.

'It's a kid, guv. Early to mid-teens from what they can see. Wrapped up in a rubbish bag.'

Mike followed his gaze to where the police surgeon knelt, directing the young woman with the camera to take still shots. She moved closely around the body, recording the ground before she stepped. Taking macro shots in situ of anything alien to grass or trees. Framing her body shots to indicate exact locations. Precise relationships.

Others stood around at the edge of the cordoned area. Watching, waiting for their cues.

Mike glanced upwards at the sky. The clouds had thickened and the air grown even more chill as they stood there. A rough shelter had been rigged to cover the site, polythene sheeting that cracked and rustled in the rising wind.

'Who found the body?'

'Man named Malcolm Fisher. Out after rabbits.' Price nodded his head back towards the road. 'He's in the car.'

Mike glanced back one more time at the murder scene, then turned towards the road.

'Let me know when they're about to move the body,' he said. 'I'll go and talk to Mr Fisher.'

Mal was drinking coffee in the back of the Area car. He was a youngish man, mid-twenties, Mike thought, though shock and pallor had aged him. He put his cup down and shook Mike by the hand. Then drew back abruptly as though not certain that had been the correct thing to do.

'Did you touch anything?' Mike asked him.

Mal shook his head emphatically.

'Like I told them other lot,' he said. 'I bent down to see and it looked like a hand, with the fingers just sticking out of the hole.' He shrugged as though still disbelieving. 'So I pulled the plastic, like, just a little way and shone my torch right inside and I saw it. Lying there. And these eyes, wide open and looking at me. And then I ran.'

Mike nodded slowly. 'And you touched nothing else? You're certain of that?'

'I touched nothing. I came in through the trees and I saw this rubbish lying on the ground like someone dumped it there.'

He shook his head. 'I only came out looking for rabbits,' he said. 'Then I saw this bloody rubbish strewn all over the place and I got so fucking mad . . . I mean, you know . . . dumping stuff like that.'

He turned to look at Mike, his expression tense and hurt.

'I kicked it,' he said. 'The kid in the bag, I mean.' He halted suddenly, breaking down, bringing up his hands to cover his face. Mike heard the words muffled through Mal's fingers. 'I kicked it. I didn't know it was a kid . . . Someone killed him and then I go and do a thing like that.'

'You didn't know,' Mike told him softly. 'You didn't know.'

Chapter Fourteen

It had always seemed to Mike that a murder investigation should be a more dramatic affair. That there should be more outward sense of urgency. Of fevered activity.

There should be people rushing from place to place, gathering clues, putting them together and snatching the answers from nowhere. Something as violent and blasphemous as the taking of another human life should leave more traces. Shake the fabric of the universe in some tangible, obvious regard.

But that was never the way of it.

Mike stood in the clinically clean room waiting for the post mortem to begin and considering, step by cautious step, just where his investigation should take him.

An incident room had been set up on the roadside close to where the body had been found. Road blocks stopped the sparse traffic. Anyone remotely local would be interviewed this morning, though even that, most basic of procedures was of little use until a time frame could be established. For that, they needed a time of death.

Price stood close by, champing at the bit far more visibly than Mike. He wanted to get on. To be out there, doing, solving, creating his own kind of organized havoc in order to get to the bottom of this.

He was angry, Mike could see that. Angry and hurt in the way that all officers became over the death of a child. That was when it became personal. That was when the case became their own.

Normally at a crime scene some approximate parameters could be established – how long the body had been there, an approximate theory as to cause of death.

In this case, with the body wrapped tight in its pathetic black shroud, the only clue had been the dryness of the grass beneath it when, finally, they had lifted it on to plastic sheeting and carried it away.

Hot days, but it had rained the last two nights. Been dry before.

At least two days, then, maybe three.

Mike sighed and tried not to speculate too much. Tried instead to concentrate on what would happen next.

Soon the pathologist would begin. A description would be circulated. Anyone seen in the area over the last few days would be found and questioned. Missing persons reports searched in detail – time consuming and, Mike knew from experience, often unrewarding.

Then, if they struck lucky, they'd find his family. His name. Get a recent photo and media time to circulate it. There'd be sightings, many of them. Most leading to dead ends or other kids unrelated to this one. Each lead would be checked, collated and rechecked. Each failure would become a personal one. Each possible breakthrough the stimulus to keep on looking. To push that little bit further.

Mike felt suddenly depressed at the prospect.

The crash of the double doors being opened and a trolley being wheeled into the room brought him from his reverie. He watched as the body still in its protective wrappings was laid on the table.

The outer coverings were peeled back. The whole package weighed and then the careful visual examination began, the pathologist speaking all the while into a microphone suspended above the table.

He felt Price move closer as the black plastic was cut away and the body finally laid out in full view. Even from where he stood, Mike could see that parts of the hand and a small area of the shoulder, had been chewed and scratched. But the face seemed untouched. Unclosed eyes staring up at nothing and the jaw slack, leaving the mouth to fall open when the body moved.

Just for an instant, Mike remembered Stevie. The shock he had felt when he'd tried to close his eyes and found the lids refused to shut, the muscles drawn into spasm after death.

'They used to put pennies on the eyes of the dead,' Mike said softly. 'To stop them from opening.' Price made no reply.

The pathologist continued with his ritual.

'Male Caucasian. Estimated thirteen to fifteen years. Height, five feet two, one hundred fifty-seven centimetres. Evidence of bruising to the right temple, left shoulder and the right side of the rib cage two centimetres above the nipple.

'You have that?' he asked, waiting for his assistant to record the marks on the body chart.

The photographer from the crime scene circled the body as she had earlier, recording each injury. Preparing to switch to video as the operation progressed.

Mike watched as they took samples of hair, swabs from nose, mouth and rectum. Examined the eyes for signs of asphyxia. Scraped beneath the short nails.

He watched as they sat the body forward to examine the back, noting the marks of hypostasis on the right-hand side. He flinched, as he always did, at the eerie sound of expelled air forced upward from the lungs and through the larynx as the body was eased forward, head lowered towards the knees and samples of the spinal fluid taken.

He stayed while the boy was washed and the X-rays taken, feeling like some anxious parent watching as their child was examined, and thinking all the time about his own dead son. But when the surgeon produced the dissecting knife and laid the body straight to make the first cut, Mike left swiftly. Striding across the room to the swing doors. Pushing through and hearing them clang loudly behind him.

Price followed only minutes later and joined Mike in the car.

'Should be bloody strung up,' he said. 'Fucking bastards. Just give me ten minutes and a length of rope. That's all they're bloody worth.'

Saturday evening

Mike sat alone in his flat and watched the press conference on the evening news, glad that this at least had been taken out of his hands.

The Superintendent read a pre-written statement. He looked grey and strained, Mike thought. Maybe he liked this kind of personal appearance as little as Mike.

'The body of a teenage boy was found at ten p.m. last night,' he said. 'It had been dumped, wrapped in a black dustbin liner, close to a spinney locally known as Bright's Wood, about a hundred yards from the B5681, as it runs between Otley and Alchester.'

The news cut to pictures of the murder scene. Police cordon, covered area, a small group of people moving purposefully about, and, close by, a long-lens view of a line of searchers moving slowly across the neighbouring field.

'The body has not, as yet, been identified but it is believed to be that of a teenaged boy, aged between thirteen and fifteen years. Five feet two inches in height with light blue eyes and sandy hair. A red sweatshirt believed to belong to the victim was also found at the scene.'

Mike watched as the camera cut once more, this time to the red shirt that had been found bundled into the bag with the dead boy. The bloodstained sleeve had been tucked back out of sight and the shirt was wrapped inside a clear plastic bag. The logo of an American football team showed clearly on the chest.

It hadn't been purchased locally. That much they did know. But the labels had been removed and a slight tear at the neck had been mended, badly, in green thread.

The sweatshirt was probably the best lead they had.

There followed an appeal for information. A hotline for informers and frightened relatives. A reassertion that everything was being done to bring the killer or killers to justice.

'This is a despicable crime,' the officer was saying. 'An act of true evil. I want to assure the public that every avenue of investigation is being pursued and that this force will not rest until the boy's killer has been brought to book.' His left hand moved unconsciously to twist the large onyx ring he wore on his right hand. Then Superintendent Jaques turned to the assembled journalists, fielding questions from the floor.

No, as yet there were no suspects.

No, the cause of death had not yet been established and, no, he couldn't comment on whether or not the boy had been sexually assaulted until all the reports were in.

Mike switched off then and leaned back in the only armchair his tiny flat contained.

'The cause of death has not yet been established,' he repeated softly to himself, then laughed grimly.

It wasn't policy, he knew, to put out over the air that the boy had almost bled to death from a ruptured artery after repeated rape. Or that someone had finished him off by pressing something with soft blue fibres over his face when he was far too weak to even try to struggle.

No, Mike thought, he didn't suppose they could really put that out over the air on the teatime news.

Chapter Fifteen

Sunday morning

Eric Pearson skimmed through the Sunday papers. Johanna brought him three of them every Sunday when she took the children out for their weekly visit to the park.

Eric didn't like the family going out en masse like that. Didn't like knowing they would be gone for two or three hours, perhaps, but it was something Johanna insisted upon doing and, these days, he didn't seem to have the energy to argue with her. Arguments required too much sustained concentration.

Eric skimmed the papers, trying to catch up on the week's news. He could hear the children and Johanna chattering away in the kitchen below and the sound of the radio coming from his eldest son's bedroom.

Eric could almost believe the world to be sane and normal once more.

Almost, but not quite.

For several minutes Eric stared at the twin images on the page in front of him before beginning on the text. The first was taken with a long lens. The slight edge distortion and the unguarded pose of the man in the centre of the shot told him that.

It was the DI who had come to his house. Nosing about, looking at his photographs.

'Detective Inspector Mike Croft,' the caption read, 'directing operations yesterday.'

Eric skimmed through the text. The finding of a boy's body out Otley way. And this man was heading the investigation.

Eric almost spat in disgust. It was the other picture that really got to him. Superintendent Jaques holding forth at a press conference the night before.

'A despicable crime.' Eric almost laughed. 'Promise they will bring the guilty to justice! Ha!' What did Jaques know about justice?

And this other man, this Croft, he was working with him.

Eric put the paper aside and stared upwards at the ceiling. He had almost liked Croft. Almost believed that he might be different. But he would be just like all the rest if Jaques was working with him.

'Corrupt as hell,' Eric said softly to himself. 'The whole damned lot of them, corrupt as hell.'

He leaned right back in his chair, his eyes still fixed to the ceiling as though trying to peer through to his bedroom overhead. At the old bed with its shot springs and its sagging mattress and at the box file that held the journal.

Jaques' name was in there. Eric knew it. If he thought hard enough he could even recall the words.

'Corrupt as hell, the whole damned lot of them. Corrupt as hell,' Eric repeated to himself.

*

Mike stood on the cordoned walkway and gazed at the empty space where the body had lain.

In the two adjoining fields volunteers and police could be seen walking in close formation, continuing their intensive search. At the edge of the wood, undergrowth had been cut back and carefully lifted aside, then sifted by hand for any random fragment that didn't belong. The wood had been subjected to the same meticulous attention.

The boy had died elsewhere. That much was certain. Had been killed and left for some time half turned on to his side and with something pressing against his right shoulder.

Later, long enough to develop marks of hypostasis but not long enough for rigor to have set in, the body had been moved, wrapped in a plastic bag with the knees curled close against the chest.

Later still, he'd been brought here.

There were two layers of plastic. The first bag had split and the whole untidy bundle that had been a teenage boy pushed unceremoniously into a second bag and tied tight.

It was hard to say more than that. Black plastic was black plastic. Mike had become something of an expert on the subject over the last few hours.

These particular black liners were of a bigger than normal size, designed for the large wheeled bins now in use in some parts of the county. For a brief time this had seemed like a lead but a dozen calls just to the local shops that opened on a Sunday had told him that it meant little.

There was not much else. Fragments of skin and hair under two of the boy's fingernails. A single dark hair clinging to the sweatshirt, and then the sweatshirt itself. The label cut out and the inexpert repair made with green thread to the shoulder seam.

Mike turned and walked back towards the car parked by the farm gate on the other side of the field. Tyre tracks had been found close to where his own car stood. Casts had been taken. Casts taken too of footprints, deeply indented in a patch of softer ground under the trees. Footprints that from their depth had been made by either a heavy man or one carrying something that weighed him down.

Mike sighed, wondering just what kind of hole this death would be leaving in someone's life.

Chapter Sixteen

Sunday evening

It began with the evening edition of the *Chronicle* carry-ing an update on the 'Bright's Wood Body', and confir-mation that the murder had been sexual in motive.

People talked about it. Of course they did. A body found not five miles from where they lived. A child, abused and murdered. Memories for such things are long, and the scandal of the Fletcher business not much more than a couple of years past came clearly to mind.

The last council-run home Fletcher had been in charge of was only three miles from Portland, in the opposite direction to Bright's Wood.

Connections were made, as connections are. Parents cast a closer eye over their children. Teenagers were told to stay together and not to walk home alone. Adults tried to whisper, to hide, that which was common knowl-edge in the papers, on the radio, shown in colour pictures on the TV news.

But it was Dora, all intent on avoiding scandal but unable to resist, who dropped the bombshell.

' 'Course I'm sure,' she said. 'We talked about it at the lunch club the other day. Pearson used to live on Malpass Street, that's where the Williams still are. And she remembers . . .'

Soon she wasn't the only one to remember. Pearson's

misdemeanour had not, perhaps, been on the scale of Fletcher's, but it was bad enough.

'He was a teacher, wasn't he?'

'Yes, some private place.'

'Little kids, they were. No older than Lizzie's two.'

'Who knows what else?'

'He was never actually charged with anything, was he, Dora?'

Dora looked uncomfortable. 'Well, no,' she said, 'but that doesn't mean . . .'

'And the wife. Staying with him when she's got kids of her own . . .'

Watching from his window, Eric knew that something was wrong. 'The natives are restless,' he whispered to himself, his voice mocking and contemptuous. He watched people moving from house to house. Neighbours visiting neighbours, grouping themselves together, glancing up at him as he stood to one side of the window, all-seeing but out of sight. Something was going on.

By six o'clock the rain had begun, driving people inside. Lightning flashed, illuminating Eric Pearson still in the window gazing out at the shocks of brightness that lit the sky and waiting for the storm to break around him. Behind him the television screen flickered. The only light in the large room, shining garishly on his children's faces.

There would be trouble tonight. Eric knew it with a certainty born of experience. But he'd be ready for them.

By nine thirty the rain had stopped. The clouds were breaking and scattering in the light wind. For a little while Eric thought that he had been mistaken. That maybe the rain would be enough to cool things for another night. But then there were voices. Two figures broke from the shadows near the kissing gate and stopped, opposite the house. Two youths that Eric dimly recognized as being local stared up at him.

'Yah, you bastard. Get your arse down here.'

'Nah, fuck it! He won't do that. Too fucking scared.'

Eric glanced further down the street. As if their shouts had been the cue they needed, doors to the houses were opening. Neighbours came out, calling to the youths either in approbation or question.

Eric moved from the window and crossed to the phone. His oldest son looked up, eyes questioning.

Eric's hand hesitated over the nine. Then, abruptly, he changed his mind and dialled another number.

'Is that the *Chronicle*? Good. If he's still in his office, I want to talk to Tom Andrews?

Rezah's key turning in the lock didn't wake Ellie. It was only the sound of his voice, calling to her to take off the chain and let him in, that drew her out of her deep, exhausted sleep.

'Oh! Sorry! I'm so sorry!' The suddenness of her awakening startled her into too much of an apology.

He hugged her to him as soon as she'd let him through the door. 'Are you all right, Ellie? You're shaking.'

She laughed, nervously. 'No. I'm fine. I'd just fallen asleep. The storm . . .' She stopped, looked over his shoulder at the scene outside. 'Rezah?'

'I don't know,' he said. 'I only just arrived.'

Ellie looked at him with frightened eyes. 'I thought, tonight. The rain.'

'The rain stopped half an hour ago,' Rezah told her. 'No, come inside. You want no part of this.'

Ellie glanced at him. He was right, she did want no part of it, but the sight of everyone gathered in the street – neighbours, kids, people she recognized as being local, others she had never seen before – all standing silent and immobile, drew her out on to the step.

Rezah left her side and went to the telephone standing on the little table at the foot of the stairs.

'What are you doing?'

'Phoning the police. Then I'll get hold of my father, tell him I'm bringing you over first thing in the morning.'

She gave him a startled look, then turned back to survey the crowd gathered in the street.

Dora stood on the footpath, hands on her hips, scowling at everyone but looking vaguely guilty. 'Bloody fools,' she muttered as Ellie came to her side. 'We should all complain to the council, get a petition or something, get them out that way. This isn't going to do anyone a bit of good.'

Ellie was baffled. She glanced up the road at the

sound of a car engine approaching. The car stopped. Two men got out, the younger one with a professional-looking camera gripped in his hand.

There were shouts from the windows of the Pearson house. The sound of a water hose spurting suddenly into life. Other voices, raised angrily in response. Ellie looked away from the two men and stared at the big house.

Then someone threw a stone and the smash of window glass shattered the night.

'There are children in that house,' Ellie whispered. 'Little kids like Farouzi. Like Lizzie's kids.'

A second window smashed and Ellie wheeled around once more to stare at the Pearsons' house.

It wasn't the adults who were throwing the stones. Children, young kids of eight and nine and ten, hurling stones and half-bricks, bottles, clods of mud, anything that could be used to smash glass, or to threaten those inside. Kids' voices, cheering as they made a hit, and the elders, parents, neighbours, the two men from the car, watching in near silence. Watching, Ellie thought, and approving.

'There are children in that house,' she said again.

'Come back inside.' Rezah took her arm. 'Ellie, come back inside.'

He made as though to draw her away, but Ellie still stared at the partly shattered windows of the Pearson house, at the figure of Eric Pearson standing behind broken glass, hurling bottles and insults out at the crowd below.

'Ellie, come inside!'

Ellie stared up at the topmost window. A small child had climbed on to the sill and peered down from its perch. A moment later the glass in front of it smashed into fragments. The child fell back. Ellie could hear it screaming. She could take no more of this. Breaking free of Rezah's hand she raced across the road, screaming at the attackers.

'What are you doing? What the hell do you think you're doing? There are kids in there. You're just a bunch of bloody cowards, attacking a house with kids in it.'

Rezah had grabbed her arm once more, was pulling her away. There were voices all around her, angry voices. Threatening.

'Get her out of here.'

'What the fuck do you think you're doing? Back off, Ellie. Or do you want to bring this down on your own head?'

'You know what that bastard did, woman? Interfered with little kids, that's what he did. And you want to defend the bastard!'

'What?' Ellie stared. 'What?'

'Still feel the same, do you? Knowing what that bastard did. Little kids, like yours and mine. He's a pervert, just like the one who killed that boy. You really want filth like that living round here?'

Ellie continued to stare, disbelief and shock etched on her features. Anger, less directed now, threatening to bring tears as the memories flooded her mind.

Rezah slipped an arm around his wife's shoulders.

An act of uncharacteristic public affection, but she barely noticed it.

Dimly, she heard Dora's voice. 'She's pregnant, Matt. She didn't know, and look at her, how upset she is.'

'We've got no quarrel with Ellie, or with you, mate.' This last to Rezah. 'But little kids. We can't put up with that.'

'The child in the house,' Ellie whispered. 'The glass broke right in front of him.'

'No one meant the kids to be hurt, love, but what about our own kids? What about them, eh?'

Ellie stared around her. The two men who'd arrived in the car stood near the house. Dora appeared in front of her, mouthing words of comfort that she couldn't understand. Rezah was there holding her tightly, supporting her as though afraid she might faint. And there was shouting. Yells from the street and others, coming from the house. A child screaming and a woman shouting out for help.

Ellie half turned back towards the Pearson house. Johanna Pearson stood just outside the door, her youngest in her arms, blood on her hands and face and, from an upstairs window, seemingly oblivious to the risk to his wife and child, Eric Pearson threw a bottle, lit at the neck with a rag fuse. It hit the ground in the middle of the crowd and exploded, sending a sheet of flame right across the path.

Ellie screamed, her hands lifting instinctively to cover her face, pushing backwards against Rezah, trying to escape the flames.

Rezah pulled her aside, dragged her back towards their house, forced her inside and closed the door.

Outside, Ellie could hear the police sirens begin to wail.

Chapter Seventeen

Monday, early hours

'Is it true, what they were saying about him? Is it true? And the little kid in the window, what's happened to him? There was glass all over. Smashed straight in front of him. He was standing there and then the window shattered and I saw him fall over backwards and I just couldn't take it any more. What they said about him – Eric Pearson. It's true, isn't it? What they said about him.'

Mike said nothing for a moment. Ellie Masouk had worked herself into such a state he wondered if she would even hear him.

Rezah sat beside her, holding her hands in both of his own, trying to calm her. The look of shock on his face and the way his hands trembled told Mike that the young man was suffering no less than his wife.

Mike decided to take the easier question first. He said, 'The Pearson boy – Daniel, I think it is. He's not badly hurt, Mrs Masouk. It seems his elder brother pulled him down just before the window shattered. He's got a few cuts and bruises, but nothing major.' He paused. Ellie Masouk was staring at him now, wet eyes fixed on his face as though looking for lies.

'Truly?'

'Truth,' he said. 'Really, Mrs Masouk, he's all right.'

She continued to stare for a moment, then dropped her gaze. 'And the other things?' she asked. 'What they said about him. Is that true?'

Mike sighed. It was the question everyone had asked him, even those declaring it to be the truth. There'd been bewilderment, undirected anger and not a little shame from everyone he'd talked to tonight. And a stubborn resolve not to point the finger at any of their neighbours as having started this whole thing.

'Where did you hear this, Mrs Masouk? These accusations about Eric Pearson?'

Ellie looked puzzled for a moment. 'Tonight,' she said. 'I mean, in the street. People shouting at me, telling me about him. About . . . about what they said he did.' She broke down again, crying softly, leaning against Rezah.

'Mr Croft,' Rezah Masouk asked, 'do you really need to talk to her tonight? My wife and I have already made statements.'

Mike looked at them both. They were shocked and tired and clearly as much in need of sleep as he was. Yes, they'd made statements, Ellie's coaxed from her almost word by word by the young WPC. Their statements had been corroborated by the other people Mike had spoken to in Portland Close. Neighbours who'd told him of Ellie's run to the defence of the Pearson child; her accusations of cowardice; her hysteria, her distress when they'd 'put her right' about Eric Pearson.

He'd been astonished at how little malice towards Ellie there had been from those who'd witnessed it all.

How little ill feeling her accusations had drawn, of the sympathy and affection that had been expressed for the Masouks, and for Ellie, upset so badly this late in pregnancy.

Frankly, such expressions of concern had bewildered Mike. Had confused the other officers on the scene too, coming as they did after such scenes of violence and intolerance. He had looked for falsity, but, as far as he could discern, had found none. The young couple and their little daughter seemed to be regarded as part of the Portland Close community, to be protected even when misguided.

Not like the Pearsons.

Mike sighed, returned to Rezah Masouk's question.

'No, Mr Masouk. If you've nothing to add, then I don't see why I should bother you any more tonight.'

He pushed himself out of the easy chair, aware of how comfortable he had become and how reluctant he was to move.

'And what they said?' Rezah asked him. 'About Eric Pearson. Is there any truth in that, Inspector?'

Mike sighed and weighed his words carefully before replying. No doubt they'd have some 'full' version of events soon enough. But it wouldn't be from him.

'Eric Pearson has never been convicted of any crime, Mr Masouk,' he said and turned to leave.

Price was waiting for him outside, leaning against the car.

'I was just about to come and get you,' he said.

'Oh?'

'Yes. Superintendent Jaques wants you back at the office.'

Mike looked surprised, glanced at his watch. Four thirty-five. 'Who dragged him out of bed?'

Price grinned, mirthlessly. 'Don't know, sir, but I hope they got their bloody heads bitten off.'

'Half the street were claiming to have been told by some third party,' Mike explained. 'And the other half now miraculously remember the fuss in the papers.'

Jaques grunted discontentedly. 'And Pearson's still shouting conspiracy?' He looked up sharply, fixing Mike with an unhappy glare. 'Anything new on that side, Croft?'

Mike shook his head. 'A lot of paperwork, sir, and not a lot said. The only thing new, as you know, is this journal Pearson claims to be in possession of.'

'You definitely think he has it?'

Mike shrugged. 'Not at the house, I wouldn't think. Not after what happened to the original.'

'What is *alleged* to have happened to the original,' Jaques corrected him.

'Quite, sir. But even if we make the assumption that the journal did exist and that Pearson has a copy, it's unlikely the CPS will accept it as new evidence. The copy can hardly be proved contemporaneous. If it was handwritten, of course, forensics might be able to give us something, but,' he shook his head, 'quite frankly, sir, it's all very circumstantial.'

'But your feelings about it,' Jaques persisted.

'My "feelings" hardly matter.'

'I'd like them anyway, Croft.'

Mike gave him a quizzical look. 'My feelings, sir, tell me that there was something more. That, in this case, Pearson may well be telling the truth.'

'You suspect a cover-up?' Jaques' voice was sharp.

Mike shook his head. 'No. Nothing as definite as that, just too many things that don't fit neatly into the pattern. We knew – the detectives involved in the original investigation knew – that Fletcher wasn't in it on his own. That he was as guilty of procurement for others as he was of abuse, but Fletcher's testimony was flawed. He lied consistently throughout his interrogations, was proved to have been lying on oath in court. He undermined his own evidence time and time again.'

'I've never understood, sir,' Price said, 'just how Pearson claimed to have got hold of this journal.'

Jaques looked surprised. 'I thought that was common currency,' he said.

Mike explained for him. 'Fletcher was on the board of governors, you know, at Pearson's school. Pearson maintains that Fletcher stole the journal. Saw it as some kind of insurance, I would guess.'

'And Fletcher gave the journal to Pearson?' Price was clearly amused.

'Pearson claims that Fletcher was afraid of the evidence being destroyed – which it was. Gave it to Pearson for safekeeping.'

'And Pearson gave it to his solicitor.'

'And the solicitor's office was broken into and gutted by fire a week or so later,' Mike finished.

Jaques frowned and shook his head. 'Frankly, Mike, the whole thing stinks. Though what can be done about it . . .' He gathered up the papers on his table, knocking them into a neat pile. The brief descent into informality had ended as abruptly as it had begun.

A knock at the door broke the moment of awkward silence that followed and a PC entered, clutching a large brown envelope.

'Just arrived by courier, sir.'

'Ah,' Jaques said. 'Good.'

He emptied the contents on to his desk and began to glance through the black and white prints.

'More photographs?'

Jaques smiled, wryly. 'Yes, Sergeant, but these are, I hope, of somewhat more use than Eric Pearson's efforts.'

Price leaned forward, curious. The events of the early hours of the morning on Portland Close were laid out before him. Mike looked too and saw Ellie Masouk, disbelief and anger contorting her pale face; Rezah Masouk reaching for her; the crowd parting, one child, arm raised to throw the half-brick that was shown poised gently in mid-flight in the next shot; Eric Pearson standing in the window, his face twisted with rage; and, in the upper window, the child's figure, arms thrown back as he was pulled clear of the window shattering around him.

'You're going to let them print these, sir?' Price sounded outraged.

Jaques actually looked amused. 'Suggesting we try to gag the press, are you, Sergeant?' Then he sobered. 'It won't look good,' he said. 'Make us out to be a bunch of bloody fools.' He stood, impatiently gathering the photographs together and thrusting them back into their envelope. 'Look them over, Price. I want names to faces. I want to know who lives there and who doesn't. I want arrests, Mike. Want to know who's been stirring up this hornets' nest and why.'

He tapped the envelope again and handed them to Price.

'I want arrests,' he repeated. 'I want this lot sorted and I want it done quickly. I know you've got your hands full with this killing, but we can't be seen to be letting violence like this get out of hand.'

Mike nodded, mumbled some acknowledgement and headed for the door.

As they left he turned to Price. 'The reporter – not the photographer – the older man with him?'

'Andrews,' Price supplied.

'Ah,' Mike said. 'I thought I knew the face. And we know that Pearson called Andrews.'

'Yes, sir. He wasn't in the office, but they got him on his mobile and sent a photographer to pick him up. Seems Pearson made it sound like a real drama.'

'And made sure it turned into one when Andrews got there.' Mike shook his head in disgust. 'I mean, bloody petrol bombs. What are we charging him with?'

'Public order offences. Got the duty solicitor in and

he'll be bailed, I expect, later this morning. You want to interview him?'

'Not if you've already had the pleasure. I'll talk to him later.' Mike frowned. 'Who spoke to Andrews?'

'PC Nelson, but he's gone off shift. He was on overtime from ten last night.'

Mike laughed. 'That's going to please accounts. Thought we were on restrictions this month. Why did Pearson choose Andrews?'

'He's dealt with him before. He covered Pearson's arrest.' They had wandered into the briefing room now and Price automatically filled the kettle for tea. 'Andrews did a series of lengthy pieces on the Fletcher trial too. Pretty vociferous, from what I remember, asked a lot of uncomfortable questions.'

He paused, dumped tea bags into mugs and perched on the edge of the counter waiting for the kettle to boil. 'Andrews seemed to think we should be digging deeper. Taking another look at all the allegations about witness harassment and the like.'

He glanced at Mike. ''Course, you won't remember, you moved here after it was all over. Right messy business.'

'And there was harassment of witnesses?'

'Do pigs fly?' Price grinned. 'Bloody right there was, but prove it . . . Most weren't what you call reliable. Scared kids. Adults who didn't want their past dragged up in court. Business associates of Fletcher's who'd do anything not to put their precious careers on the line. Easy to intimidate any of them.' He shook his head.

'Well, guv, if there's nothing else I'm going to grab a couple of hours' sleep.'

Mike nodded, then frowned, furrowing his brow. Just what was going on here and how deep was he going to have to dig to find out? More to the point, were the residents of Portland Close right, in one degree at least? Was the body found in Bright's Wood part of this whole shabby deal?

Chapter Eighteen

Tuesday morning

A fresh, rain-drenched breeze was blowing, taking the edge of heat off the day as DI Croft drove towards Portland Close.

Monday's action had slowed after mid-morning. Mike had tidied up the paperwork, filed his reports and dealt with the new day's routine, then gone back to his flat and caught up on some sleep, leaving others to collate and cross-reference the flood of calls that had come in about the dead boy.

There had been no real developments. The case had, so far, generated nothing but a mass of statements, an increasingly large pile of random debris picked up by the search teams, all of which had to be labelled, examined and shipped off to forensics. And a mass of taped phone messages. Parents with missing kids. People who thought they'd seen something; a boy matching the description. A girl with a sweatshirt just like the one found. Two men, walking the fields near Bright's Wood on the previous Thursday night.

Apart from a possible lead on the chain of sports shops as far as afield as Edinburgh and Birmingham stocking the sweatshirt, there had been little of consequence. It was not even certain which night the body had been dumped, though the pathologist reckoned on the boy being dead for about a week by the time he had been found. Certainly not less than four days. Blowflies had settled on the body, getting into the bag through the holes torn by the foxes. They had laid their eggs but the maggots had not yet hatched.

It was the best time-frame Mike could hope for. Four to seven days. A big gap of lost time.

The evening had been spent back at the office, reading and re-reading the records of the Fletcher case and of the events of the last few weeks on Portland Close as well as being brought up to date on the murder.

His mind teemed with facts and names and events . . . and missing pieces.

Fletcher was guilty. Mike couldn't doubt that; but the others he had named?

Fletcher had spoken, repeatedly, of widespread and networked pornography. Of children abducted, abused, even killed. Fletcher had claimed to be only the tip of a massive iceberg and a relatively innocent tip at that. If you could call the repeated and long-term physical and sexual abuse of children supposedly in his care anything of the sort.

Was this boy a victim of a pornography ring? Or was it a random opportunist killing?

Was Fletcher lying? Mike didn't know. Instinct told him, as it had told others involved in the investigation before him, that there was a horrifying amount of truth in what Fletcher had said.

Mike glanced sideways at the copy of yesterday's paper on the passenger seat. At Andrews' report of events on Portland Close, together with three of the images he had seen spread out on the Superintendent's desk:

Ellie Masouk, caught in mid-flight; the child, white faced, in the Pearsons' window; Johanna Pearson, her youngest child in her arms, standing at the front door, her face shocked and startled, the flare from the blast of the petrol bomb burning out almost a half of the rest of the image.

Andrews' account of events had been interesting. He'd described what had happened, reviewed the Fletcher case, asked all the questions Mike had spent the last few days asking himself and left his verdict open. The last paragraph, a denouncement of modern society and a demand that the police take further action, was standard and expected.

The story shared space on the front page with an update on the boy found in Bright's Wood.

Mike sighed. Something Fletcher had said in the taped interviews he had listened to stuck in his mind. He reached across and pushed the tape into the cassette player. Fletcher's voice, educated, its local accent carefully expunged, spoke to him.

'You seem to think it's impossible, don't you? That kids just don't disappear. That no one could get away with it for as long as I've said it's gone on. But I ask you – how many kids go missing every year and never turn up again?

'What we've taken is just a fraction. Just scraping the top, and a body's not such a hard thing to get rid of. Not so hard at all.'

He'd refused to say more, though they'd pushed him for details. For names, places and the ways and means of disposal Fletcher seemed so certain of. But he'd clammed up. Refused to say anything after that, and his words had been buried in the mass of documentation the case had generated.

They troubled Mike, though, those words. Reminded him of something Tynan had said to him a year ago, about how many children disappear without trace.

He'd not known then, not wanted to play the numbers game. But he knew now and the facts, coupled with Fletcher's words, had shocked him more deeply than he had thought possible.

Digging around, he'd found figures from the Children's Society for 1987. 'We keep better figures for lost dogs than we do lost children,' Tynan had once told him.

In 1987 alone some 98,000 minors had gone missing. Of those, thousands had never been accounted for again.

Mike saw, in his mind's eye, the families behind the statistics. The pain and the tears. The fear generated by imaginations that could only give shape to the worst of thoughts. Families who couldn't even grieve for a death – and, Mike knew, that was tough enough.

What would it have been like if Stevie hadn't died? If, one day, he'd just not been there. Not dead, not alive, but in some limboland that Mike could never reach.

Angrily, he shook the thoughts from his head.

He wasn't in the business of staging a one-man campaign against the world's lost causes.

But Pearson knew something and so did Fletcher and they, Mike decided, most definitely fell within the confines of his pitch.

Chapter Nineteen

Tuesday morning

John Tynan turned his car into the long drive. He could see the house up ahead, a big Victorian place set within a circle of flowerbeds and green lawns.

'Nice,' he commented.

Beside him Sam nodded. 'It's a good place,' he said.

John glanced sharply at him. 'Do you regret leaving here, Sam?'

The younger man shook his head. 'It's not something to regret,' he said. 'I just don't have a place here any more, Mr Tynan. You don't live a lie just 'cause it's a comfortable life.'

John smiled. It was a nice rule. He didn't know many who would keep to it.

He parked the car in front of the house. Double bay windows arched outward. Large windows with the curtains pulled well back allowed the sun to flood into the two large front rooms.

The two men walked slowly up to the front door. It stood open, exposing a large tiled hall. A pokerwork plaque hung above the door.

' "Suffer the little children",' Tynan read.

Sam nodded. 'That's what the Lord said, to let the little ones go to him and be saved.' He glanced at Tynan, his face betraying his awkwardness, as though he found it hard to explain his old home. 'It's a kind of a motto, I guess.'

'You must be John Tynan.'

John and Sam both turned. A man climbed the steps behind them, hand extended towards John.

'David Laughton,' he introduced himself, then nodded at Sam. 'Please, come in. Come in.'

It was cool inside, cool and dim, as Laughton led them out of the sunlit hall and towards the back of the house.

John, looking around him, caught glimpses of large, simply furnished rooms, polished woodwork and neatness. The house had a freshly cleaned air to it.

Behind them, two small children thundered down the stairs into the hall and ran outside giggling. Laughton smiled. 'Lessons over for the day,' he said. 'We don't keep them inside too long on days like this.'

'Do you have many children here?' Tynan asked him.

'There are twelve in all under sixteen and three more not yet reached their majority.'

Tynan raised an eyebrow. It was such an old-fashioned thing to say. 'Under eighteen?' he asked.

Laughton smiled. 'Oh no, Mr Tynan. Here our children remain our children until they are twenty-one. After that they make some choices for themselves. Don't they, Sam?'

He looked sideways at the younger man, who flushed and looked down at his feet.

'And they accept that?' Tynan questioned.

Laughton emitted a brief burst of laughter. 'Those

are our rules, Mr Tynan. I don't imagine it does them any great harm, do you?'

'I don't know,' Tynan said, frowning. 'It must be tough to be treated like a child when the rest of the world would see you as an adult long since.'

Laughton smiled again. 'Those on the outside expect their children to grow up too fast, Mr Tynan. We protect our own here.'

John said no more. He glanced sideways at Sam, who refused to meet his eyes but continued to stare at the floor, shoulders hunched miserably.

Laughton had led them through to the kitchen. 'Can I offer you anything?' he asked.

'Thank you, no,' Tynan said. Sam's discomfort was growing by the minute. He had no wish to prolong his agony.

Laughton turned to the younger man. 'Your stuff is out there, in the storeroom, Sam. It's all boxed up, just the way you left it.'

Sam Pearson murmured some kind of thanks, then disappeared rapidly through the back door.

Laughton paused for a moment, then said, 'How's he getting along, Mr Tynan?'

John gave him a surprised look. There was genuine concern in the man's voice and a somewhat anxious look in his eyes.

'John, please,' he said. 'And he's doing fine, Mr Laughton. He's a very pleasant, very genuine young man. You should be proud of him.'

Laughton peered at him for a moment, as though

looking for some deceit. Then he nodded, appeared to relax a little and sat himself down at the kitchen table.

'I'm glad of that. Very glad. It can't have been easy.' He glanced across at Tynan and then enquired, 'This girl he's marrying . . .' He laughed, suddenly. 'I'm sorry. Mr Tynan, I've no right to ask, have I?'

John smiled at him. 'Please, call me John,' he said again. 'I've not met her personally, but I hear she's a nice girl, and her family certainly seem to have taken Sam to their hearts.'

Laughton nodded. He looked relieved. 'He deserves to be happy. I only wish it could have been here that made him happy. To have one of our own leave like that . . .' He shook his head. 'It was like a bereavement, having Sam decide to go.'

John looked at him curiously. 'It isn't the first time, though, surely? Well, I know it's not. Sam's uncle and his family . . .'

He broke off as Laughton got to his feet. Laughton was clearly displeased, his mouth set in a tight line. 'That, Mr Tynan, was a different matter. An entirely different matter.'

Tynan gave him a questioning look, hoping that he would continue, but Laughton seemed unprepared to say more.

'The publicity can't have been pleasant,' he said placatingly.

Laughton glared at him. 'What that man did was sinful. He had a wife and children. A home. He was a part of our community, trusted, with a place of trust on the outside as well. And he did that.'

'Nothing was ever proved,' Tynan said mildly.

Laughton glared at him. 'Many things can't be proved, Mr Tynan. Many things, but they are truth none the less.' He sighed. 'We never told Johanna and the children that they must leave. We would have cared for them, protected them, no matter what it cost us.'

'Cost you?' Tynan asked.

Laughton glanced at him. 'Johanna was not an easy woman,' he said slowly. 'She caused disturbance. Questioned the Elders and caused friction with the other women.'

'Oh?' Tynan asked, then, 'It must be difficult, living communally like this. I don't think I could manage it.' He laughed, briefly. 'Too cantankerous and too fond of my own way, I'm afraid.'

Laughton allowed himself a smile. 'I don't think anyone finds it easy all of the time,' he said. 'But Johanna and Eric . . .' He shook his head wearily. 'Sam tells me you've found them?' He didn't sound as though he considered that a desirable thing.

'It didn't take much doing.' John reached into his jacket pocket and pulled out Monday's *Chronicle*, handed it to Laughton. The other man took it reluctantly and stared at the front page.

'More trouble,' he said. 'Everywhere they go we hear there's trouble. And you're taking Sam into this? Don't you have any sort of conscience, Mr Tynan?'

He thrust the paper back at Tynan, his lips once again pulled taut with disapproval.

'Sam's a grown man,' John said slowly. 'He makes his own choices and, if he feels he has to take his father's things to his father's brother, then that choice is his.'

'And you think Eric Pearson will make him welcome? Or that it would be any good for Sam, even if he does?'

'I doubt it,' Tynan said. 'But it seems to me that Sam needs to shed his old life completely before he gives himself to the new. I make no judgement about this set-up, Mr Laughton. If it produces young men like Sam, then there's probably good in it, but Sam makes his own choices now and there are things he needs to know and things he needs to do. This is one of them.'

Laughton frowned at him and shook his head. 'Eric Pearson brought shame on our house,' he said. 'He'll bring shame on whoever touches his life.' He pointed at the paper in Tynan's hands. 'That shows what kind of trouble he causes, Mr Tynan.'

A movement behind him alerted them to Sam's return. 'I think you'd better go now. You know the way out, Sam. I wish you well.' Then he was gone.

Sam looked at Tynan, his face apologetic and embarrassed. 'I'm sorry, Mr Tynan,' he said.

John smiled. 'Here, let me help you with that,' he said, taking one of the boxes Sam held. 'Now, let's get going, and get this stuff to where it belongs.'

*

Rezah Masouk was coming out of his house when Mike Croft arrived at Portland Close. Rezah had a suitcase in one hand and what looked to be a carrier bag stuffed with teddy bears in the other.

Mike eyed the baggage thoughtfully. 'Is anything wrong, Mr Masouk?'

Rezah shook his head. 'I left word at the police station,' he said, 'in case you needed to speak to me or to Ellie.'

'You're leaving?'

Rezah laughed briefly. 'It looks that way, Inspector. We're staying at my parents' home for a few days. All of this . . . mess, it isn't good for Ellie.'

Another man and a young woman came out of the house. The man was older than Rezah, but there was a strong resemblance between them. The woman wore Western clothes but her head was covered by a black veil that completely hid her hair. They looked curiously at Mike.

'This is my father, Inspector Croft, and my sister.'

The older man extended a hand. 'I am pleased to meet you, Inspector.' He glanced at Rezah. 'You have everything? Good.' He nodded briefly, and went with his daughter to get into the car.

Mike asked, 'And how is Mrs Masouk?'

Rezah frowned slightly. 'This has done her no good, Mr Croft. Three years, almost, we've been here and everything's been fine, and now all this.' He sighed. 'I've left her with my mother while we came to collect some things.'

Mike nodded. 'I can understand you wanting to be

out of it.' Then, 'Tell me, Mr Masouk, the people round here, you've never had any problems with them?'

'You mean, Inspector, has there been harassment because I'm not whiter than white and I've stolen an English woman?' He laughed briefly at Mike's expression. 'No, please, Inspector. I do know what you mean, and, no, we've had no problems. I don't know of anyone who has . . . until now.'

He put the suitcase and the bag in the boot of the car, then reached into his back pocket and withdrew a large manila envelope.

'This is what I call problems,' he said, handing it to Mike.

Mike withdrew the single sheet of paper and read it, frowning.

'The council are applying for an injunction,' Rezah said. 'A restraining order.'

Mike could hear the anger in Rezah's voice. He handed the letter back.

'We've all got them,' Rezah went on. 'The entire street. And we did nothing, Inspector. We wanted peace and quiet. We had no wish to be drawn into this, whatever it's about.' He shook his head, bewildered. 'I don't want to tell Ellie about this,' he said.

'Mr Masouk,' Mike began, wanting to reassure him, 'we have nothing in our reports to suggest that you or your wife took part in any of the stone throwing. In any of the violence. Your wife acted out of concern . . .'

'And ended up with this?' Rezah shook the letter

angrily. 'With this threat to take away her home if there are any more reports of harassment or vandalism.'

'Nothing will happen, Mr Masouk. There's no suggestion of your involvement.'

'Isn't there, Inspector? I think the council and court records are going to be showing otherwise, don't you?'

Mike said nothing. There didn't seem much point. He stood and watched as Rezah Masouk got into his car and started the engine. Then he made his way, reluctantly, towards the Pearson house.

'He's Moslem, you know.'

Mike was taken by surprise. 'I'm sorry?'

'Masouk,' Johanna Pearson said. 'Moslem.'

Mike was nonplussed. 'Is that relevant, Mrs Pearson?'

Johanna snorted as though the reply should have been obvious. 'Don't you listen to the news, Inspector Croft?'

'When I can.'

'Then you'll know the damage they're doing. Conversion at all costs, Inspector. Conversion by the book or by the sword. It's all the same to them.'

'I don't think Mr Masouk is set to take up the sword, Mrs Pearson.' Mike was genuinely astonished. 'And all religions have their extremists.'

'Live and let live. Is that it, Inspector Croft?'

'Whenever possible,' Mike said. 'There are people

always willing to do harm, no matter what religion they belong to.'

'And that makes it all right?'

Mike sighed. 'Mrs Pearson, I don't think this is the time for religious dialectic, do you?'

It was her turn to look surprised and Mike took full advantage. 'I see you have new windows, Mrs Pearson.' He went over, puzzled by the slight distortion of the view outside, and tapped on the glass. Then looked questioningly at Johanna.

'Oh, they didn't put glass in this time. It's some sort of unbreakable plastic,' she said, her voice rich with satisfaction. 'Let the little bastards try and break those.'

'And you think they will?' Mike asked her.

Johanna snorted rudely. 'Oh, they'll try again, Inspector. They'll try again to frighten us and they'll go on trying. But they won't succeed. Oh no. We'll stand firm.'

Mike looked thoughtfully at the woman. 'What are you hoping to gain?' he asked her softly. 'Why is your husband so intent on stirring all of this up again?'

'The guilty should be punished,' Johanna said stoutly. 'It's justice that matters. I intend to make them pay for what they did to Eric. To all of us.'

She paused then and let her gaze travel over the shabby room with its ill-matched furniture; its lack of any sense of home. Mike could see how weary she looked, how great the strain must have been these past years, following Eric Pearson from place to place. Facing so much turmoil. So much pain.

He said gently, 'You must love him very much, Johanna.'

She turned on him, eyes blazing as though he'd said something insolent and cruel. Then the anger died, swiftly, as though she no longer had the strength to maintain it.

'He's father to my children,' she said. 'The man I married and made my vows to. And I believe in his innocence, Inspector, believe that those men framed him, sought to discredit him because of what they knew Fletcher had told him.' She moved closer to Mike. He could feel the tension in her body even without being close enough to touch.

'If I didn't believe in him, Inspector, believe that all they said about him was lies and more lies, do you think I would have left our home and brought our children to be with a man capable of abusing them? Is that the kind of woman you think I am, Inspector Croft?'

Steadily, Mike returned her gaze. 'I believe you did what you thought was right,' he said. 'But what about the children, Johanna? Can it be right to make them suffer like this for a matter of principle you'll maybe never be able to prove?'

Johanna Pearson turned away from him, her shoulders trembling, back rigid, holding in her pent-up anger. 'The courts will decide, Inspector. We'll make our case when the time comes.'

Mike sighed. It seemed of no use to reiterate that the Pearsons' so-called evidence might not even make it into court, and would likely be discounted even if it did.

He would have given a great deal for a brief look at the journal, but there was no hope of that. It was defence evidence, exempt from right of disclosure.

Below them, a banging on the door and a shout announced Eric Pearson's return. Johanna moved towards the stairs. Children's voices sounded, three or four of them all talking at once, as Eric made his entrance.

Mike was about to follow Johanna down the stairs when a car pulling up in the road outside the house attracted his attention. John Tynan? What was he doing here?

Mike stood and watched as John and a younger man got out of the car and began to take boxes out of the boot.

Sam Pearson, by any remote chance? Mike wondered.

He made his way downstairs and opened the front door before John and his younger companion got to it.

'John?'

'Well, hello there. This here's Sam, you remember I mentioned him to you?'

Mike nodded. Eric Pearson's voice, angry and questioning, broke into the conversation.

'Just what do you think you're doing?'

Mike stood aside, pressing himself against the wall in the narrow hallway.

Eric Pearson stared out at the two men standing on his doorstep.

'Hello, Uncle Eric,' Sam said.

*

Eric Pearson was clearly far from pleased.

Grudgingly, he had allowed John Tynan and Sam to come inside and shown them through to the kitchen, where they had placed the boxes on the table.

'My father wanted you to have these things,' Sam told him. 'He said there were some of his and some things that you'd left behind.' He hesitated, clearly confused by the lack of response from his uncle. He said hesitantly, 'You did know that my father had died, didn't you?'

Eric glared at him. 'How could I have known?' he said. 'And it makes no matter. The whole damned lot of you died as far as we were concerned, the day we were driven out.'

For a moment Sam stood, staring at his uncle, lost for words. Then he gathered his dignity about him and said quietly, 'Well, I've done what I came to do and that's an end to it. I'll say goodbye now.' He nodded politely at Johanna and headed for the door.

'I'll see you out,' Johanna said vaguely.

John glanced at Mike, then followed them. Mike heard him say, 'I'll leave you my card, my dear, just in case you want to talk to Sam again.'

Eric Pearson looked at the boxes on the table, a curious expression on his face. Mike knew he had been completely forgotten as Eric Pearson slowly began to unpack the boxes and assemble the contents on the kitchen table.

Chapter Twenty

'So, what was in the boxes?' Jaques asked.

Mike shrugged. 'Nothing more or less than you might expect. A few books. Poetry mostly. A nifty selection of ties; rather too bright for Eric's taste, I would have said, and a plastic bag full of photos.'

'Oh?' Jaques sounded ironic.

Mike smiled. 'No, sir, family snapshots, mostly taken at the house in Otley by the look of it.'

'Hmm.' Jaques frowned. 'Anything else?'

Mike shook his head. 'Bits and pieces. Some of their mother's jewellery, nothing valuable and the sort of trinkets people keep around them. Nothing significant.'

Jaques sighed. 'So he didn't exactly play the loving relative?'

Mike shook his head. 'No, sir, but if you ask me I think that's just as well. Sam Pearson's probably better off making his own way.'

'You could be right.' Jaques glanced down at the sheet in front of him. 'But this other matter, Mike. This request to see Fletcher. What do you hope to gain from it?'

'Probably not a great deal.' Mike frowned briefly. 'Fletcher made several claims while he was being interviewed but wouldn't substantiate any of them. I'd just like to know if a spell inside's softened him up any.'

Jaques gave him a shrewd look. 'And that's all?' he asked.

Mike shrugged. 'The truth is, I don't know, sir. There's just things I'd be happier about if I could confront Fletcher personally.'

'You think we missed something?' Jaques' voice was sharp.

'I don't know,' Mike said, refusing to be intimidated. 'But Fletcher's been inside more than a year now. Almost two if you count the remand, and it's just possible that having time to think might have made him more prepared to put detail to some of the claims he made. And this boy we've found. It fits with the kind of story Fletcher was spinning. I have to look at everything.'

Jaques stared at him for a moment or two longer, then said, 'I'll set it up, but I doubt you'll get much out of him even now. Arrogant bastard, he was, all the way through. Almost as though he saw himself as being above the law in some way. Like he expected all the time for something or someone to come along and get him off. Never seen anyone look so surprised as Fletcher did when the jury came back with a thirteen-count guilty verdict.'

Mike nodded. 'But then,' he said, 'he claimed all along to have friends in high places he'd drag down with him if he looked like going under. Maybe he figured they'd be so scared of what he could say that they'd move mountains to get him off.'

'Maybe so. Instead of that, his so-called friends let him swing.' Jaques nodded as though suddenly making up his mind. 'All right, then. You talk to Fletcher and report back. But my feeling has to be that you're wasting your time.'

Mike shrugged but decided to make no comment.

'Thank you, sir,' he said, and left the office.

'And just what are you doing?'

Maria sounded amused. She stood in the doorway, leaning against the wooden surround, her lips twitching with half-controlled laughter.

Mike glanced up, then smiled and put the book he was holding aside.

'Catching up on some reading,' he said.

'So I see.'

She crossed the room, kissed him and then reached out for the nearest of the books that Mike had scattered all over the low table and looked at the title.

'Is this to do with the Fletcher case?' she asked.

Mike leaned back on the sofa and clasped his hands behind his head. 'Could be,' he said. He stretched wearily. 'God, but this makes depressing reading.'

She perched herself on the table edge and began to examine the books. Mike watched her. He enjoyed watching her.

'You've certainly covered some ground,' she said. '*Satanic Abuse* to *Nursery Crimes* and beyond.' She smiled at him. 'Any of it make sense?'

'Less and less,' he said, laughing rather bitterly.

Maria smiled, stroking the spine of the book she held with a long finger. Then she sat down beside him on the small sofa, kicked off her shoes and wriggled her toes with a deep sigh of satisfaction.

'It would help if I knew what you were looking for,' she said, 'then you might not have to ransack my bookcase to find it.'

Mike looked startled, then glanced about him at the mess he'd created – books on the table, on the floor. Scraps of paper with page numbers scrawled all over them. Strips of newspaper sticking out at all angles between the pages, marking references he thought he might have a use for.

'Sorry,' he apologized. Maria ignored him, closed her eyes and leaned back against the deep Chesterfield-style arm of the sofa, swinging her long legs up on to Mike's lap and clearly preparing to unwind.

'This is getting to you,' she said. 'This thing with Fletcher.' She opened her eyes and looked at him sharply, her dark eyes curious and more than a little anxious. 'Mike, do you have to push it this far? The case is closed, Fletcher's inside and from what I've heard of this Pearson character his new evidence is likely to be no more than wishful thinking and hot air.'

'And if it's not?' he asked. 'What if Fletcher wasn't bluffing? He talked about something very organized. Widespread.' He paused, gestured helplessly. 'He talked about kids being killed, Maria. About them being abused and tortured and their bodies dumped. Just like the boy we've found. I keep asking myself how many more are there? If Fletcher was telling the truth, how many other kids have there been raped and killed and dumped like this one?'

Mike looked at her, his eyes showing the strain and his mouth drawn into a tight line. 'I don't know how much truth there was in what Fletcher claimed,' he said. 'But I do know that I've got to find out.'

Maria nodded slowly. 'All right,' she said. 'But you should start with what we can tell for certain before you go dashing off chasing maybes. I mean,' she gestured towards the scattered books, 'how much do you really know about all this?'

Mike sighed and began, automatically, to massage her feet.

'To be honest, not nearly as much as I thought I did.' He gestured towards the books. 'I mean, when the Cleveland furore was at its height a few years back, this whole thing of sexual abuse became something everyone was talking about.' He laughed bitterly. 'I mean, it's like these things go in fashions. All the media hype, everyone that was anyone – or thought they were – having an opinion about it and, well, it seemed to me, anyway, that there was sweet FA they could agree on.' He shook his head. 'It was something you couldn't get away from.'

'And that bothered you?'

He gave her a wry smile. 'Yes, doctor,' he said, 'that bothered me.' He paused, trying to get his thoughts in focus. 'It wasn't just the thought of kids suffering that got to me. And it wasn't that I hadn't met up with this kind of thing before. I'd dealt with my share of rapes and sexual assaults and all the trauma that went with them.'

He paused again, aware that, maybe, he sounded glib and unfeeling. Maria continued to regard him, eyes thoughtful, noncommittal.

Mike stumbled on, feeling totally inept. 'It was the effect, the broader effect it was having on people. I mean people who had never given it much thought, beyond the notion that "interfering with kids" was wrong. Before Cleveland it wasn't something anyone talked about. Just another of those things that happened elsewhere. To other people.'

He could see her mouth begin to twitch, the corners dimpling. 'Go on,' she said.

He shrugged, suddenly very awkward. 'So many people I talked to, it's as though they suddenly felt the ground rules had changed.'

'In what way?'

He gave her a sideways glance, amused and a little disturbed at how easily she fell back into being Dr Maria Lucas even off duty.

Maria recognized the look. She laughed, eased her feet off his lap and got up, heading towards the bedroom. Mike followed her, then lounged on the edge of the bed watching contentedly while she changed into jeans and sweatshirt and dragged a comb through her short, tight curls.

'We'd got friends,' he said, 'with kids quite a bit older than Stevie. They must have been, oh, I don't know, about eight and ten at the time. Well, the parents were invited to the school to hear this talk given by one of our lot. I seem to remember they dragged in a fatherly-looking DC for the job. And they planned to show this film called . . . *Not Always Strangers*, or something like that. The school was trying to decide whether or not to show it to the kids.'

Maria glanced at him again. She was foraging in her sock drawer to find a matching pair. 'I remember the film,' she said, then frowned as though trying to recall it. 'Something about a neighbour who groped one of his kid's friends, wasn't it?'

Mike gave her a slightly startled look. It wasn't quite the phraseology he would have used, but, yes, it must be the same film.

'Well,' he said, 'these friends of ours, she'd got a part-time job. Cleaning or something, just a couple of hours a day. Jim would get home from work just before she left and take over with the kids till she got back. He'd let the two girls have their friends round to play and start getting dinner ready. You know. But not after seeing the film. After that, he was scared to have any of the other kids in the house unless his wife was there, and he wasn't the only one. Maggie told me about someone she worked with. He was suddenly scared to play with his own children, you know, the way fathers do, tickling and just generally fooling about. It seems he'd been watching a documentary or something on incest and that someone on the programme had pointed out just what a fine line there was between normal play and impropriety.'

'Impropriety!' Maria laughed, suddenly.

Mike scowled at her and stood up. 'I don't happen to think it's funny,' he said. 'I'm talking about something that can ruin a life for ever and you think it's godamned funny.'

He left the room, made his way to the kitchen and began to fill the kettle, shockingly aware of just how pompous he had sounded. Maria had laughed at his rather coy choice of words, he knew that. Not at his feelings or at those of the children involved.

The truth was, he still found it difficult to speak objectively about anything that involved children. He would try. Make serious attempts to distance himself, but each time the general came back to the specific. The specific became someone he knew, or might know, or could recognize and care for.

Grief about the world's children became grief about Stevie. A pain that was as raw now as when first inflicted.

He heard her enter the kitchen behind him. He carried on with his side of the conversation as though there had been no interruption, knowing that she would take her lead from him. For now.

'And then I ended up at this conference,' he said. 'Spent three or four hours looking at diagrams of where and how to recognize a child that had been abused. Watched a film of the kinds of therapy they were using and got lectured on the problems of leading the witness.'

'Pity it was so long ago,' Maria remarked. 'You could have had fun with false memory syndrome too.'

Mike turned and gave her a slight smile. 'And there was a video. These little kids playing with anatomically correct dolls.' He could feel his mouth curling with distaste and was uncomfortably aware of Maria's gaze.

'That bothered you a lot,' she said.

Mike nodded. 'Though I'd be hard pushed to tell you why. It just seemed so unreal. All so unrelated to what we were really doing. Just technical stuff. As though something like that could be pinned down and categorized.'

Maria grinned at him, the corners of her mouth twitching again. She said, her voice full of ironic tones, 'I get what you mean, Mike. It's the same all over. Make the paperwork so much easier if we could identify the IC1 sexual abuser or the IC3 would-be rapist.'

Mike sighed, began to make them coffee.

'But it doesn't work like that, does it?' Mike said. 'What one person can learn to cope with, even turn around and take strength from having survived, another person might end up topping themselves over.' He gestured irritably towards the other room. 'And those damned books didn't help. Half the so-called experts can't even decide what the facts are. There's some woman seeing Satan's hand in everything and some other guy talking about societal reforms and lowering the age of consent. And it's all nicely quantified and written up in neat technical language. What it doesn't tell is how the victims feel. What damage it does and how likely they are to be abusers themselves because of – What did they call it? – "dysfunctional emotional responses" or some other damned rubbish.'

Maria listened for a few minutes more as he railed

on. His anger at so many unrelated things spilling out. She knew better by now than to try to call a halt.

Finally, he seemed to run out of words, or at least out of breath. He paused, staring down into his coffee mug, a puzzled look on his face. The image of the sandy-haired boy lying in the mortuary floated into his mind.

'It matters to you,' she said. 'So you'll run it ragged till you get your answers.'

He looked up at her, surprised, as always, that she should be so accepting of him, of his obsessiveness.

'And as to understanding,' she went on, 'I don't think you need any books to tell you what grief is like. You take something from someone by force, they'll grieve for it. They'll dream about it and they'll wake up sweating like a pig, just the way you do, because they've just gone through it all over again.'

He stared at her, shocked for a moment that she should throw his own pain back at him. Surprised again that she should also be so right.

Tynan sighed contentedly. He took a drink and placed the glass down carefully, centring it deliberately upon the beer mat, then glanced about him as though seeing the pub for the first time. 'Doesn't change much, does it, this place?'

Andrews laughed. 'The Fisherman? No, it doesn't change, thank God. There was talk of installing a juke-box back in the sixties. Almost started a riot, it did. They've had the sense to leave it be ever since.' He paused, allowed his gaze to travel over the small, some-what elderly crowd packed into the public bar.

'Croft's a good man, John. I like what he did in the Ashmore case. Cares more about the job than the career and that's rare enough these days, either in his profession or in mine.'

'But?' John asked him.

'Who said there was a but?' Andrews smiled, then sighed. 'It's not a but, John, it's a worry. He'll stick with this thing till he's cracked it.'

'Figure you know that already.'

Andrews nodded. 'I don't like the smell of it, John. Not any of it. Fletcher's where he should be, and if you ask me Pearson should be cell mate with him. Thought so at the time, and I think so now. And that Mike Croft of yours is heading for a fall if he pushes this thing too far.' He paused, took another swallow of his pint.

'He'll not back down,' John said again, the pride evident in his voice.

Andrews smiled at him. 'Pity you and Grace never had kids of your own,' he said. Then laughed at John's startled look.

Andrews drained his glass, then got to his feet, preparing to leave.

'You know, of course, that there was talk about Superintendent Jaques?'

John shook his head. 'What kind of talk?' he asked.

'Oh,' Andrews frowned, 'nothing you could place bets on, John. Just talk. He and Fletcher knew each other socially and Fletcher made a lot of noise, demanding to see Jaques when he was first arrested.' He shrugged. 'Like I say, John. Nothing certain. Anyway, I'll be in touch. Just tell that boy of yours to watch his back.'

Ellie sat up suddenly and put her hand on her chest, feeling the rapid thudding of her heart.

It was months since the nightmares had woken her, but the events of the last few days had been so unsettling it was no wonder they should come back now.

The house was quiet.

Beside her, Rezah slept deeply. Across the room in the travel cot Farouzi grumbled in her sleep and turned over.

Dimly, through the wall, Ellie could hear her father-in-law snoring and there was just the faintest hum of late-night traffic to be heard as it raced swiftly along the main road, far enough away to be almost soothing.

Ellie lay down again, images still in freefall at the edges of her memory. She lay, staring at the ceiling, listening to the late-night sounds of the house, the faint creaks and moans of cooling timbers and settling floors.

Rezah felt warm beside her and his steady breathing invited sleep.

Ellie turned over on her side and settled back close to him. She knew what had brought the nightmare this time and with it the dread she had lived with for such a very long time.

It was what they had said about Eric Pearson. The things they had accused him of and, despite that policeman's claim that Pearson had never been charged with anything, Ellie knew that in her mind he would always carry with him the taint of possible guilt.

It was what they said that brought it back to her. That, and sleeping in a strange house, where the floorboards creaked just the way they had done in her parents' home.

Creaked when her father came up the stairs after her mother had gone out. Creaked just outside her bedroom door when he paused and knocked before coming in. And then creaked again as he crossed the room to where she lay in bed.

Ellie could feel her heart thumping, hear the echo of it as she pressed her ear closer to the pillow.

Cold sweat stood out all over her body, chilling her in spite of Rezah's warmth.

Ellie closed her eyes, but she could still see her father's face, feel his hands gripping her shoulders and his breath, hot against her cheek.

'It isn't me,' she whispered, keeping her voice low, making her words barely more than breath. 'It isn't me.' Just like, as a child, she had said over and over again in her head until, almost, she could believe in it.

'It wasn't me!' Screamed out loud at her mother, stony-faced and disbelieving, blaming Ellie for what the man she loved had done.

'It wasn't me,' Ellie whispered, angry now rather than afraid.

'None of it was me.'

Chapter Twenty-One

Tuesday late evening

It was the moment Mike had been both seeking and dreading.

'We've got the boy's parents,' Price told him, his voice cracking up slightly over the bad phone line.

'You sure?' Mike demanded.

'Well,' Price conceded, 'there's still the formal ID. Jaques wants you there. But they know about the sweatshirt. About the label being cut out and the green stitching on the neck, and he went missing at the right time for it to be him.'

'Shit!' Mike whispered. 'OK, OK. What time's the ID?'

'Soon as you can make it there, guv. They've driven down. He'd hitched all the way from Birmingham, guv. Daft kid. He used to come on holiday round here. I suppose he thought it was always going to be like that, like some long holiday.'

Mike could hear the tension in Price's voice even over the line.

'Half an hour,' he said. 'I'll be there in half an hour.' He paused for a moment, then asked, 'Do we have a name?'

'Ryan.' Price told him. 'Ryan Sanderson. Fourteen years old. Just fourteen fucking years old.'

*

Price stood next to Mr and Mrs Sanderson. Mike faced them across the body of their son.

Ryan lay in the little chapel close to the mortuary, swathed to the chin in a white sheet, his head was covered with another, leaving only his face and a curl or two of sandy hair visible.

'You're certain that this is your son?' Mike asked gently. But the woman's stricken face and soft moaning and the man's sudden pallor told him all he needed to know.

'Come on, love,' Price said. 'We'll get you some tea.' He began, gently, to coax them from the room, his arm slipping around the woman's shoulders.

Mike stood a moment longer looking down at the boy's pale face. White even against the whiter sheets.

'You got any kids?'

Mike looked up. Mr Sanderson had paused in the doorway and was staring at Mike with a mixture of anger and resentment in his eyes.

'Have you got any kids?' he asked again. "Cause if you have then you'll know about it. Know it isn't always easy. You know. They get out of hand now and then and . . . you know . . .' He paused, wiping his eyes with the heel of his hand, then straightening himself deliberately. 'He was never a bad kid, though. Not really. Not a bad kid.'

Mike stared back at him. I lost my son too, he wanted to say. I know what you're going through.

But he couldn't ever say that. Not to this man. Not to his wife. Not to anyone.

He sighed deeply and then moved around the body to stand with the other man close to the door.

'Your wife needs you now,' was the best he could manage.

Chapter Twenty-Two

Wednesday morning

Netisbrough Head was just over an hour's drive from divisional HQ in Norwich.

It had been a pleasant drive, the air cool and slightly damp from early morning rain and the sunlight still hazy and undecided.

By the time Mike and his sergeant reached Netisbrough, the wind had strengthened and changed direction. Now it veered from seaward and as the coast road climbed up on to the headland Mike could see rainclouds massing on the horizon.

Less than an hour, he guessed, and there would be rain. Sea rain, fast driven and falling straight and hard as stair rods, soaking anything it hit in seconds.

The grey light gave a mysterious look to the headland. There were stories about this place. Mike had yet to find any spot in the region that didn't have stories told about it. But this place, they said, had been the haunt of wreckers, the cove beyond the headland the grave of many ships and men.

Mike only half believed it. He still couldn't get it out of his head that wreckers were something born in Cornwall and had no rights being this far to the east.

The wrecks were easier to believe in. Much of the coast seemed to be shielded by sand bars and mud flats not so far beneath the surface that a ship couldn't be driven aground on them. Many, he knew, had been broken by the tides and half swept away long before the alarm was raised.

Price had been unusually silent on the way here. Mike had been left very much to his own musings.

Up ahead, the road veered sharply to the right, following the line of the cliff. For the merest instant, as they turned into the bend, there seemed to be only sea beneath them, a grey, churning ocean fifty feet below. Then they circled back towards the left and looked down on Netisbrough prison, sprawling like some five-armed octopus below them.

Mike experienced a moment of disappointment. The threatening, storm-laden day. The disturbing aspect of the cliff. The grey dimming of the light, all had built his expectation for something far more Gothic than this slouching example of all that was wrong with modern architecture.

'Copied a Yankee design,' Price said. It was the most coherent thing he'd contributed in the long drive.

'Oh?' Mike found that he was glad to break the silence.

'Yeah, some big southern state penitentiary.'

'Not Yankee, then.'

'Sir?'

'Southern state,' Mike explained patiently. 'Confederate, not Yankee.'

Price gave him a puzzled look. 'Same thing, isn't it?'

he asked. Then lapsed once more into a bilious-looking silence.

Mike left him to vegetate, concentrated instead on the view ahead of them.

It did have an American look to it, or at least the chain link topped with razor wire and the look-out towers spaced at equal intervals along its length reminded Mike of US penitentiaries he'd seen in films.

A closer look, as the side road they were now on began to run parallel to the fence, showed him that most of the towers were left unmanned, personnel replaced by cameras facing in towards the prison and out towards the road. But, then, Netisbrough was hardly high security. Setting aside the one secure wing, in which Fletcher was detained, the place was low risk, housing more on remand than anything else.

'Get your head together, Sergeant,' he said, pulling in at the gate and stopping the car at the gate-house.

Price awarded him a withering look. 'It's not just the head, sir,' he said. 'Think I got up with someone else's stomach this morning. It sure as hell don't feel like mine. I had a bit to drink after I left you last night,' he confessed.

Mike grinned at him, then wound the window further down and announced himself at the gate.

Fletcher was brought into the interview room about ten minutes after Mike and Sergeant Price had settled themselves there. He seemed none too pleased. He barely spoke after the first introductions and listened in silence as Mike played back to him tapes of his previous interviews.

Mike had ample time to take a good look at him, and found himself surprised by the ordinariness of the man.

It wasn't a new feeling. Irrational though it was, Mike had often found himself examining those he arrested in the half-expectation of seeing some sign; some physical clue to whatever went on inside.

Fletcher gave no more outward indication than most. He sat at the table, his head resting on one hand, face turned slightly away from the two policemen, watching the tape machine as though he too looked for visual clues.

Fletcher was beginning to show his age. Photographs Mike had seen taken only a couple of years before showed him as a man defying his fifty-plus years. Now he seemed to register all of them and more.

He looked fit enough, his body showing the hours Mike had been told Fletcher spent working out. His grey hair was thinning, receding from the forehead, and a bald patch, like a tonsure, was developing at the back of his head. He'd not, Mike noted, fallen into the trap of combing loose strands of hair across in an effort to hide it. Instead, his hair had been cropped short all over, adding to the monastic look.

His eyes, on the couple of occasions he had deigned to look at Mike, were light blue, intelligent.

He had given the impression of a man who summed things up very quickly, who had assessed Mike and his companion with a single swift look and decided they were beneath his attention.

Arrogant, Jaques had called him. A sentiment echoed that morning by the prison governor and one Mike felt inclined to be supportive of.

The tape ended and when Mike made no move, this time, to replace it, Fletcher turned to look at him.

'And?' he said, gesturing lightly towards the recorder.

'You made certain claims,' Mike said. 'Then you refused to ratify them. Why was that, Mr Fletcher?'

'Mr, is it?' Fletcher laughed bitterly. He reached out and picked up the cigarettes Mike had left on the table, shook one free and lit it, pocketed the rest.

'Words,' he said. 'Just so many words. What makes you sure they count for anything?'

Mike regarded him thoughtfully for a moment, then he said, slowly, 'You don't strike me as a man who wastes words, Mr Fletcher.'

Fletcher laughed out loud this time. 'Waste my words,' he said. 'That's a good one, Inspector, that really is.'

Mike felt, rather than saw, Sergeant Price shift irritably at that. He was clearly growing impatient with the whole charade. With Fletcher, sitting there like he'd not a care in the world; with his guv'nor for letting him lead the whole show. He said, 'Come off it, Fletcher. We've not come here to play your games.'

Mike cut him off. 'You've an appeal coming up. I can't believe your brief's not advised you to give a little.

All these claims you're making and not a damned thing to back them up.'

'You think your so-called friends give a shit about you, Fletcher? All they care about is their own hides,' Price put in. 'Stood by and let you take the rap, came out squeaky clean in every investigation we ran on them. And you. You sat there day after day, making claims that you could drown the whole damned lot of them, and what did you end up giving us? Not a thing. Not a fucking thing.'

Both Mike and Fletcher turned to look at the younger man. Fletcher continued to sit, regarding him steadily with his calm blue eyes, drawing deeply on the cigarette. Mike could sense that he was ruffled.

He took his lead from Price.

'Then there's this famous journal. Supposed to prove your point, wasn't it? Prove that you were just the pawn taking the blame for the bigger fish? Promised to protect you, had they? What went wrong, Mr Fletcher? Did things get too hot for them so they needed a sacrifice?'

He paused, then asked thoughtfully, 'Was that what Eric Pearson was meant to be?'

'That fool!' Fletcher's voice was contemptuous. 'He knew nothing. Just liked to think he did. Wanted to be an insider for once.' He shook his head as though unable to believe that anyone could be so stupid. 'A loser, that man. Right from the word go. Only thing he ever did was to father kids on that bitch of a wife of his.'

'A loser, Fletcher?' Price questioned. 'Funny, that, and here's me thinking it was you ended up inside.' He paused, turned innocent eyes on Mike. 'Seems we got it wrong, Inspector. Maybe that was Mr Fletcher's plan all along, get himself banged up.' He looked back at Fletcher, who was stubbing out his cigarette on the table edge. 'Got something good lined up for you when you come out, have they, these friends of yours? Be up for parole in maybe seven, eight more years.' He leaned over, thumped Fletcher lightly on the shoulder. 'Still be a young man, won't you? I mean, not quite ready for your pension.'

'Don't you touch me!'

Fletcher had risen to his feet, knocking over his chair, all semblance of calm gone from his features.

The transformation was swift and startling.

'Sit down, Mr Fletcher,' Mike said quietly.

'Something wrong, Fletcher?' Price jeered. 'Too old for you, am I?'

Fletcher leapt for him, his face scarlet with rage. Price dodged smoothly, putting the table between them. The two guards outside the door burst in. Mike rose to his feet and shouted for silence.

'Now sit down!'

Fletcher, reluctant, his breathing deep and heavy, picked up his chair and sat down hard on it.

Price made a show of straightening his tie, then seated himself again on the table edge. Mike waved the officers away.

'Now let's begin again,' he said. 'In your interview, March third 1994, you claimed to have been witness to a murder.'

'I wasn't a bloody witness. I never said I was fucking there.'

Mike raised an eyebrow. 'You led us to believe, Mr Fletcher, that you witnessed this event.'

Fletcher reached into his pocket for the cigarettes and lit another one.

'I never claimed to be a bloody witness,' he affirmed once more.

Mike nodded, as though weighing this up. 'Accessory, then,' he said, making an elaborate note on the pad he had on the table top.

Fletcher stared at him.

'Perhaps you'd like to tell me about it, then. This murder you may or may not have seen. I have all day, Mr Fletcher, and if that's not enough time I can come back again.'

Fletcher stared at him, then turned his gaze on some spot in the corner of the room, blew a long stream of smoke from between pursed lips.

'I have nothing to say,' he declared.

Mike ignored him.

'Then,' he said, 'when we've finished with that, we'll move on to the small matter of procurement, a few points I want to review. For my own satisfaction, you understand. A few minor things I'd like you to tell me about.'

He paused, noting the look of distaste that curled Fletcher's lips.

'In detail, of course, Mr Fletcher,' he said. 'In as much detail as you can give. We wouldn't want to miss anything, now would we?'

He settled back in his chair as though preparing for a long wait.

Fletcher gave him a long, cold look. 'Go to hell,' he said.

Price was gnawing on the side of his thumb, worrying at a bit of loose skin. He'd maintained a studied silence all the time they had taken to leave the prison compound and for the car to climb back up the long hill on to the cliff. Only when they had topped the rise and the view opened out before them once more did he speak.

'Any chance of stopping for some lunch, guv?'

Mike grinned. 'Hangover gone now, has it?' His grin broadened as he saw the offended look that swept across Price's features.

'Bound to be somewhere,' he said placatingly. Then, 'Well, what did you make of him?'

Price glanced at Mike, frowning slightly. 'I don't know,' he said. 'Likes to think he's cool. In control of things, but, you ask me, he's scared shitless about something.'

Mike nodded. His own impression had been similar. In the three hours they had spent with Fletcher the man had said very little. Had recovered from his outburst and settled for fielding Mike's questions. Fencing questions with questions with almost political skill. Or simply smoking, silently, staring into space as though Mike and the sergeant no longer existed for him.

Despite that, though, Mike was certain that their

presence had unnerved him. That Price's little jibe about rewards that might await Fletcher at the end of his sentence had, maybe, not been so far from the truth.

'Scared of what?' he asked. The question was rhetorical.

'His so-called friends, I suppose. But what I don't get, guv, is why all the half-hints and misinformation he fed to our lot if he wanted his friends to protect him? And, if he figured they'd sold him out, why not just drop them all in the shit for real instead of just creating bad feeling all round and generally queering his pitch both ends up?'

Mike laughed briefly and shrugged. 'Trying to keep both sides in play, I suppose,' he said. 'And in the end, he won neither.'

Mike frowned. And then there had been that comment made just before they left. Possibly the most fruitful thing to have come out of the entire morning: Northeast of Otley. Five miles. A turn off the main road on to a dirt track that led to a derelict farmhouse, the land owned now by one of the big frozen food combines and the house deserted.

Fletcher had talked about a well . . .

'I think we'll take a little detour on the way back,' he said. 'Via Otley. See if we can find that place he talked about.'

Price grinned and settled back more comfortably in his seat. 'Nice pub out that way, sir. Miller's Arms, serves hot food all day and a damned good pint.'

'Otley it is, then,' Mike nodded. 'Otley it is.'

*

Ellie had caught sight of Johanna Pearson walking between the aisles of frozen food and had hurried to the end of the delicatessen and out of view. It was a shock when she saw her again, this time walking straight towards her, pushing a trolley slowly between the rows of canned goods, her face a study of concentration.

Ellie began to move away. The last thing she wanted right now was some sort of confrontation with Johanna.

Then Johanna Pearson looked up. Her face registered recognition and, to Ellie's dismay, she began to walk towards her.

'Good morning, Ellie,' Johanna said.

'Er, good morning,' Ellie managed.

She glanced away, embarrassed, began to move on, but Johanna had hold of her arm.

'Please,' she said, 'don't rush away from me. I'd like to talk.'

Talk! Ellie stared, as though Johanna had suggested something incredible. She glanced around, suddenly afraid they might be seen, then squared her shoulders angrily.

'All right,' she said. 'But I really don't think we have anything to say to each other.'

'Are you afraid of me, Ellie?' Johanna asked her.

'Of course I'm not!' Ellie burst out, her voice carrying more anger than conviction.

Johanna nodded slowly. 'Come, then,' she said, and led the way towards the supermarket restaurant.

*

'How can you go on living with him, knowing what he did?' asked Ellie, once they were seated at a table.

'He didn't do it.' Johanna paused and glared at her. 'I know Eric. We grew up together, he was the first and only man I ever wanted. Eric did nothing.'

She leaned across the table and seized Ellie's hand. 'Help me, Ellie. You're well liked. Well respected, and people will listen to you. Help me to tell people that they're wrong about Eric.'

Ellie gazed back at her. 'I can't,' she managed to whisper. 'I can't do anything, Johanna. You must see that.' She shook her head vehemently. 'I don't have any influence, Johanna. We just want to live quietly. Just get on with our lives.'

'And you think I don't? You think I like what's happening to my marriage? To my children?'

'No! No, of course I don't, but I don't see . . .'

Johanna rose to leave, apparently having said all she planned to say. Then she turned back to look at Ellie.

'I know you, Eleanor Masouk. You might remember that. I saw you in the public gallery at your father's trial.' She paused, noticing Ellie's pallor. The blood draining even from her lips.

'Eric pointed you out to me,' she went on. 'We sat through the whole thing, Eric and I. The whole thing. I remember, I even felt sorry for you.'

Ellie stared at Johanna's back as she walked away, feeling the life she had built over the last few years crashing about her.

Wednesday 1 p.m.

Jaques had come to hate the telephone. He avoided taking calls, avoided answering it himself, created excuses until he was certain that others were noticing his distaste and wondering about it.

This time, the phone was ringing as he walked through the front door. He called out to his wife, hoping that she would get to it first, but she shouted back to him, 'Get that for me, will you? I'm seeing to the oven.'

Jaques stood for three more rings, hoping that whoever it was would ring off, or that his wife had the answerphone set.

Instinctively, he knew who it was. Fear and disgust coiled themselves in the pit of his stomach and bit hard.

'Did you hear me, love? Can you get that?' his wife called to him again.

Angrily, Jaques snatched at the receiver. 'Yes!'

'You took your time.'

'Just say what you have to say and piss off.'

'Language, Jaques. And after you let us down so badly.'

'I did what I could.'

'Did you, Jaques? Did you really? But they found it, and now they've got his face splashed all over the TV and papers. You're getting sloppy.'

'Go to hell.'

He slammed the phone back down on to its cradle and stood staring at it. Almost at once it began to ring again.

'I heard that DI Croft went out to see Fletcher this morning.'

'What about it?'

'You could have blocked it. Delayed it at least.'

'And arouse his suspicions! He's no fool.'

'Which is why he shouldn't be allowed access to Fletcher.'

There was a brief pause, then the voice said, 'My friends tell me that Fletcher hasn't been himself at all since the visit. That he's having an attack of conscience, maybe.'

'He won't talk,' Jaques said with more conviction than he felt.

'You'd better hope he doesn't, for your sake and for his. And for your Inspector Croft.'

Jaques' wife had come through from the kitchen. She stood in the doorway, regarding his obvious distress.

Jaques took a deep breath and tried to regain some composure.

'I'll speak with you later,' he said. 'We'll sort the whole thing out then.'

He replaced the phone gently and forced a smile to his lips.

'Work,' he said. 'Only just come off bloody duty for a quick lunch and they still won't let me be.'

Chapter Twenty-Three

There was more heat in the day than Mike had expected. The rain had come and gone while they had been at Netisbrough and by the time the two of them reached Otley the sun had burned the rest of the cloud away, leaving only blue heat and the damp rich smell of wet greenness flooding into the car through the open windows.

The farm had taken time to find, set back off a side road and surrounded by well-grown trees and unpruned hedges.

Mike pulled the car to a stop in what had once been the back yard of the house. The warm damp hit him as he got out of the car. The air was very still. The scent of earth, rotting wood, and the last of the flowers left in the overgrown beds rose up around them.

'Shame to see places like this when there are folks needing homes,' Price said unexpectedly. 'I mean to say, guv, the house looks sound enough, seems stupid not to sell it or at least rent it out.'

Mike nodded thoughtfully. He crossed the yard and pushed his way through the dense undergrowth, making for the line of broken-down fencing just visible behind the mass of nettles and rambling roses.

He swore softly as the thorns bit through his shirt

sleeves, and brushed irritably at the cuckoo spit and spilt pollen that clung to his clothes.

Beyond the fence were flat fields. Broad swathes of land, densely planted. The same on the other side – they'd seen that driving up – and probably out at the back, too. Featureless flat lands, made for the use of combines and mass market needs, and here, this little house and its garden, a lost island in the middle of it all. Neglected and left to rot.

Mike glanced around him at the ragged undergrowth. He could make out the lines of borders and narrow pathways, just wide enough to give access to the beds.

If there was a well here, where would it be? Close to the house?

He went back to where Price was pacing about the yard, poking at things with a long garden cane he'd found and glancing about him with an air of dissatisfied curiosity.

'A well,' Mike asked him. 'Where would they dig a well in a place like this?'

'You're asking me? Christ, guv, where I come from we've got hot and cold running and full gas central heating.'

Mike laughed. 'So, take a guess.'

'Be close to the house,' Price said, looking around. 'You'd not want to be carrying water far.'

'But there's nothing in the yard . . . What's that?' He pointed to the small outbuilding at the side of the house.

'Outside loo, one of the old kind with a hole in the bench and a bucket underneath.' He grinned at Mike's look of distaste. 'It took a while to get indoor plumbing round here. I had an aunt out at Otley, they only got theirs in the mid-seventies. Till then it was the loo seat, the bucket and the dilly cart.'

'The what?'

Price grinned again. 'Dilly cart, we used to call it. Came round to collect the . . . er . . . waste once a week or so. I remember when I was a kid and used to stay with her. It stank to high heaven when the dilly cart came.' He laughed, shaking his head and clearly remembering with the perverse pleasure that comes with knowing something is long gone. 'It's not likely the well would be close to the outhouse, is it?'

He had a point.

Mike glanced around once more but was reluctant to investigate further. Already, in his mind, this was scenes of crime territory. He wasn't happy about poking around like some half-trained flatfoot.

'Well, sir?' Price asked him, clearly bored now and ready to eat.

'Lunch,' Mike said, to Price's evident relief. 'That place you were telling me about. Then we'll get back to base, talk to Jaques and see if we can get some men out here.'

Price nodded, then grinned wryly. 'Nice, that,' he said. 'Spot of gardening on a hot summer afternoon.'

'I'll make sure they bring the deck chairs,' Mike said, mirthlessly.

Wednesday 10 p.m.

Tynan shrugged, Mike could hear it over the phone. 'I don't know, Mike, he didn't seem to want to go in for specifics, just told you to watch your back. And he doesn't like Superintendent Jaques too much either. Seems he was a friend of Fletcher's.'

'Fletcher had a lot of friends, John. Bad judgement doesn't make them all guilty.' He paused, taking this new information on board.

'Well, I'll see you Friday, then,' Tynan said. 'Give my love to my favourite lady, will you, Mike?'

'Will do, John. See you soon.'

He put down the telephone and crossed to where Maria sat on the small sofa. 'John sends his love,' he said.

She smiled. 'He tell you what Andrews said to him?'

Mike raised an eyebrow. 'Way ahead of me again, are you?'

She laughed. 'He called earlier, wanted to know if he'd catch you here tonight'.

He nodded, settled back, contented and very tired. The wall clock with its slow-ticking pendulum told him it was a little after ten, but it felt much later. Not that it had been a hard day; it just felt as though it had been a long one. His prolonged interview with Jaques, late this afternoon, reporting on what Fletcher had and had not told him, had just added to his sense of frustration.

'So, Jaques wouldn't play?' Maria asked him, seeming to read his thoughts as she so often did.

Mike shook his head. 'He's got a point, of course,' he said, trying to be generous. 'It's off our patch, would require the co-operation of the Otley division and pull men we really can't spare.' He shrugged wearily. 'And Fletcher's track record really doesn't encourage anyone to take him seriously. It could just as easily be another of his games.'

'But you don't think so?'

'No, not this time. It was strange, but he behaved as though it was almost dragged from him. No, I'm not sure what I mean either.' He frowned, trying to get a handle on things. 'He spent the entire time we were there *not* telling us anything, waited until we'd practically made it out of the door before he told us about the house.'

It had been odd, that, the way Fletcher had spoken so hurriedly, so urgently, as though afraid that someone else should hear. Then clammed up again, simply demanded to be taken back to his cell.

'Yes,' Mike said again, 'I believe there's something in what Fletcher said, and I think we should at least look for that bloody well. Got to admit, though, it would make a damned good place to hide a body.'

Maria laughed. 'So, now what? You work on Jaques?'

'I work on Jaques.'

The telephone rang again, its sound shrill and insistent, cutting through the peace of the room. Mike knew, even before Maria answered it, that it was work.

'Jaques,' she mouthed at him, handing him the receiver.

Mike took the phone and listened in silence. He replaced it on its rest with the exaggerated care typical when something troubled him. When he turned back to Maria, his face was strained.

'You've got to go?' she asked him.

He nodded. 'Out to Netisbrough,' he said. 'It's Fletcher. They found him hanging in his cell about an hour ago. The governor wants to know what I said to him this morning that made him want to kill himself.'

Chapter Twenty-Four

Wednesday midnight

The coast road out to Netisbrough was unlit and almost deserted this late at night. It was close to midnight by the time Mike reached the high cliff overlooking the prison compound now laid out below him, its outline drawn in lights like some elaborate funfair ride.

Fifteen minutes later he was standing beside Jaques and his superior, Chief Superintendent Charles, in what had been Fletcher's cell.

There was little in the tiny room to give any sense of what had gone on there. Neatly made top bunk, bottom one unoccupied, shaving gear, soap and other toilet articles on the top one of two shelves, books and a pad of writing paper, a couple of pens on the lower one. Nothing pinned to the walls, nothing visible that wasn't, clearly, in its designated place. An environment already made impersonal by its very nature, made all the more so by the lack of input from its inhabitant. By the apparent lack of desire to make any kind of mark.

It reminded Mike of the Pearsons' living room. That same sense of impermanence, of someone just passing through. That might have been accountable in the Pearsons' case, moving on so many times in a few short years. But Fletcher was likely to have been here for a long time. Tied into a system that did little to accommodate personal difference. In such circumstances, most people would do anything just to delineate their territory, state their sense of self.

Here, there was nothing.

He walked over to the far wall, turned, looked at the top bunk. A strip of cloth still hung from the end of the bed, cut ragged by the penknife that had been used to free Fletcher's body. He moved over to the bed, comparing its height with his own. Fletcher had been almost as tall, an inch shorter than Mike maybe.

'He did it from here?'

The puzzlement must have shown in his voice. Jaques said, 'Seems he was determined. Must have leaned into the noose till it pulled tight, then, as he lost consciousness, his weight would have done the rest.'

'Is that possible?'

'Anything's possible, Mike,' Jaques snorted irritably. 'If you're desperate enough.'

'You looking for something else, Croft?'

Mike glanced over at the speaker. It was the first time Chief Superintendent Charles had spoken to him since he had entered the cell.

'I don't know, sir. It just doesn't look right. I would have said that Fletcher was worried about something when we spoke to him, but not suicidal. No, definitely not that.'

Charles shook his head. 'That's what the governor keeps saying,' he commented. 'Certainly he wasn't considered high risk. He wasn't on the potential list.'

He paused, thoughtfully, then went on. 'You're right,

though, something's not kosher.' He glanced around the room, taking in its furnishings and its few personal oddments as Mike had done earlier. 'The way he was found, Mike, it puts a little doubt on the suicide angle.'

'Oh?'

'Hmm. Could have been an accident. Could be something else.'

'An accident?' Mike asked.

Jaques laughed but there was no humour in it. Charles was already out of the door. Jaques followed him. It was left to Price, standing on the landing, leaning idly against the safety rail, to explain. He grinned at Mike and told him in an undertone, 'Seems they found him with his pants round his ankles and his dick hanging out, guv.' Mike gave him a sharp look. Price continued, relishing the details. 'I've heard tell, that it, er, increases the sensations, guv. Gives you a real high. Adrenaline rush or something, being that close to copping it. Kind of —'

Mike silenced him with a gesture. 'OK,' he said. 'I get the picture.'

'They figure maybe he got a bit too excited, got himself so wound up he didn't realize how far gone he was.' Price was unwilling to be put off.

Mike nodded again. 'I got your drift the first time.'

They were following the senior officers down the stairs now, their feet ringing on the metal steps. It appeared that an interview with the prison governor was next on the list. Mike was not relishing the prospect. Price's thoughts were clearly running the same track.

'Bit of a naff deal, though, isn't it, guv? Not a peep out of him in all this time. Model prisoner, they said he was. Then the day we come to see him, this happens.'

He sounded so affronted that Mike had to smile. He nodded thoughtfully. 'You'd rather he'd waited a few days, would you, Sergeant? Just to keep the records straight?'

Price frowned and looked across at Mike, his lips parted ready for protest, then he saw Mike's wry smile and grinned in return.

'Got to admit, sir,' he said, 'it is bloody lousy timing.'

'And this farmhouse. You say the two of you went out there today?' Charles asked.

Mike nodded. 'I reported back to Superintendent Jaques. Asked about the possibility of ordering a full search.'

'It's not on our patch and we don't have the manpower,' Jaques put in quickly. 'To get something like that done, on the vague say-so of someone we know to be a pathological liar. Well, sir, it seemed not to be worth the effort at the time.'

Mike frowned. 'I wouldn't have called Fletcher a liar, sir,' he said. 'It was more that he wouldn't back his statements up than that we found them to be falsehoods. And surely, sir, the finding of Ryan Sanderson's body puts something of a different complexion on things.'

Charles nodded slowly. 'Well,' he said, 'this afternoon I would probably have agreed with you, Jaques. We're under-resourced and heading over budget as it is. But in the light of what's happened, both with the Sanderson boy and now with Fletcher . . .'

'If we could find the well, sir,' Price put in, 'we'd have some idea of whether or not there's truth in it. No well, no go, and it's likely to be close to the house. Probably wouldn't take that much finding. And it might make the difference, sir, between Ryan Sanderson being one random killing and something one hell of a lot more serious.'

Charles nodded thoughtfully. 'I agree,' he said. Then, 'Jaques, I want a preliminary search made of the house and the immediate surroundings. If the well is there, then I want that searched, see what we turn up. Then we'll review the situation.'

Jaques nodded. 'Yes, sir,' but he was clearly unhappy. Having cast the prospect off as a wild goose chase, he was reluctant, now, to take it on board again.

'And do I put it out as suicide or accident? Either way, it reflects badly on everyone.'

Charles turned his attention back to the governor, who had put the question. He sat behind his desk looking weary and disconsolate.

'We wait for the path reports to come in,' he said. 'No point in jumping the gun.'

'What have you told the next of kin?' Mike asked quietly, his sympathy going out to whoever had ended up with that job.

'There's no one close,' Charles said. 'His wife left him five years ago and he's estranged from his brother.

The parents are dead. The brother's been told it looks like suicide.' He shrugged. 'Under the circumstances, it seemed kinder.'

Mike nodded.

'There's a daughter,' Charles went on. 'We're trying to get an address.'

Charles turned his attention back to the governor and returned to discussing the best way to present Fletcher's death to the media. Mike stared down at his feet, slumping back in his chair and gazing thoughtfully at the scuffed toes of his old brown shoes.

He shifted uncomfortably. The chair in which he sat was not made for slouching. Wood, with low curving arms. It looked like a refugee from a dining set, this one the carver, wheel backed and with a hard seat. He sat up straighter and gazed, instead, at the well-worn, dark-grey carpet.

What had been going through Fletcher's mind that morning?

Mike didn't believe for one instant that Fletcher had lied about the farm, about the bodies he swore were concealed there. Mike wished he could believe that Fletcher was, as Jaques had accused him, a pathological liar, but it didn't fit.

And if he wasn't lying – if there was some measure of truth in his hastily uttered, swiftly regretted words that day – then what else could be truth? How many more deaths had there been?

Mike sighed heavily and glanced about him.

Jaques, Charles and the governor were still discussing

the politics of events. Drafting a statement. Price sat listening, clearly bored, his fingers steepled together in front of his face as though framing a shot.

The room was painted a depressing pale green. Heavy curtains of a darker shade hid the windows. Filing cabinet, desk, small side table decked out with coffee mugs, milk and sugar on a brushed aluminium tray. Bookshelves, a couple of certificates in a dark corner and three cricketing prints on the wall opposite the door.

The usual jumble of paper and pens, in-trays and envelopes arranged across the desk and a letter opener, made of bone, which the governor played with absent-mindedly as he talked.

Mike finished his inventory and went back to staring at his feet, legs stretched out in front of him.

In his mind he went once more through the items in the cell: bunk to the left of the door, chair just beside it; small table across in the far corner; two shelves above it; shaving gear, toilet things, books, writing pad, pens.

What books? There were two that Mike had taken note of, spines facing towards the room, lying on their sides. A Western novel and a D.H Lawrence, *The White Peacock*.

And the writing things.

'Did he send many letters?' Mike asked suddenly.

The others turned back to him.

'I can find out,' the governor told him. 'Important, is it?'

Mike shrugged, noncommittal. He could feel Jaques'

eyes on him, narrowed with suspicion, trying to discern the direction of Mike's thinking.

'And there was no note,' he said, thinking aloud.

'No, I've already told you that.'

'The notepad, on the shelf,' Mike asked. 'Was that checked?'

''Course it bloody was,' Jaques said irritably. 'Nothing on it.' Then he frowned. 'What are you getting at, Mike?'

Mike shook his head. 'I'm not sure.'

'Well,' Charles said, 'it wouldn't hurt to have the notepad sent down to forensics, run it through an electrostatic test.'

Mike nodded.

'You think there *was* a note?'

'I'm not convinced it was suicide, sir.'

'Then, what? Accident?'

Mike hesitated, unsure that he wanted to commit himself. Then, 'No. I'm not convinced of that either.'

Charles gave him a hard look. 'It's a possibility we have to consider,' he said slowly. 'But if you think someone helped Fletcher on his way, why look for a suicide note?'

'I'm not, sir. Not exactly.' He paused, feeling his way forward. 'It crossed my mind,' he said, 'that Fletcher might have had second thoughts about what he told us. Or that he might use having told us something to put pressure on one of his so-called friends on the outside.'

'And that someone in here saw him writing it and knew he'd told you something?' Charles finished for him.

Mike nodded slowly, not certain that was what he meant exactly, but it would do for starters.

The governor was frowning. 'That's a serious charge, Inspector.'

'But not beyond the realms . . .' Charles added.

'No. Regretfully, it's not.'

Charles rubbed the side of his nose thoughtfully, shifting his glasses and massaging where they had pinched the skin.

'OK,' he said. 'Have the notebook shipped off to documents, have them run the ESDA. Then tomorrow I want that farmhouse looked at.'

He got to his feet quickly, as though suddenly impatient with the whole thing.

'Meantime,' he added, 'I suggest we all get off home and try and catch some sleep.'

Chapter Twenty-Five

Thursday morning

Eric Pearson heard of Fletcher's death on the local radio news. He heard it over breakfast, the voice of the reader only just cutting through the noise of his wife and children, all talking at once as Johanna served breakfast and poured tea.

Fletcher was dead.

At first the thought came alone; the shock of it driving everything else from his mind.

Then the companion to it, driving hot upon its heels and taking over.

There would be no appeal. Fletcher was dead. The appeal was no longer required.

Eric Pearson's evidence would not be heard in court.

The overwhelming sense of anger, of failure, was more than Eric could comprehend. Almost more than he could bear.

Fletcher was dead and it was all over.

Across the table Johanna gazed at him curiously. She had been too intent on seeing to the needs of her brood to take much notice of what the man on the news had said.

'Fletcher's dead,' he told her. 'The news . . .'

He couldn't continue, the words stuck in his throat. Johanna got to her feet, her eyes fixed on his face, body tense. Then, slowly, he saw her begin to relax. Her shoulders and back unbend as though a weight had been lifted from them. He saw relief in her eyes. A glint of hope appeared that had not been there in such a long time.

'Then it's over,' she said softly. 'We can forget all of this, Eric. Forget the court case and that damned journal and get on with our lives again.'

Pearson glared at his wife. The muscles of his jaw tightened. 'Over!' he whispered. 'You think it's over! No, woman, it's not over. I'll have my say either in the court or out of it. I'll not settle until I have.'

He was on his feet now, heading towards the door. The children had fallen silent, surprised by the novel sight of their parents arguing like this.

'Why?' Johanna demanded. 'Why must you go on like this? We could make a new life here, or if not here some other place where no one knows us and we can begin again. I'm tired, Eric. Tired of always being on the outside. Of having no friends, no neighbours, no one to turn to. Of having to be suspicious of everyone who comes near the house.'

Eric turned on her, his body shaking with anger. 'You think you could make friends round here?' he demanded. 'Here? Among the stone-throwing louts and foulmouthed vandals we've met so far? Is that who you want friendship from? Those, those ... nothing people who live round here? Is that who you want our children mixing with?'

Johanna stared at him, stunned and angry.

'No,' she said softly, 'that's not what I want, Eric. I just want an ordinary life in an ordinary street, somewhere I can let my children play outside without being afraid for them all the time.'

'And you think you'll find that somewhere like this?' He shook his head. 'You're crazy if you do, Johanna.'

He took a step towards her, quiet now, but all the more menacing. 'There's me and there's our children, Johanna. We're the only ones you can depend on; the only ones you need.' He seemed to soften suddenly, reached out and patted her arm.

'We must see justice done,' he said quietly. 'Fletcher may be dead, but there are still those whom God and the law have not yet punished and it's in our hands.'

Then he left, pausing only to take his jacket from the peg in the hall.

Johanna sat down once more. The momentary flood of relief had given way to case-hardened despair.

'Eat your breakfast, loves,' she said, her words automatic.

Maybe Eric was right, she thought. Things were never going to be simple, never peaceful until this thing had run its course. And maybe she was being selfish. After all, not being charged with something was not the same as being judged innocent. And it was right that Eric should want this thing brought out into the open, want his innocence confirmed.

She sighed. But these last years had been so hard.

'Eat up,' she said again, her voice artificially bright. But she sighed inwardly. Dear Lord, she thought, you didn't tell me any lies when you said that this path was rough.

Mike and his team had been at the farmhouse early, the dew still heavy on overgrown foliage.

He watched as the four men he'd been assigned began to cut back the dense undergrowth closest to the house.

It took the joint efforts of both himself and Price to force the door open on its rusted hinges. Disturbed dust rose to meet them. Upstairs were three rooms. The end of the largest had been partitioned off and converted into a tiny bathroom.

Downstairs, two rooms and a small kitchen. The front door opened straight into the main living room. Built-in cupboards both upstairs and down. Wooden floors on both levels. A layer of dust and cobwebs, which looked as though it had spent years settling, covered everything. Mike glanced around the last room.

'Doesn't look like anyone's been in here since the last tenants,' Price commented.

Mike nodded. The house could wait. 'Let's get back outside,' he said.

The day had warmed up considerably and the last of the dew burnt away. Mike was amazed at the transformation. Tall plants, hacked down and raked aside. The full line of the wooden fence exposed. The shape of the once-neat beds now clearly marked and the heavy scent of damp herbs filling the air.

He and Price began to cross the yard when a shout

accompanied by a loud crack drew them round to the side of the house.

'What the—!'

They arrived in time to see two officers pulling one of their colleagues to his feet.

'You've found it?'

The man grinned. 'Damned near fell into it, guv. Watch your step, sir.'

Mike moved closer. The well was camouflaged by the undergrowth and the officer hadn't seen the wooden cover, green with slime and partly rotted, until he'd put his foot on it and almost fallen through.

He traced the edge of the wooden cover with his fingers. Overgrown and half rotten it might be, but the edge was clear, his fingers able to slide beneath the lip all around, and when he pulled gently he could lift it free.

He carefully eased the broken wood aside and peered down into the hole. He could see nothing but blackness.

'So he wasn't feeding us a line,' Price said, the expression in his voice somewhere between excitement and awe.

Mike looked up at him. 'And if he didn't lie to us about this . . .'

Andrews' call came late afternoon. Mike had been back at the office from midday, leaving Price to co-ordinate with SOCO. There was nothing much he could do, bar get under people's feet, so he'd come back and tried to clear some of the stuff cluttering up his in-tray.

It seemed to Mike that he spent more time these days shuffling paper than he did out on the streets trying to solve crime.

Andrews' call was a welcome break.

'I had a visit,' Andrews told him, 'from a mutual acquaintance.'

'Pearson?' Mike guessed.

'The very man.'

'And our friend wanted?'

'Mostly someone to shout at, I think. He did plenty of that. Rather narked with Fletcher, he was. Seemed to think Fletcher had let him down in some way, killing himself and all.'

'Don't tell me,' Mike said. 'He's mad about the appeal not going ahead.'

'That, and other things. The truth is, I'm inclined to think he's just plain mad.'

Mike laughed.

'He brought something with him,' Andrews went on. 'Pages from this journal Simon Blake is supposed to have written, implicating Fletcher and others he was supposed to be involved with.'

Pages from the journal. Mike was intrigued. 'He wants you to publish it?'

'If he does, he's on a loser. Paper like the *Chronicle* doesn't have the funds to fight the libel case we'd end up with. Anyway, this thing's just a photocopy and JP Blake died of a heart attack more than a year ago.'

'You know Pearson claims that Fletcher gave the journal to him?'

'Yes,' Andrews said. 'Supposed to be insurance for Fletcher. He couldn't be sent down without implicating the rest. So, I ask myself, why wasn't it produced at the trial? Why wait till the appeal?'

'The original was burned before the trial. A fire in the solicitor's office. You remember that?'

'Hmm.' Andrews said. 'So why not produce the copy then? Surely it would have had a better chance of being judged admissible evidence then than now?'

'I don't know,' Mike told him. 'The journal was mentioned during the CPS assessment and so was the photocopy, but there were doubts about either being genuine. The author of the journal was a highly respected JP and it was known he probably didn't have too much longer to live. His heart had been very bad for a long time, from what I can gather.' He laughed briefly. 'And I'm not sure any of us could fathom Fletcher's motives for half of what he did.'

'Meet me,' Andrews said. 'Say about eight o clock, I'll be tied up till then.'

'Suits me fine,' Mike told him.

He glanced up as the office door opened. Jaques stuck his head round, saw Mike talking and came in quietly. Sat down.

'At eight, then.' Mike confirmed. He listened carefully while Andrews gave him the name of a pub he thought would be a good place. Directions for getting there. Mike scribbled them down, then rang off.

'Just came to tell you,' Jaques said. 'They've lowered some poor sucker down that well of yours. There's about a foot and a half of mud in the bottom there. It could take us days to clean it out.'

Unaccountably, Mike felt disappointed. He'd hoped for something sooner. But that, so often, was the way of things.

For several minutes Jaques stood looking at the telephone, twisting the ring round and round on his finger. Then he picked up the receiver and dialled.

'Yes, yes,' he said in response to the impatient reception from the man on the end of the line. 'I know it's not the time and place but you wanted to know when he'd be alone. Well, I've got a when and a where, but for God's sake be discreet.' He took a deep breath, then gave the location of Mike's meeting with Andrews. 'He'll come in on the Fernley Road. That's the way he's been told to go.' Jaques hesitated for a moment, then went on. 'But look, he knows nothing.'

'Yet,' the voice argued, 'he knows enough to go on digging. Knew enough to provoke Fletcher into spilling his guts. He'd been writing the whole bloody thing down when my people found him, all ready to give to his brief. And take it from me, my friend. We go down, you won't be far behind us.'

Jaques' hand was shaking when he replaced the receiver. How had he got into this? It had started so simply. So stupidly. A few photographs. A rather indiscreet episode with a girl who knew what she wanted even if the law told her she didn't. Somehow it had all gone downhill from there. First he'd been afraid of losing his job and destroying his marriage. That had kept him silent – and, God knows, he told himself, I truly love my wife. Then he'd got in way too deep.

The first one had wanted it. Wanted it as much as he had . . . But then there had been the others.

Jaques closed his eyes trying not to remember.

At any point, early on, he could have backed out. Faced the scandal and walked away with some part of his life intact.

But he didn't have the courage then. Couldn't face the blame, the loss, everything that would have gone with it.

And it had been so easy with Fletcher. Supply had been so easy . . . He wiped the palms of his hands across his face.

No more of this. He could take no more. He had to find a way out and he had to find it soon.

It was well after eight by the time Mike neared the pub Andrews had specified. The last half-mile or so took him along a narrow lane overhung by tall, mature trees, their shadows heightening the twilight.

He halted the car at the junction at the end of the lane, checking Andrews' instructions. Glancing to the left, he smiled, seeing the pub sign at the next bend in the road.

He was about to slip the gears and make the turn when the sudden roar of a car engine, coming up fast behind him, distracted his attention.

'What the —!'

The car screamed by him and swept away to his right, its occupants, three youths, shouting from the windows. An empty lager can thrown from the window bounced off the bonnet of his car.

Mike cursed, automatically taking note of the make, blue Sierra, and registration, in half a mind to give chase. He dismissed the idea as soon as it occurred to him. There'd be a phone at the pub – he could call control from there and report it.

He shifted the car into first and pulled out, watching the pub come into view, sandstone and flint, low, gabled roof. A small garden off to the side with swings for the kids.

Nice, he thought. Quiet, out of the way and pleasant. A good place to meet.

There were no parking spaces in the car park, so Mike pulled the car on to the verge opposite the pub. Another car was drawn up on the grass a little further along.

Andrews? He hoped the journalist had not grown tired of waiting.

The evening air was sweet and warm as he got out of the car. Idyllic English summer, he thought – singing birds and blue skies, greying with the twilight, the distant sound of cows mooing. Maria said he was a closet romantic; on evenings like this he figured she was right.

He locked the car, his mind wandering distractedly over the events of the day and the prospect of a cool beer. Dimly, he could hear the sound of a car engine. He reminded himself to report the car that had passed him at the junction. He glanced sideways, to his right, as the engine noise grew louder, then stepped back swiftly as the same car came into view once more.

'Jesus!'

Mike stepped back further on to the verge. The car sped faster towards him. There was a brief moment of disbelief before it hit, sending him reeling backwards, somersaulting into his own vehicle. He heard the metallic clash as the blue Sierra gave his car a glancing blow. Then a sharp explosive pain in the centre of his back as he made contact with the metal.

Blackness pooled in across his mind as the dimming sound of the engine drifted out.

Then nothing. Mike was unconscious even before he hit the ground.

Chapter Twenty-Six

Friday morning

It was so hard to focus. When he opened his eyes the light seemed too bright. Images, swirling just out of reach.

And he had what felt like the biggest hangover life had ever created.

'Mike.'

He could hear the voice, realized now that he had heard it before, calling his name, but couldn't quite figure out where it had come from.

'Mike.'

This time he opened his eyes again. Patterns of light and colour swirled in front of them, slowly coalesced.

'Maria?'

He felt her take his hand. 'You're going to be all right,' she told him.

He could hear John now, as well, somewhere off stage. Hear the voice, but not the words.

He made a supreme effort to squeeze Maria's fingers. Wasn't certain that he managed it. Then everything faded out once more.

Next time Mike woke his eyes could focus. It still hurt like hell to turn his head even a fraction, but he had the vague memory of things being much worse.

He inched his aching head sideways to look at the figure by the bedside. Maria sat in a high-backed hospital chair, her head lolling against a balled-up jumper she'd wedged against her shoulder.

He lay watching her for several minutes, trying to figure out where he was and why. Hospital, he decided. The smell alone would have told him that. The why part caused him more problems.

He had a dim memory of an engine, a car engine, the sound rushing towards him. Then Maria woke and looked at him and he stopped trying to fathom it out; concentrated on trying to smile.

She took his hand again. 'Mike.' She sounded relieved.

'You been here all the time?' he asked her. His voice sounded croaky, as though he'd not used it in a long time.

Maria smiled at him, the relief on her face clear this time.

'I've been here. So has John for most of it.'

'John?' Her words hadn't quite sunk in. He found himself looking around for the older man.

'He's not here right now. Gone to have lunch with Tom Andrews.'

'Andrews?'

Maria waited for a moment. 'The journalist you were supposed to be meeting,' she said, filling in the gap that yawned in his memory.

'Andrews. Yes.'

Mike concentrated very hard, or as hard as the pain

in his head would allow. Andrews. Andrews called him, arranged a meeting. He'd driven out there.

'The car.' He moved sharply, instantly regretted it. 'God! My head.'

'Bad concussion.'

'The car,' he repeated. 'Blue Sierra. I remember the licence number.'

Maria smiled. 'It's all right,' she said. 'We know all about the car.'

Mike closed his eyes. 'How long have I been here?'

'Since last night. It's almost midday.'

He absorbed that slowly. Last night. The car, hitting him. That flash of pain, then nothing.

'Concussion?' he asked.

Eyes still closed, he felt Maria nod. 'That and three broken ribs – they'll be the next to start hurting – a broken wrist and leg – simple fracture, five inches below the knee – and bruises like you wouldn't believe.' She sounded cheerful about it. He opened his eyes and regarded her suspiciously. Saw she was smiling at him, her eyes glinting with mischief.

'You're enjoying this,' he accused.

She shook her head and laughed. Leaned closer and kissed him full on the mouth.

'No,' she said. 'I'm just so bloody relieved. When your Sergeant Price called last night I didn't know what to expect. Anything's better than the things my mind made happen on the way down here.'

He grinned weakly. 'Glad you're here,' he whispered,

realizing with a shock just how glad he really was. Then, 'Marry me?'

'No.' She bent forward and kissed him again. It was amazing, Mike thought, just how much of the headache a kiss could take away. 'Maybe later,' she said. 'Now, go back to sleep.'

Mike had his eyes closed again and barely even heard her words.

The next time he awoke it was to the sound of voices. Children, adults' voices that he didn't recognize. He opened his eyes slowly.

Visitors. The man in the bed opposite seemed to have his entire family in to see him.

Mike watched them, an older woman sitting herself down at the bedside, a younger woman trying to keep control of a toddler and a slightly older child, on their hands and knees and chasing each other around under the high bed. A teenage boy, looking awkward and out of place, staring around the ward, clearly at a loss as to what to do or say.

Slowly, it registered that there were other voices, ones he did recognize, approaching down the length of the ward. Sergeant Price and Superindendent Jaques appeared around the partition that divided the ward into bays, filling the small area with their presence and their noise.

As if these new visitors had brought the awareness with them, Mike suddenly realized that his ribs were hurting him, that his wrist ached and his entire body felt sore and tender. Worse than all of that, his bladder was very full and shrieking urgently for relief. It didn't look as if he was going to get it in any hurry.

Jaques, looking solemn and official, seated himself beside the bed. Price leaned against the partition.

'How are you feeling now?' Jaques asked him. 'I was here before, but you were well out of it.' He shook his head. 'Well out of it,' he repeated. He paused and regarded Mike with an interested, appraising air.

'You're looking better,' he said. 'Damned lucky, of course. They tell me you were hit at an oblique angle.' He gestured with his hands, angling one against the other as though to demonstrate. 'Lucky,' he repeated. 'That bloody car had hit you straight on' – he paused again to demonstrate, this time driving the fist of one hand into the palm of the other – 'well, we'd have been visiting the morgue, not the hospital.'

Mike glanced across at Price. The sergeant was grinning at him. 'We found the car,' he said.

'Oh?'

'Abandoned in the middle of Norwich about an hour later. Been reported stolen about six o'clock. Joy riders, we reckon, with too much booze inside them.'

Mike nodded. 'Any ID?' he asked.

'Not a thing, yet,' Jaques told him. 'It's being dusted for prints but it might be a while before we get a match. *If* we get a match.'

Mike sighed. He tried hard to get his thoughts into some kind of order. 'The well?' he asked. 'Did they find anything in the well?'

'As yet, bugger all that's any use to us,' Jaques told him. 'Remains of a dead cat and an old shoe. An adult's shoe, about size eight, they reckon,' he added at Mike's half-hopeful look.

'I see.' Mike said, deflated. He'd been certain they were on to something.

'Anyway,' Jaques went on, 'that's not your concern now. You'll be on the sick for a good few weeks with those ribs.'

He got to his feet, official visit clearly over.

'Don't worry about a thing, Mike,' he said. 'We'll get the buggers. You just get yourself fixed up.' He nodded, as though to affirm his words, and straightened his jacket, making himself ready to leave.

He nodded briefly to Price, then left with the most perfunctory of goodbyes. Price pushed himself off from the partition, preparing to follow.

'Beautiful bedside manner,' he commented.

Mike did his best to laugh.

'You take care of yourself,' Price told him. 'I'll be in later'. He smiled briefly and departed.

Maria took Price's place beside the partition.

'Thought I'd keep out of the official way,' she said. Then, a slightly anxious look crossing her face, 'Are you all right? Want some painkillers or something?'

Mike nodded. 'That would be good,' he said. 'And a nurse with one of those bottle things or a bedpan would be even better.'

*

'He's looking a great deal better,' Maria told John, the satisfaction evident in her voice.

John smiled into the receiver. When she had called him the night before, with some vague story about Mike being badly hurt, John had been devastated.

'I'm so glad, my dear. I'm taking Andrews along to see him. It is open visiting on that ward, isn't it?'

'Yes, John, till eleven, I believe, but don't make it too late, he's still pretty groggy.'

'Don't worry, my dear, we won't keep him up. You're driving back to Oaklands tonight?'

'Yes, Chandra's taking care of my patient list today, but I've a full diary for tomorrow and I've got to arrange for everything to be re-scheduled when they let him out.'

'You'll bring him here, of course. His room's all ready.'

'Thanks, John.' He could hear the relief in her voice. 'That would be a great help. And I've a few days' holiday still due to me . . .'

'Then I'll expect you as well,' he said, his mind busy already with planning meals and wondering who had a camp bed he could borrow.

'Do we know when they'll let him out?'

'Hmm, they'll keep him over the weekend, I should think. It was bad concussion. On the other hand, they need the bed and I'm well qualified to look after him. I'd make a guess at Monday.'

'Monday,' John repeated. 'Right, I'll sort everything out. Don't you worry about anything.'

He said goodbye to Maria shortly after that and stood beside the telephone a few minutes more, thinking.

Tom Andrews had described the entire incident to him when he'd seen him earlier. The car, Andrews had said, had come out of nowhere. Mike had stepped back to get out of the way, but the Sierra had seemed to follow him up on to the verge before pulling back across the road and powering away.

'They meant to get him, John. I'm convinced of that,' Andrews had told him. 'Even if the police are listing it as a simple non-stop RTA.'

John had thought long and hard about Andrews' assertion. The man could be mistaken, of course. His view from the mullioned pub window would have been narrow and awkward. Maybe he thought he had seen things happen in a certain way, when in fact the car might have swerved across the road, skidded, maybe, rather than been driven at its victim.

But John couldn't convince himself. Andrews had spent a lifetime observing, gathering facts and assimilating them into sense-making patterns.

But if he wasn't mistaken?

Was this 'accident' in some way connected with what Mike had been working on?

Andrews had asked the same question. Neither he nor John had come up with an answer.

*

It was, despite John's promises to Maria, very late by the time he made it to the hospital, and when he did it was without Andrews.

There was no mistaking, though, that late as it was Mike was glad to see him, feeling better enough to be bored, having slept enough to be sleepless and in bed long enough to be sick of it.

'I thought Tom Andrews was coming with you,' he asked when their greetings were over.

'He was,' John confirmed. 'I got a call from him about an hour ago. Seems someone broke into his office at the *Chronicle*, set fire to the place.'

'What! They're certain it's arson?'

'Sure as they can be yet. I don't know any more than that. Tom was on his way to me when he found out. They got hold of him on his mobile and he was heading back to the office when he phoned me.'

Mike was silent for a moment. 'So you don't know if anything was stolen?'

John shook his head.

At the other end of the ward the staff nurse was dimming the lights, gently hustling the late visitors out.

'Looks like I'm going to have to leave you,' he said. 'Sorry Mike, I should have come earlier, but first Tom was delayed, and then that happened.'

The staff nurse had reached the end of Mike's bed now. She stood, checking his records and politely waiting for John to take his leave.

'It is very late,' she said gently.

John nodded and got to his feet. 'I'll be back tomorrow,' he promised. 'And I'll bring Tom in with me.'

''Bye, John,' Mike said. He watched his friend walk down the ward, his mind already clouded with thoughts.

What was going on?

He sank back into the pillows and tried to get to sleep. Trying to avoid the blue Sierra that kept speeding through his dreams.

Chapter Twenty-Seven

Saturday morning

'You've made the papers.' The staff nurse told him. 'Here, let me help you back into bed and I'll leave the paper on the locker for you.'

Mike was grateful for the help. They'd allowed him to get up and go to the toilet, even have a wash, provided he didn't lock the door, but the whole process had exhausted him more than he thought possible. He allowed the nurse to ease him between the sheets and rearrange his pillows for him, then lay back against them, trying to convince himself that he was doing well really. That there would be a time, not so far off, when he wouldn't have a head that kept opening and closing like a repeatedly slamming door and ribs that wouldn't clamp up on him, like sharp claws digging deep into his side, at the slightest overstretch.

Still, he thought, look on the bright side. They'd said he could probably manage a bedbath later. Mike found himself looking forward to the possibility with almost childlike anticipation.

With difficulty he reached out for the paper that the nurse had left on his locker.

He grimaced, not certain he welcomed this fifteen minutes of fame.

The report itself was an eye-witness account of events

outside the Fox Inn, written by Tom Andrews himself and describing in vivid detail the shock and horror as he and others watched the car slew across the road and hit Detective Inspector Croft. Of their feelings of outrage when they realized that the driver didn't even plan to stop.

What, Andrews questioned, would have happened if the incident had occurred at a more remote location? If help had not arrived on the scene when it did?

'You're quite famous,' the staff nurse told him, coming back with his painkillers. 'We've had no end of calls, people wanting to know how you are and the like.' She smiled brightly at him, then left him once more, bustling off to attend to the man in the opposite bed.

Mike looked ruefully back at the paper. He couldn't blame Andrews for the report, of course. An eyewitness account of an accident involving a policeman in a hit and run was far too good to miss out on. All the same, he felt, he really could have done without it.

The article finished with a résumé of Mike's career, mentioning specially the child murder case he had been involved with the year before. Mike found himself described as an 'imaginative and conscientious officer, of which the force could be proud'.

He folded the paper up, article to the inside, embarrassed by the fuss, and glanced around, feeling both awkward and amused, wondering who else had seen it.

Mike's thoughts were broken by a woman's voice speaking his name.

'Mr Croft?'

He looked up. 'Mrs Masouk?' Ellie was the last person he would have expected to see.

'Um, I, I mean, I hope you don't mind me coming, Mr Croft. Inspector.'

'Mike,' he said.

She smiled, shyly. 'Can I sit down?'

'Oh, please.' She wasn't alone, he noted. A woman stood behind her, regarding Mike with a kind of anxious curiosity. He smiled encouragingly at her, watching as she drew up a chair and sat down, a little apart from Ellie, as though to give her privacy but still to make her presence felt.

Ellie had seen him looking. 'This is Fatima,' she said. 'Rezah's sister.'

Mike nodded remembering having seen her on Portland Close.

'It's ante-natal day,' Ellie was explaining. '''Tima comes with me, or Rezah's mother. I don't like coming on my own.' She paused, obviously uncertain, now she was here, that she'd done the right thing.

'I saw, in the paper, about your accident. I thought, well, I thought . . . How are you feeling?'

She bit her lip and looked anxiously into his face.

'Feeling well enough to be bored,' he assured her. 'And it's very kind of you to come, Mrs Masouk.'

She smiled then. 'Oh,' she said, 'please call me Ellie. Everybody does.'

Fatima moved restlessly. 'Your appointment's in half an hour, Ellie,' she said.

Ellie nodded. Then turned back to Mike.

She looked pale, Mike thought, and there were dark shadows under her eyes as though she'd not been sleeping. She bit her lip. Then, folding her hands together in front of her, like a child about to recite from memory, she began.

'I was only eight years old when it started,' she said, 'when my mum went out and I was left on my own with my dad.' She had lowered her head, but now she glanced up at Mike as though assessing his reaction. Mike tilted his head slightly, keeping his expression neutral, professionally concerned.

'He used to come into my room,' she said. 'First of all it was just games, he'd tickle me, just play games just like all my friend's dads did with them. Then it started to be different.' She hesitated, clasped her hands more closely, the knuckles white with the pressure. 'Then he started touching me. Kissing me like I'd seen him kiss my mum. Making me touch him. He'd tell me that he loved me, that I was special to him, and,' she glanced up swiftly once again, her eyes pleading, 'he was my dad, Mr Croft, I wanted to be special to him, but . . .' She looked away again. 'I didn't like the rest of it. He scared me and he hurt me and it got so I'd do anything not to be on my own with him. I'd kick up a right fuss when my mum went out to work in the evenings and my dad would tell her that I was spoilt. But I just got so scared, being on my own with him, knowing what he'd make me do and what he'd do to me.'

'Why didn't you tell your mum?' Mike asked gently.

Ellie lifted her head and he saw that her eyes were wet.

'I did,' she said softly, 'and my dad went mad. Telling my mum that I was just attention seeking, just trying to make trouble. And he kept demanding, in front of my mum, to know who'd told me about things like that. About sex. About all the things he'd made me do. Shouting at me, saying that he wanted to know how I knew about them. And my mum believed him.' She shook her head sadly, then said, 'She loved him, you see. They'd been happy before I came along. I don't think they ever really wanted kids. I came between them.'

'That's no excuse for what he did,' Mike said. 'How long did this go on for, Ellie?'

She looked at him properly this time.

'I was fifteen,' she said. 'He'd kept on doing it to me all that time, started having proper sex with me from when I was about eleven and I'd given up on trying to tell anyone.' She hesitated for a moment, as though unable to explain why she hadn't tried to get help.

'I was scared of him,' she said softly. 'Scared of what he might do. He'd threaten things and then do some of them. He broke my arm once because I said I was going to talk to my teacher about him. Broke my arm and then took me to the hospital, said I'd fallen off the swing in the park. Acted so concerned I knew they'd never believe anything I said against him, and he said he'd do worse.' She looked away from him once more. 'I believed him,' she said simply, 'and in the end I couldn't fight him any more.'

Mike was silent for a moment. He glanced across at Fatima but the young woman was impassive, her expression impossible to read. 'And when you were fifteen?' Mike asked quietly.

'I got a boyfriend,' Ellie said, 'and my dad caught us kissing. He went mad. Dragged me off home and up to my room. Started hitting me and yelling at me, then he told me to get undressed. I told him no. It was the first time I'd said no.' She paused again, her voice now awed and softened. 'I thought he'd kill me,' she whispered, 'he was just so angry. He started tearing at my clothes, saying that if I liked it so much then he'd give me more. He was shouting so loud he didn't hear my mum come home from work. When she got upstairs he'd got me pinned to the bed with my clothes half off. She saw it all.'

'What did she do, Ellie?'

Ellie shook her head. 'Sent me to stay with my aunt. Then she came after me and we both stayed there for a few days then found this grotty little flat.'

'She didn't go to the police?'

Ellie laughed bitterly. 'She loved him. She didn't believe it was his fault. Said it was mine. That I'd strung him along.'

She shook her head, the tears standing in her eyes again. 'She even went back to him for a while and I stayed with friends, relatives, anyone who would have me.'

'And then you met Rezah.'

Ellie nodded.

'I had to tell him,' she said, 'and he had to tell his

family. I thought they'd want nothing to do with me, but they've been great.'

Fatima reached out to clasp Ellie's hand. Ellie wiped the tears from her eyes, then said, 'I read about things, after I'd left home. All the reports I could find and the books on the kind of thing that has happened to me. And I went to counselling for a while. It helped, you know, to know I wasn't the only one.' She paused for a moment. 'But you know the worst bit? It was finding out just how many kids that are abused go on to abuse their own kids. I read about this girl who had a baby and she had to be taught the right ways to touch it and to look after it because she had nothing in her own life to tell her how.'

Fatima squeezed her hand, gently. 'You're a first-class mother, Ellie.'

Ellie gave her a pale smile. 'It was daft, I guess. But I spent the first six months after Farouzi was born jumping out of my skin every time someone knocked on the door. I thought, any time now they're going to come to my house and take my baby away. They're going to say I'm unfit to be a mother because my dad did that to me and I can't know the proper ways to do things.'

She looked at Mike. 'Oh, I know. It sounds daft. It *is* daft, but at the time . . .'

Mike nodded, trying his best to understand.

He didn't know what to say to her.

Ellie got to her feet awkwardly. Again she smiled shyly at Mike. 'I wanted to tell you,' she said, 'because of Eric Pearson.' She hesitated, as though not certain that he understood. 'It brought it back, you see. We'd been happy there and then he came along and spoiled it.' She laughed, the sound wry, self-effacing. 'I guess that must sound selfish,' she said.

Mike shook his head. 'No, not selfish. Very natural, I would have said.'

She nodded briskly, her movements becoming more businesslike, more controlled. 'Well, I hope you'll be better soon, Inspector Croft.'

'Thank you,' he said, uncertain now, how to respond. It seemed that nothing more was needed. Ellie made her way down the ward towards the exit.

Fatima Masouk hung back. Evidently she had something to say.

'There's something she didn't tell you,' she said. 'The real reason she had to come here today.'

She flicked her gaze down the ward towards Ellie, then looked back at Mike.

'Her father was arrested about three years ago. But it wasn't for what he did to Ellie.'

'Oh?' Mike said, puzzled now.

'Ellie's maiden name,' Fatima said to him, 'was Fletcher.'

Chapter Twenty-Eight

Saturday morning

Eric Pearson left home early, pulling the reinforced front door closed with a bang and pushing at it two or three times to make certain it was shut fast.

The last few days had been relatively quiet. They'd had kids shouting at them from the street and even the occasional rock hurled at the windows, only to bounce back at those who'd thrown it. And telephone calls that began with laughter and ended in silence. Those upset Johanna, he knew. They left her with the feeling that people could get to them even inside their fortified house. That worried her deeply.

Eric had reported everything, of course. Had kept detailed notes on everything that happened and had recorded every phone call made to the police, using a stick-on microphone hooked up to a tape deck.

Simple, but it worked and they couldn't deny his reports, not with the tapes to prove them.

The police had made their presence felt on Portland, increased foot patrols and instigated a drive-past in the area car every couple of hours. Eric didn't really feel that was enough, but it was better than nothing, he supposed.

He was aware, every time he went out, of the twitching curtains, of the eyes watching him, and, on three or four occasions, of some of the local yobs following him when he went shopping; something Johanna had suddenly refused to do.

It bothered him, of course. But no way was he going to be broken down by that kind of pressure. No way. Eric knew himself to be in the right and, although Fletcher's death meant that there would be no appeal, he would still have his say.

He had thought better of Andrews, though. Really hoped for a more positive response from the man. After all, he was a journalist. And hadn't Eric presented him with a story well worth the telling?

Shrugging his shoulders inside the loose fit of his summer jacket, Eric dismissed Andrews from his mind.

He'd paid the man back for his lack of interest. A good cleansing thing, was fire. And anyway, he had other ways of doing things now.

From the second-floor window of their house, Johanna watched Eric as he made his way up the hill.

He'd lost weight, particularly over these last few months. His clothes hung on him, his trouser belt had to be pulled tight enough for the waistband to ruckle up and his jacket would have fastened double breasted if she'd added the buttons.

He barely touched the food she set before him every day. Had to be reminded to eat, or he would simply sit at table, staring into space, oblivious even to the children's noise. And his hair had faded almost to grey, losing the reddish brown colour that the three older boys had inherited from him.

Even his eyes had paled, and his lips seemed almost bloodless, the way he kept them pressed in such a stern line.

It was so hard, Johanna thought, to remember the vital, hopeful young man she had fallen in love with all those years ago.

Johanna looked down at her hands, at the narrow wedding band and the broken nails she no longer had the will to care for. And she wondered where it was all going to end.

Price drove through the farm gate to find the SOCO team already at work and half a dozen officers combing their way through the cut-down flower beds.

He was running a little late, having stopped off to call the hospital and check on Mike. The incident had shaken him to an unexpected degree. He'd slept badly and felt like death. Learning that Mike had had a good night and was feeling 'much more comfortable' was only limited help.

Price got out of his car into the moist heat of the summer morning and breathed the ripe scent of scythed grass and hacked greenery that rose all around him.

One of the SOCO had heard his car and stood waiting.

'Glad you're here, I was about to have a call put out for you.'

He led the way round to the back of the house and pointed to where three more of his team, in white overalls stained with green and soiled with wet mud, pored over a patch of cleared earth that Price had at first assumed was just another uncovered flower bed.

'We found this and one other over there.' The SOCO gestured. 'Patches of disturbed ground. This one the most recent from the look of it.'

'Recent? How recent?'

He squatted down, Price beside him. 'We've had a good summer. Hot and wet, great growing weather.' He grinned. 'You can see that from the jungle this place has turned into. But here . . . We saw it this morning when your lot cut back the undergrowth.'

Price stared. He doubted he'd have noticed the difference straight off, but yes, now it was pointed out, the plant growth was different. Small creeping things he couldn't name with tiny flowers had spread themselves across the surface, vying with tufts of Ground Elder. But compared with the surrounding luxuriance it was nothing.

Price held his breath. 'You've reported this,' he said at last.

'Yes, called in as soon as we spotted it. Your Super – Jaques, isn't it? – said you were on your way.'

Price nodded. 'You said there was a second area?'

'Yeah, but we've not touched that yet.'

Two of the SOCO were spreading polythene sheeting at the side of the uncovered ground. Price watched, hardly daring to look away as they began, layer by layer, to scoop the earth aside. Working with the same skill and attention the pathologist had used on Ryan's body. Each stripped-back layer photographed and analysed, sifted carefully on to the plastic sheet.

Give me a shovel, Price wanted to say, impatient with what he knew was their necessary thoroughness. Let me get in there. Instead, he nodded, got to his feet.

'Call me the moment you find *anything*,' he said. Then stalked off out of their way.

Tom Andrews and John Tynan had arrived at the hospital just after ten to find Mike sitting in a chair, his injured leg stuck out on a rest in front of him and his heavily plastered wrist lying on a pillow across his lap.

With his good hand and the fingers of his hurt one, he was trying hard to manipulate the pages of a broadsheet newspaper and failing miserably, bashing his plastered wrist against the arm of the chair in his attempts to straighten the pages.

It hurt. Mike swore.

'Is that any way to greet visitors?' John said, laughing.

Mike's face brightened. 'John! It's good to see you. I'm going crazy in here.' He extended his good hand to shake Andrews', pushing the newspaper aside and almost hitting his wrist again, then wincing as his ribs complained at his too-rapid movement.

'I've got to get out of here,' he said plaintively. 'Find

yourselves some chairs or something and then talk to me!'

John laughed again. Andrews captured a chair from the other side of the ward and John seated himself on the edge of the bed.

'You're looking a lot better,' he said, his tone both satisfied and relieved.

'I'm feeling it. Really. Just so damned frustrated. Still, it could have been a lot worse.' He turned to Andrews, who had just planted the chair close by and sat himself down.

'I heard about your office,' he said.

Andrews shrugged. 'Office is too grand a word for it. I've got a partitioned-off cubby hole. We're all egalitarian and open plan these days. Only good thing about it was that I had a half-share of the big window. Or I did have until someone threw a brick through the window and a home-made petrol bomb after it. A quick-thinking colleague with a fire extinguisher dealt with it before it spread.'

'The building was occupied?' Mike asked, somewhat startled.

Andrews nodded. 'We don't always work regular hours in our game any more than you do in yours,' he said. 'Fortunately, no one was hurt and there was very little damage done. It only just had time to set the smoke alarm off and the sprinkler's on an override switch.' He shook his head. 'Either fire or water damage could have just about finished us.'

'Anybody see anything?' Mike asked him.

'Couple of people saw a man running away from the front of the building. Not a lot to go on, really. About five six to five eight, they reckon. Skinny, short grey hair and wearing a dark sweater.' He shrugged. 'I've got my theories, though.'

Mike looked speculatively at him. 'Our friend Eric Pearson?' He sighed deeply and shook his head again. 'Be hard to prove,' he said. 'And why?'

Andrews leaned back in his chair, his hands steepled thoughtfully. 'He wasn't best pleased that I didn't want to publish. Seemed to think I'd jump at the chance.'

'I don't suppose . . .?'

Andrews drew himself up with a slightly guilty start. 'Oh yes. I'm sorry. He reached into his inside jacket pocket and withdrew a few sheets of paper, gave them to Mike.

Mike read them in silence, then turned his gaze on John. 'You've seen this?' he asked.

'Yes. Quite a love life this man had.'

Mike skimmed the pages again. The sexual description was graphic and detailed and disturbingly erotic, evoking the softness of his lover's skin, of kisses flavoured with wine. Of the caress of hands and mouths and the most intimate of touches. In reading it, Mike felt himself to be blundering through someone's most private moments. He looked up at Andrews, puzzled.

'It's erotic,' he said. 'I wouldn't have said pornographic. I agree, it's not the kind of thing you'd want someone else reading, but . . .'

'Eric claimed that the boy was under age,' Andrews

231

told him, 'and that the pages that follow on from this make that plain. He also claims that Fletcher told him Blake had the boy killed, buried him at some old farmhouse.'

Mike's look was sharp, then he frowned and shrugged.

'Fletcher said a lot of things. So far we've proved none of them.'

'Let's just pray it stays like that,' John said quietly.

Ten thirty saw Eric Pearson emerge from a local print shop, carrier bags bulging with paper tightly clasped in his arms. He glanced left and right along the length of the street as though worried he'd been observed, then dashed across it, almost running, or as close to running as his baggage would allow.

His next stop was the main post office. He arrived breathless and somewhat flushed, pushed his way through the double swing doors and headed towards the stationary racks. Ten minutes later saw him with a pile of neatly addressed envelopes perched awkwardly on a corner of the counter.

Eric knelt down and emptied the contents of the two carrier bags on to the floor, stacking the paper into two unequal piles, then began to push ten or so pages from one pile, one from the other, into the envelopes.

It didn't take him too long. He worked swiftly, almost impatiently, not troubling that he creased some of the pages and crushed others sideways in his haste to complete his task. All the time, he glanced about him as though expecting to be stopped before he finished.

Then he sealed the envelopes, drawing his tongue across the flap, wrinkling his face like a child at the unpleasant taste. He paused now and then to moisten his lips and hammer at the envelope seal with his fist, driving each one against the floor to make certain it was glued tight.

Then the stamps, each envelope weighed and posted. Sent on its way.

Eric paused at the post office door, a tiny smile curving his lips.

He held one bag, about half full. There were still things to do before he went home. But it was all right, he thought to himself. He'd make certain they would listen to him now.

It had taken almost an hour to remove just over a foot of earth. Price had occupied himself by getting in the way, giving unwanted advice, poking about in areas already searched and generally punishing everyone for his inability to speed things up.

Now though, he would have given a great deal to be still unoccupied.

'God above,' he whispered softly as he stared down into the narrow depression scraped in the earth. Only a small part of the head had been uncovered, bone protruding though torn gobbets of rotting flesh. Strings of mud brown thread, he realized must be hair, sprang out from

233

the ground. The stink of decay smothering the scent of green that had earlier filled his lungs. He cleared his throat.

'How long has it been here?'

'Can't say yet. We need the police surgeon and the pathologist. Can't do much without their say-so.'

Price nodded. 'I'll call in,' he said. 'Tell them we've another murder on our patch. Jaques'll just love this.'

'Who knew you were coming to meet me?' Andrews asked.

Mike smiled. 'Don't you think you're going a bit too far?' he asked. 'You're suggesting it was a set-up.'

Andrews shook his head. 'You're not stupid, Mike, and you're not naive. You've got to see it's possible.'

Mike exhaled slowly. What Andrews had put into words had been at the edge of his thoughts all along.

'Price,' he said. 'I saw him just before I left Divisional. And Jaques, he was there when you made the call.'

'Anyone else?'

Mike shrugged. 'Undoubtedly,' he said, 'Price could have mentioned it, or Jaques, and the canteen was full when I talked to Price. Anyone could have overheard.'

'Well,' Andrews said thoughtfully, 'I guess our best hope is to track down the driver or one of his friends. See what they have to say for themselves.'

'I'm not that much into conspiracy theories,' Mike said with a shake of his head. But his words sounded hollow and unconvincing even to his own ears.

'Did John tell you,' Andrews asked him, 'that your superintendant Jaques and Fletcher were friends at one time?'

'Yes, I did,' Tynan said. 'But as Mike pointed out, that proves nothing in itself.'

Andrews hesitated for a moment. 'Even so, in your place, Mike, I'd be careful what you say to him. If Pearson's to be believed, he's also mentioned in the journal.'

Chapter Twenty-Nine

Saturday afternoon

Sergeant Price ducked into the ward at about one fifteen.

He parked himself beside Mike's locker and began to unpack the contents of two large carrier bags.

'Told you I'd be back,' he said. 'Got a bit held up, though. Maria dropped these off,' he added. 'Said she'd be in about five but you might want these now.'

Mike watched with amusement as packets of biscuits, crisps, a bottle of blackcurrant cordial and various items of underwear disappeared into the drawers and cupboards. He'd been trying to eat lunch, pushing something that claimed to be chicken fricassée around his plate and wishing that someone would bring him a cup of tea.

Price's final production, a large blue flask full of the stuff, very hot and very sweet, seemed like the answer to a prayer.

'Thinks of everything, your lady,' Price remarked, pouring a cupful for Mike and purloining one of the apples from the bowl of fruit he'd just brought in. 'She says you get picky when you're bored. Eat yourself silly,' he observed thoughtfully, looking at Mike with an interested air. 'So, I thought, just to save your waistline I'd give you something to think about.'

'You've found something?' Mike demanded.

Price grinned. 'Yeah,' he said, shifting from the

uncomfortable chair and flopping down on the edge of the bed, his mouth full of apple. 'But not in that bloody well.'

'Tell me,' Mike demanded. He abandoned all pretence of eating the fricassée and pushed the bed table aside, reaching over to grab some fruit instead.

Price took his time, infuriatingly, chewing thoughtfully on a piece of apple before he said, 'Well, so far as we can tell, allowing for the two foot of mud at the bottom, there's bugger all down that well. Or if there is, then it's . . .'

'Stuck in the two foot of mud and refusing to be dredged out. I get the picture.'

Price grinned again, clearly enjoying his boss's frustration. 'What we have got, though, is two patches of recently disturbed earth round at the back of the house. Looks like someone's been digging,' he added, as though doubting Mike had got the point of it.

'And?' Mike demanded.

Price shook his head. 'We found a body, guv, part decayed, buried no more than a foot down. Been wrapped in black plastic. The SOCO had to pull a bit of it away to find out what we'd got. God, the stink!'

'So, Fletcher was telling the truth,' Mike whispered.

'Looks that way. And there's another thing, guv, you were right about that notebook of Fletcher's. You know the one we found in his cell?'

Mike nodded.

'Well, we got the results of the ESDA.' He pulled a folded page from his back pocket with all the flourish of a magician conjuring rabbits, then hopped down from his perch on the side of the bed.

'List of names,' he said, 'and places, times and dates and what looks like a detailed confession addressed to his solicitor.' He grimaced slightly. 'We've only got a part of that, though. Seems it ran to two pages and the first one muddied the detail on the second. The list, that's more promising. We've got our collaters office liaising with a half dozen other divisions over this, and guess what?'

Mike looked expectantly. 'Our computers won't talk to their computers,' he said.

Price laughed. 'Apart from that.'

Mike smiled, but his eyes were grim and tired. He noted that for all Price's hyperactive enthusiasm he too looked strained and weary below the surface expression.

'They're all missing persons,' he said. 'And they're all kids.'

'Take a look, guv,' he said. 'See what you can get out of it. But for Chrissake, don't let Jaques know. Official line is, you're out of it. Case closed. Inspector Croft invalided out.'

He took another bite of apple and shook his head, not able now to conceal the worried look around his eyes.

'You ask me, guv,' he said, 'there's someone out there much happier now you're out for the count and a hell of a lot of people determined to see you stay that way.'

*

Eric felt that he had been truly imaginative in the way he had done things. He had thought carefully about where and how to distribute the photocopied pages from the journal.

A half hour of calling directory enquiries the night before – he'd worry about the phone bill later – had supplied him with addresses for the main regional papers, a selection of the nationals and a half-dozen radio stations.

To each of these he had posted ten or so pages from the journal, together with what he had termed 'A Deposition', outlining the problems he had encountered in trying to make his voice heard.

He had included a full and open accusation of those in authority, the police, the courts, the local powermongers. Outlining how they had ignored his testimony. Ignored the facts. Allowed Eric and his family to be persecuted, driven from one place to the next, stoned and assaulted. Disbelieved by everyone, because of one unproven mistake in Eric's own life. How, by their own blindness and corruption, those who should have put justice first had left Eric Pearson and his family without protection. Persecuted and reviled.

Eric saw his cause as having almost Biblical importance and millenarian implications. How could God fail, in the final analysis, to bring justice to those that disregarded the law and so persecuted the very people who tried to bring the wrongdoers to notice?

To Eric it was inconceivable that justice – his total,

absolutist, unswervable view of justice – would not in the end prevail.

And if God needed a little help along the way? If there were those who chose to ignore what was right? Then Eric had shown himself more than ready to be the one acting as intermediary.

Eric didn't hear the voice of God in his head. If someone had suggested such a thing he would have been outraged. The hearing of voices was something endured by the mad, the insane. By those poor misguided souls who needed help and comfort. Needed locking away somewhere safe and peaceful, out of sight and sound of the rest of humanity.

No, Eric didn't need to hear the word of God. He knew His wishes. Knew them; felt them deep within himself.

Eric knew that his actions had brought pain to his family. Lost him friends, his home, even the work as a teacher that he had truly loved. But it didn't matter.

All of that would soon be over. It just needed one more push. One more try. And when Eric Pearson's story had been told, when the corruption amongst the powerful had been revealed, and when it was publicly known what Eric and his family had been through to get their story told, then everything would all be right. Then Johanna and the children would be happy and they could go home once more. The Children of Solomon would be proud to welcome them back once again. There would be no more nightmare. No having to comfort the little ones when they woke with bad dreams. No blame from Johanna.

They would have the old days back again.

Eric went through the swing doors of the public library. His bag was almost empty now. He'd lost count of the number of places he had gone to that afternoon, leaving little stacks of paper; extracts from Blake's journal and copies of his own Deposition at the town hall, two of the branch libraries, book shops, cafés, anywhere he could think of where people might gather.

He glanced swiftly about him in the library. The counter staff were busy, customers lining up to have their books checked in or out. A couple more people pushed heavy trolleys stacked with books between the shelves.

Where would be the best place?

Looking around again he saw a table, close to the check-out desk and covered in leaflets.

He walked over to it, diving his hand into his bag and pulling out a thick sheaf of paper.

Briefly, he scanned the leaflets on the table. Night school courses, 'know your rights' advice for the unemployed. Adverts for local concerts and events.

With a sweep of his hand, Eric cleared himself a space right in the centre of the table. He placed his own sheaf of papers between a stack of roughly photocopied sheets advertising a Scouts' 'summer fayre' and neatly folded orange sheets issued by the local tourist information.

He laughed softly to himsef as he carefully placed a smaller stack of paper next to the first. His 'Deposition'.

It was a good choice, he thought, sitting his words next to adverts for local tourist attractions. Very soon it would be Portland Close that would draw the visitors. A tourist site. A centre of interest for anyone concerned with truth and justice.

Eric allowed himself the pleasure of visualizing the journalists, the newsmen, the civil rights agitators who would soon be beating a path to his door. He smiled broadly, nodding happily to himself. 'That'll show them,' he said aloud. Yes, that will show them all.

As he left the building, still unobserved by the counter staff, busy dealing with the line of customers trying to beat early closing time, Eric's only regret was that it was Saturday. That even though his letters would have caught the post, already be in the system, already unstoppable, no one would read them until the Monday morning.

He sighed, a little let down by the thought. That almost certainly meant an evening and an entire day of waiting before the action really began. Unless, of course, someone picked up one of his hand-delivered messages and acted on it sooner.

That thought had him smiling again. Eric felt light of heart and satisfied with a day's work well done.

He set off for home, stopping on the way only to buy a reel of tape from a stationer's. He still had about a half-dozen copies of his Deposition left. He could go out, late tonight, tape them up at the local shops and at the bus stops along the main road. Maybe even to the door of the local police station. The thought amused him so much that Eric Pearson laughed out loud.

They would listen to him this time. Eric would take pleasure in making certain of that.

It was around dusk before the body at the farm house was removed, lifted carefully along with the adhering mud on to a white sheet then wrapped in a body bag and carried away.

Digging had begun in the second area, slow and precise under the harsh false daylight of the dragon lamps.

Chapter Thirty

Saturday evening

Jaques had decided that he didn't want to go home. Home was a comfortable place where his wife, a pretty woman to whom he had been married fifteen years, would be waiting for him. A place that held all the things that mattered but which, right now, was the last place he felt able to go.

It wasn't that he didn't want, desperately, to be there. Rather that he couldn't face his wife's questions. Her concern if she realized something was wrong. Her desire to help him.

He tidied his desk carefully, placing papers in neat, orderly stacks. Pens and pencils in the side drawer. Telephone, calculator and plastic stationery trays placed just so, parallel to the edge of the desk. He slipped a long brown envelope into his pocket and switched off his office light for what he knew would be the last time. Then he left the police station, pausing for a moment in the front office as though to check the day book.

Outside it was raining. Just a light drizzle, enough to mist the windows of his car and make the roads feel greasy and insecure. Jaques drove, heading without thought from the centre of town to the rundown streets and derelict warehouses that backed on to the canal. Almost before he noticed where he was he had stopped in front of the terraced house where Ryan had died. Jaques got out and stood motionless, facing the boarded windows and the blank front door.

Further down the street, lights glowed from behind drawn curtains and faint sounds reached him of over-loud music. This end of the street, though – this end was scheduled for demolition. The row was boarded and deserted and the bend in the road made it hard for anyone further down to see who went into the house and who never came back out. It had been perfect, Jaques thought. So close to ordinary people and their boring, ordinary little lives and yet set apart just enough to be almost invisible.

He turned abruptly and walked back down the street towards the canal. He stood on the bridge, staring down at the dark water below. At water clogged with weed and the random supply of rubbish people dumped there and which sank into the thick, cloying depth of mud and clay at the bottom.

Rather like that damned well, he thought. Vaguely, he wondered what it would be like to drown.

Chapter Thirty-One

Saturday evening

'And will she get over it?' Mike asked. 'Really get over it, I mean. Or will there always be things bringing the memory back to her?' He paused thoughtfully. He had told Maria about Ellie's visit and about what had spurred her into telling him about her father.

'We can't wipe out our own memories,' Maria told him softly. 'We can bury them, think the pain of them is gone for ever. Even shove them into a mental hole so deep we're not even aware that they were there in the first place, at least not on a conscious level. But, no. I don't believe we can ever really get rid of them.'

Mike looked doubtful. He felt very tired now, and, welcome as Maria's company was, he knew that what he really wanted was to go to sleep.

It was as though the events of the last couple of days since his accident had finally caught up with him. He knew that he'd been trying very hard to make a good showing. Not to let on that not only was he physically very uncomfortable, but mentally he was deeply shaken.

Here he was, lying in a hospital bed with broken bones and a headache that still wouldn't completely say goodbye, growing more and more aware that he had been profoundly lucky.

Images of his own mortality kept impinging on his

consciousness and he felt, at times, absurdly close to tears. Angry with himself, he tried to drive all the negative and frightening thoughts from his mind and to concentrate on Maria.

'I think she's doing a remarkably good job of getting her life together,' Maria told him. 'She isn't blocking her feelings or trying to hide them away somewhere. She's actually trying to do something with them.'

'And that's good?' Mike asked. Then, 'Yes, I suppose it is, isn't it?'

'You look very tired,' she said.

'I am.' He swallowed spasmodically, feeling the tears threatening again. He looked for distraction. 'And you,' he asked, 'have you had to deal with many cases like Ellie's?'

Maria continued to look thoughtfully at him. 'A few,' she said. 'Not quite like Ellie Masouk. I've had women referred to me by rape crisis centres and social services. A few men too.' She laughed at Mike's look of surprise. 'But I've only ever dealt with adult survivors, not with kids. That's just not my field.'

She leaned forward, resting her elbows on the side of the bed and speaking quietly. 'You've got to remember, Mike. You can't see this as a sex thing. It's about power, just the same way as most rapes and sexual assaults are about power. And it's often not the sex part that does the damage.'

He frowned at that, his look sharp. 'You can't condone that kind of thing, surely. I mean, having sex with kids is wrong. No one can argue with that.'

Maria laughed softly again, refusing to be intimidated by his tone. 'Taking something by force is wrong. Dominating and demeaning the rights of another human being is wrong. Mike, I've had a woman come to me severely traumatized because her father locked her in a dark cupboard whenever she was naughty. Can you imagine that? A two year old, shut away in a dark place she couldn't get out of. Knowing that however much she cried or screamed or hammered on the door she wouldn't be let out until her father thought she'd been punished enough. Someone who was supposed to love her and protect her, betraying every ounce of trust she put in him.'

She sighed and shook her head, slowly. 'However you look at it, Mike, it's the power game that's wrong; not just how it's expressed. Not just the fact that it's sex or violence or any other permutation.'

'But,' Mike said stubbornly, 'you can't think that sex with under-age kids can ever be right.'

'Under what age?' Maria challenged. 'Under sixteen, under fourteen? Under twenty-one? Mike, I'm not trying to play devil's advocate here, but the idea of what age is right for sex is largely a cultural thing.'

She glanced across at him, noting his stony expression. 'In other parts of the world girls are married at fourteen or even younger.'

'Well, I don't think that's right either,' he declared irritably.

Maria shrugged. 'Maybe not,' she said, 'and I'll go as far as saying that the thought of an adult having a

sexual relationship with a very young child appals me.'
She grinned. 'Very unprofessional, I know.'

Mike allowed himself a half-smile.

'But there are so many borderline cases, where it's
hard to know what's right. You can't deny that kids have
sexual feelings. That they explore what makes them feel
good maybe long before they even know what to call it.'
She grinned. 'I'll bet when you were six or seven, you
got told off for playing with yourself!'

'I did not!' he declared, his anger so out of proportion
to the statement that Maria laughed affectionately.

'No, no,' she said. 'Of course not.' Then, 'Mike, I'm
not suggesting you had any notion that what you were
doing – OK, what *little boys* that age tend to do is
consciously sexual. But the beginnings of awareness are
there and by the time kids reach adolescence . . .'

Mike was glaring again, clearly very uncomfortable
with the whole track of the conversation.

Chief Superintendant Charles dumped the bundle of
papers on the desk and glanced up as Price walked
through the door carrying yet more. Fragments of Blake's
journal, so carefully assembled and photocopied by Eric
Pearson were spread across the desk and spilled on to
the floor.

'These were in the Central Library, sir,' Price said,
sitting his bundle on top of the rest. 'The librarian dropped them off at her local nick on her way home.'

Charles sighed. 'So that's five locations so far,' he said. 'Busy little boy our Mr Pearson's been.'

He pulled out a copy of Eric's Deposition from the middle of the stack and read it through again.

'You think we should have men stationed on Portland?' Price asked.

Charles frowned and shook his head. 'Can't spare the men,' he said shortly, 'but you'd better increase the patrols and I want any calls from there graded one.' He sat down at the desk and motioned Price to do the same. 'Right,' he said. 'Let's see if we can put this thing together, find out what all the fuss is about.'

Price sighed deeply and sat down. Even as a kid he'd hated jigsaw puzzles.

'Did I ever tell you about Sophie?' Maria asked him.

'No, who's she?'

Maria sat back and crossed her legs, allowing Mike a tantalizing view of smooth thigh. 'Sophie was a woman we inherited at Oaklands, when it became part of the community programme. She'd been there for years. Oaklands was one of the old-fashioned asylums and by the time our lot took over she just didn't know how to survive anywhere else.'

'Is she still there?' Mike asked.

'Oh yes. We sorted out her benefits for her and managed to fiddle things so she does little jobs in the kitchen and the garden.' She shook her head, sadly. 'She's not stupid, Mike. One time, she might even have been a bright kid, but sixty years of being an inmate in the old Oaklands probably didn't do a lot for stimulating her mind. But she's all there when it comes to remembering why she ended up in the nut house.'

Mike laughed and Maria smiled back at him. 'Why was she there?' he asked.

'Sophie was shut away because society, in its infinite wisdom, saw her as a moral defective.'

'A moral what? I mean, why?'

'She got pregnant,' Maria told him. 'At fifteen years old and by a man almost twice her age.'

Mike frowned at her. 'I'm not sure I—'

'Sophie was in love with him. Whatever we might think about the morals of the man, who was married, it turns out, and didn't want to know when she found herself in trouble, Sophie loved him. She'd been having sex with him for the best part of a year before she was caught out and, from what she tells me, enjoyed every minute of it. She wasn't coerced or threatened, Mike, she was in love.'

'With a man twice her age who probably knew every trick in the book. What chance would a kid like that have to say no? What could she possibly understand about it?'

'She didn't want to say no, Mike. I asked her that. I tried to put pressure on her to admit that this man had persuaded her in some way, that she was in denial. But I don't think she was. Would you have been so shocked if the lover had been a kid her own age?'

Mike glared at her. 'It isn't right,' he said. 'It isn't decent.'

'Says who?' Maria challenged him. 'In Greece, for instance, a "civilized", "modern" European country, a good age for a man to marry is thirty, thirty-one, and they think nothing of marrying a girl of sixteen or seventeen. There's nothing wrong in that. It's a cultural thing here that tells us there is.'

'I'm not convinced,' Mike said. Very much aware that he didn't *want* to be convinced. That all this talk of children, of sexual feelings in those he thought of as too young to even have a right to know about such things made him deeply uncomfortable.

He thought of Stevie, his own son. Of the crush Stevie had had on the teenage girl who lived next door. Stevie had been only ten years old at the time, the girl a pretty blonde of seventeen. She only had to look at the boy and smile to have him blushing and stammering, hardly able to say a word to her.

They had laughed about it at the time, he and Maggie, but what was going on in Stevie's head? Were they sexual feelings he'd had? Mike sighed. Innocent as Stevie's feelings had been, well, yes, he supposed they were. But that didn't mean he had to like it.

He scowled angrily at her again, his thoughts still with Stevie.

Stevie had died in a hit and run accident. It would have been kind of ironic, wouldn't it, if he, Mike, had been killed the same way.

He could feel the tears threatening again. Tears for

Stevie and all the lost promise that his death represented, and for himself. Tears of pure fear and shock. Mike swallowed hard, determined not to show what he could not help but see as weakness.

He was uncomfortably aware that Maria was watching him closely, noticing every passing emotion, every fear and every part of his relief. He cleared his throat, making a show of coughing and changing his position in the bed. His ribs hurt him abominably and he felt so desperately tired.

'Price brought in the results of the ESDA test,' he said.

'Oh?' Maria accepted his change of subject without a blink. 'Does it tell you anything?'

'I don't know. It's a list of names and dates. MISPAS – you know, missing persons.'

Maria nodded. She'd got used to the jargon.

'It could mean anything or nothing,' Mike went on. 'Fletcher could have compiled the list from what he knew or he could have got the names from news reports, I suppose.'

He was too tired to think straight. The fact was, he thought nothing of the sort. Fletcher had compiled that list from knowledge.

Maria got to her feet and bent over to kiss him. 'I'm going now,' she said gently. 'You get some sleep. I'll be back tomorrow.'

Mike smiled weakly at her and returned the kiss, squeezing her hand and thinking how lucky he was to have this woman, even if she did have some strange ideas.

He was drifting into sleep even before she had left the ward, running through, in his half-dreaming mind, the list of fifteen names and dates. And of places. Four locations in all, set against the names. And of bodies buried in a farmhouse garden.

Jaques parked in a side street opposite the hospital and sat for some time watching the main entrance. Suicide by drowning, he had decided, was not something that he could face. The thought of cold water closing over his head, of his feet and legs dragged into the depth of stinking mud, had been too much. He had returned to the car and driven to the hospital, with the vague thought of seeing Mike.

But it was late, he thought. Much too late.

Maria had left the hospital by the main entrance about fifteen minutes after he arrived. He recognized her tall, elegant figure crossing the hospital forecourt even from a distance. He watched her cross towards the car park and then pass out of sight between the cars. If she had left Mike, then it really must be late, much too late tonight.

His mind shifted on to a different tack. Had Charles found his letter yet? Would he have read it? He sighed. Charles might not even be at the nick. Probably home in bed, well out of this mess.

Jaques toyed with the idea of going back into work. Taking the letter from where he had left it and burning it before it could be read. After all, he'd been lucky so far. Maybe his luck would hold for just a little longer.

Starting the car engine again, Jaques dismissed the idea. It was too late now, no matter how you looked at it. Jaques wasn't certain whether he should be frightened or relieved by the thought.

Chapter Thirty-Two

Saturday evening

Eric seemed unable to settle to anything. He had spent the evening wandering from room to room, half heartedly picking up a book and reading a few pages, or joining the family for a moment or two in front of the television before taking himself off again.

The children, engrossed in a comedy film, had taken little notice of him. They were well used to Daddy 'mooching about', as Johanna called it, and the film had been far more exciting than their father's mood.

It was good, Johanna thought, to hear them laughing. Behaving like ordinary, untroubled children, if only for a little while. Half an hour ago, she had hustled the eldest of them off to bed, checked on the youngest and then gone down to the kitchen to make tea for herself and Eric.

And here she was, she thought sadly, sitting with a pot of cold, stewed tea, still waiting for Eric to come and join her.

Time was when this last part of the evening, with the children in bed and a brief while left to spend alone together, had been the most precious part of their day.

What had happened to them? Johanna wondered. To the closeness and the love they had once had for one another? She sighed deeply. Everything, it seemed, had been sacrificed to this burning need Eric had within him. In time, even she and the children had been consigned to the heat of it.

Sadly, Johanna began to climb the stairs up to the living room. She could hear Eric pacing about up there, could hear the television still chattering to itself, and the slight, comfortable, going-to-sleep movements of her children in the rooms above.

Standing at the head of the stairs, Johanna watched for a moment as Eric paced back and forth, along the length of the back wall, pausing every so often to peer out into the dark beyond the uncurtained window.

He didn't hear her come into the room, didn't hear, either, as she shut off the news broadcast showing some new slaughter, neighbour against neighbour, in some other part of the world.

Johanna crossed the room towards him, catching a glimpse of herself in the black mirror of the window. How old she looked, body still slim despite bearing so many little ones, but the face lined and wounded, as though only the saddest parts of it could still function and smiles were long forgotten.

'Eric,' she said, laying a gentle hand on his arm.

Eric Pearson jumped as though he had been stung, his expression in the dark window at once startled and enraged. Then his expression softened.

'Oh,' he said. 'It's you.'

He turned away from her, pacing along the other wall this time as though to break what little contact she still claimed with him.

'What is it, Eric?' she asked him softly. 'Come and talk to me about it. I'll make some fresh tea and we can talk it through.'

He turned to look at her, but only for a moment. Then he shook his head and looked away.

It seemed, to Johanna, that there had been no more than bare recognition in his eyes. No love, no concern, no contact.

Johanna felt the pain of it rising to her throat, threatening to choke what little life she still had a hold on.

Sighing, she let her gaze travel around the shabby, messy room. She should tidy up, really. At least pick up the children's toys, or straighten the magazines.

Her gaze came to rest on the cardboard boxes that Sam had brought over.

Eric had set the boxes in the corner of the room after his first brief look through them, and then left them there.

She went over, bent down and began poking about inside.

'Why don't we unpack these, Eric?' she asked, forcing a little brightness into her voice.

This time he didn't even glance at her.

'Maybe later,' he said, then turned towards the window once again.

Johanna stared at him a moment longer; then decided that if Eric didn't want to look, well, she might as well. Anything was better than this, following Eric around the house, waiting for him to speak to her.

It took two trips before she had the boxes down on

the kitchen table. It would be nice, she told herself, to look through these things. Memories of happier times. Of what seemed like a lifetime ago.

She began to empty the boxes out on to the kitchen table, imagining that Eric was there beside her, sharing the memories with him, whispering softly.

'Oh, Lord, Eric, do you remember this tie?' she whispered, covering her mouth with her hand to suppress the laughter. 'Frank bought it for Judy's wedding, wore it with that old pin-stripe suit of his. You remember, don't you? We all laughed so much. Elder Thomas said that all he needed was a violin case and wingtip shoes and he could double for Al Capone.'

She paused, her face lighting with the memory. Judy's wedding, on a summer morning. The late mist just rising on the lawn and the bride so beautiful in her long blue dress with flowers in her hair.

There should be photographs in here, Johanna thought. Photographs of Frank and Judy and the rest, posed, laughing and exuberant on the gravel drive in front of the house.

Eagerly, Johanna began to sort through the plastic bag of photographs, pausing now and then to look more closely at one or two of them. The faces, the smiles. 'Oh,' she murmured, 'how young we all looked back then.' She wiped the tears away and, smiling softly to herself, laid the photographs aside. Later, she would take them to bed with her, show Eric. He'd be bound to take notice then, tucked up comfortably in their bed. Certain to relax enough to want to talk, to remember all the good times with her.

Smiling properly now, she dived her hand into the box once more, deliberately not looking, like a child with a Christmas parcel, trying to discern the surprise by touch alone.

Round and cool, heavy in her hand. Ah, yes. She knew what that was. Johanna lifted the object out. The mille fleur paperweight Aunt Em had been so proud of. 'Real Victorian, she used to swear it was. Do you remember, Eric?' She turned it in the light, examining the little flowers and geometric patterns set within the clear glass. 'And you used to tell me off,' she said, 'because I always thought the blessed thing was so ugly.' She giggled, suddenly childlike, and plunged into the box once more.

Books and trinkets emerged, to be examined and then strewn across the table. Aunt Em's pearls – 'Wonder if they are real, Eric.' A couple of heavily bound gold-blocked volumes of poetry. 'Keats and Shelley, my dear. Never went anywhere without one of them, did he? Not that he ever went anywhere anyway.' Three or four more brilliantly coloured neckties. 'He must have spent a fortune on these over the years.' She laughed. 'Dear old Frank. Never without his tie. Old suits, baggy trousers and shabby cardigans, but always a tie.'

She wiped her eyes once more, not realizing until now how much she grieved for Eric's brother and his wife. Both gone now, and never even the chance to say goodbye.

'And look at this, Eric.' She lifted the last item from

the box. About eight inches high and dark brown with swirling patterns scraped into its clay body. Frank's owl. 'Swore it came from Peru, didn't he? But we knew Judy bought it in that little craft shop we went to.' She paused. 'Now where was that?' Johanna shook her head as her memory failed her. It really was an ugly thing, but Frank had liked it, and Judy had bought it for him, which would have made it special no matter what. Frank had loved all the children growing up in the House of Solomon and Judy, after her dad had died and her mother wasn't able to cope, had become like another of Frank's own.

Thoughtfully, Johanna tilted the owl backwards to peer into its beaky face, feeling, as she did so, something moving inside.

She shook it, puzzled for a moment, then turned it upside down, smiling to herself again.

There was a slit in the bottom of the owl, there to release the gases during firing. The kids used to post things into it; then cry when they couldn't get them out again.

Holding it above her head and peering into the narrow slit, Johanna shook the owl again, curious to see what would come out. Whatever it was seemed to be jammed fast. Taking a vegetable knife from the kitchen drawer, she tried again, poking the tip of the knife into the hole and trying to coax out whatever was inside.

It took time and patience, but Johanna had both. Wiggling the tip of the knife backwards and forwards inside the slit, she gradually managed to draw the edge of the object down. With a little jerk, she pulled the knife free. A thin sliver of what looked like brown plastic poked out.

'Now what's that?' Johanna murmured to herself, setting to work with broken fingernails to draw the strip the rest of the way out.

In the end, there were three of them lying on the table. Brown strips of photographic negative, a little scratched from her efforts with the knife.

For a moment, Johanna stared at them, all trace of her smile now gone, her face tight and wounded once again.

Somehow, Johanna guessed what she would see, even before she lifted them to the light.

DCS Charles looked warily at the envelope with his name on it.

'This must have been left for you, sir,' the desk sergeant said to him. 'It was stuck in the day book. No one saw it till the shift change.'

Charles thanked him and took the envelope, waiting for the sergeant to leave before he opened it. 'It's from Jaques,' he said, looking at the neat handwriting on the front of the envelope.

'Jaques,' Price breathed. 'Oh, boy.' He glanced at the mess of paperwork lying on the desk. Jaques' name was in the journal. Descriptions of Jaques' involvement with Blake and Fletcher and the rest were laid down in the greatest of detail. And Jaques wasn't at home. His wife hadn't seen him since the previous morning.

And now this letter.

Impatient now, Charles ripped open the envelope and read the few lines written on the sheet of paper.

'It's an address,' he said.

Price was on his feet, reaching for the paper.

'You know where this is?'

'Yes.'

'Take some back-up,' Charles told him, his face grave.

Chapter Thirty-Three

Sunday, early morning

It was clear, just from the way Jaques walked down the length of the ward, his footfalls quick and decisive, that he was not a happy man.

Mike gave him an expectant look and invited him to sit down. Jaques didn't. He remained standing, his hands thrust deep into his pockets, fingers jangling keys and loose change, his voice as tense and abrupt as his footsteps had been.

'I can't stop,' he said, 'and besides, I've just seen breakfast about to be brought in. Wouldn't want to interrupt.'

He paused, frowning, then sat down after all, leaned forward to rest his hand on the side of Mike's bed in what was, for Jaques, an outstanding show of intimacy.

'Just wanted to be the one to tell you, Mike. Courtesy, you understand, but this thing's got bigger than any of us thought.' He sat back and rubbed his face with the palms of his hands.

'You look tired, sir,' Mike commented.

'I am, Mike, I am. It's been a long night, you know. Anyway, it looks like internal affairs will be taking over from here on in.'

'What . . .?' Mike was taken aback.

Jaques silenced him abruptly. 'You'll be laid up for a

good while yet, so it's no longer your worry ... You've heard about the body?'

Mike nodded.

'Puts a different complexion on things,' Jaques went on.

'Mike, we've not always seen eye to eye, I know, but we've rubbed along pretty well, haven't we?'

'I should say so,' Mike said, wondering where this was leading.

'And I know you've always been one to give a fair hearing, even to the likes of Eric Pearson.'

Mike frowned. 'Everyone deserves to be heard, sir, whatever our personal feelings might be,'

'Quite so, quite so.'

He rummaged in his pocket and handed Mike a few sheets of folded paper. Mike took them. Jaques sat fidgeting until Mike had finished reading. Then he said, 'Well, what do you make of it?'

Mike separated the pages. 'This,' he said, 'is part of Blake's journal. And this,' he fingered Eric Pearson's Deposition gingerly as though it might bite, 'is not going to endear him to the residents of Portland Close.'

Jaques snorted rudely. 'No, no, I don't suppose it will,' he said. He got to his feet and took the paper back from Mike, folding it tightly before replacing it in his pocket. 'Look,' he said. 'I know this is not where you want to be, but that's just the way of things sometimes. You try your best to keep things going and then it all blows up in your face.' He stood hesitantly beside the bed as though wanting to say more. 'I just came to keep you informed, Mike. Nothing official, you understand,' he said at last.

Mike nodded, puzzled now by Jaques' attitude. 'Thank you, sir,' he said. 'I appreciate that.'

Jaques straightened himself up and shuffled his feet as though impatient to go but still having something left to say.

'Just get yourself better, Mike,' he said. 'Take your time and don't try to come rushing back before you're ready.' He nodded, as though satisfied that he'd got the message right.

'Just take your time,' he said again, and then he left.

Mike watched him walk down the ward, listening to the swift footsteps and taking note of the rigidity of Jaques' back.

'Now,' he said softly to himself. 'What was that all about?'

The door was forced, the hydraulic ram smashing the lock from the frame. The uniformed officer with the ram kicked the door open. Then he and the other two men accompanying Price streamed ahead of him into the house, two running up the stairs and the third heading towards the downstairs rear.

The front door opened directly into the living room. A second room could be seen beyond and off that, the small kitchen.

The stairs were hidden behind a panelled door leading off from the corner of the room. The windows still had their original sash boxes and the tiled fireplace, now with an ugly modern gas fire sitting in front of the arched grate, also looked untouched from the time of first building.

There was newspaper on the wooden floor, old and yellowed, between the front door and the opening to the other room. His gran had done that, Price remembered. Put newspapers underneath the carpets when they were laid. Said it helped them last longer. Stopped them rubbing against the floor.

He moved through to the middle room just as the third officer came back from the kitchen.

'Bathroom tagged on to the back of the house,' he said. 'Back door's locked and there's no sign of a key. Want me to force it?'

A shout from upstairs cut across Price's reply. He ran up the steep, narrow stairs, his feet echoing on the uncarpeted wood.

'In here, sir.'

It was the smallest room at the back of the house. There were new locks on the door. On the outside. Price eased himself past the other officers standing silently in the narrow corridor. He pushed the door fully open and stepped inside.

'Jesus!'

There was very little in the tiny room with its single window. Just the smell of stale urine making the air foul and a single bed with an old mattress lying at an angle across it. A mattress with a wide, dark, brownish stain spread across its width.

*

Jaques never quite made it back to his car. He'd not hurried, instead walked slowly across the hospital fore-court with the steady, purposeful air of one determined on a direction but in no major rush to get there.

'Sir.' The young PC stepped in front of him, the look on his face almost apologetic as though he couldn't quite get his head around this arrest of a senior officer.

Jaques glanced up at him, then sideways at the other officer who had suddenly appeared on his other side.

'I'd like you to come back to the station with me,' the young officer began. 'DCS Charles . . .'

'Would no doubt want the job done properly!' Jaques glared at him. His mind already pushed beyond reason, this lack of protocol annoyed him excessively.

It was the second, older officer who stepped forward and read him his rights. Who made certain he was cuffed and led to the waiting car with the minimum of fuss. His words echoed in Jaques' mind as they drove away. 'Accessory to murder. Accessory . . .'

Sighing, Jaques leaned back as well as his cuffed hands would allow him.

'Sloppy!' he announced suddenly, directing his words at the younger officer driving the car. 'Very sloppy. Don't read a man his rights, his brief would have a wonderful time with you on the witness stand. That's if it ever makes it as far as court. Technicalities, you know, always watch out for the technical foul.'

He lapsed into silence then, bemoaning to himself the carelessness of youth, shaking his head sadly in disbelief at it all. 'Still wet behind the ears,' he murmured softly.

Chapter Thirty-Four

Sunday morning

Maria had stayed over at John Tynan's after visiting Mike. It was the weekend, nothing for her to go back to Oaklands for, and it cut a full hour off the travelling time to the hospital.

Neither of them had hurried to get up and it was almost nine before they had got round to breakfast.

The peace of the Sunday morning was shattered by the piercing ring of the telephone. John fairly leapt into the hall to snatch it up, Maria following him, their instant, twinned thought that it must be the hospital.

John lifted the phone to his ear, then shook his head at Maria, a puzzled expression on his face. Satisfied that it wasn't the hospital, Maria went back into the kitchen. From the hallway she heard John say 'yes' a couple of times, then, 'Well, I wouldn't be too happy about that, my dear,' then 'yes' again and the phone being placed back on its cradle.

'You'll never guess who that was,' he said as he came back in.

Maria raised an eyebrow, her mouth quirking at the corners in a slight smile. 'Who?' she asked.

'Well, that was Johanna Pearson. Wanting to know

about our Sam, she was, and if I could give her his address.'

'I take it you didn't,' Maria said.

John smiled. 'Listening in to my conversations, are you? No, I didn't. For one thing I didn't think it would be fair on Sam, to maybe have her turning up with no warning, and the other thing is, she'd have had a hard time getting out there with no transport. It's not exactly somewhere you can get a bus to.'

Maria laughed wryly. 'Not many places you can these days,' she said. 'So? What are we going to do?'

'We?' John said. Then he smiled broadly. 'We, my dear, are going to telephone my friend Embury and warn him to be expecting visitors. Then we're collecting Johanna Pearson and driving her out there.'

'Oh?' Maria questioned. 'And you think that will be fair to Sam, do you? Landing us *and* Johanna Pearson on his doorstep on a Sunday morning?'

John looked thoughtful and began to butter his toast, scraping the knife across the cold surface, making patterns in the yellow butter.

'She sounded distressed,' he said. 'Said there were things she had to talk to Sam about without Eric being there.' He looked across at Maria, his old blue eyes slightly guilty, a little embarrassed.

'She was almost in tears, love. You could hear it in her voice, and a woman like Johanna Pearson doesn't cry for nothing, I'm sure of that.'

Maria regarded him steadily for a few moments, then she reached across the table and squeezed his hand.

'You're a nice man, John Tynan,' she told him. 'Now, when do we leave?'

Dora's Sunday morning mood had been shattered by that single sheet of paper taped roughly to the lamp post on the back path.

She had been on her way to the shops. The big store had started to open on Sundays a few months before, and, despite her feelings that it maybe wasn't altogether right, Dora had taken to 'forgetting' little items on their Saturday shop, just for the pleasure of wandering around the half-empty store.

And now she had found this. This cruel, unfair letter, or whatever it could be called. Taped up here for all the world to see; for all the world to read that man's accusations.

It wasn't fair! It was cruel! How could this man say things like that and, worse, tape them up in a public place for anyone to see.

No way could Dora just stand by and let this happen. The police should know. And the neighbours. They couldn't let that terrible man get away with this.

Dora re-entered the Close just as Johanna Pearson left it. The two women passed within feet of each other, but the distance between them could just as well have been a hundred miles.

Each woman looked the other way, though Johanna couldn't help but notice the look of anger and distress on Dora's face.

Johanna glanced back swiftly as she passed through the kissing gate and on to the back path, noting the crumpled paper Dora clutched so tightly in her hand. Trying to dispel the sense of dread closing in on her.

Johanna had told John not to come down into the Close to pick her up. She would meet them, she said, in the car park close to the shops.

Maria and John had said little on the drive there. It seemed hopeless to speculate about Johanna's sudden desire to see Sam. It must, Tynan had said, be something to do with the things that Sam had brought over to them; but he couldn't make any guess about what.

'Maybe it's all just getting too much for her,' Maria suggested. 'Maybe, with Sam being the only family she's got, she's looking for some kind of help from him to get her and the kids out of this.'

John shook his head, concern creasing the corners of his mouth.

'I hope not, love,' he said. 'Sam's got his own life to lead without Johanna and her tribe butting in. And I can't see Eric welcoming him. He'd see any help Sam tried to give as blatant interference, and the boy could do without Eric maybe causing trouble for him.'

Maria nodded thoughtfully. 'I guess you're right,' she said.

They sat in silence for a few moments longer, then Maria asked, 'Is that her, John?'

John looked over to where Maria indicated. A

woman in a brown skirt, white blouse, and, despite the heat, what looked like a tailored jacket, was advancing on them. Johanna walked quickly, her flat shoes planting themselves firmly on the pavement and her long skirt flapping. She moved anxiously and hurriedly, allowing only the swiftest of glances as she crossed the road and strode towards them.

'Who is this?' Johanna demanded, looking askance at Maria.

'Maria Lucas.' Maria introduced herself, extending a hand across the back of the car seat.

Johanna ignored her. 'I hope it won't take us long,' she said. 'I can't leave the children.'

'Is Eric not there?' John asked her.

Johanna's look was piercing and accusatory, as though he had no right to ask.

'Oh yes,' she said. 'Eric's there.'

Then she turned her gaze to the passing world outside the window and chose not to speak again throughout their entire journey.

It was around ten thirty when DCS Charles arrived at the hospital.

'We've arrested Jaques,' he said without preamble. 'Seems this man Pearson knew what he was about with that damned journal of his.'

'Jaques was mentioned,' Mike whispered. Then frowned. 'But to arrest him just on the strength . . .'

Charles was shaking his head. 'Suspicion of murder,'

he said. He sat down heavily on the hard plastic chair at the side of Mike's bed. 'Led us to a house, back side of those derelict warehouses on Canal Street. We're waiting for confirmation from forensics, but first impressions are the Sanderson boy was killed there.'

Mike stared at him for a moment, absorbing this. 'Jaques was here, earlier this morning,' he said slowly.

'We picked him up as he left. He said he wanted to confess to you, but didn't have the nerve for it. Seemed to think that you would understand him . . .'

'Understand him! God almighty.'

Charles held out a placatory hand. 'Easy, Mike,' he said quietly. 'He's not exactly what you might call rational at the moment. The surgeon reckons we're going to have to get him sectioned.'

'Sectioned!' Mike was outraged. 'So he can plead diminished responsibility? Get a nice easy place in some low-security psychiatric unit!' He shook his head in bewilderment. 'God almighty,' he said again, as words appeared to fail him.

'You can appreciate,' Charles was saying slowly, 'this puts rather a different light on our Mr Pearson. Looks like he'll get his time in court, after all.'

Mike laughed bitterly, not sure what to think about that one either. 'He'll just love that,' he said. 'Just love it.' He paused and looked sharply at Charles. 'Jaques wasn't the only one in the journal, was he?'

Charles took a deep breath and shook his head. 'No, Mike,' he said. 'Unfortunately, he wasn't. This is only just beginning. We're rounding up everyone named in that bloody journal. Don't have a lot of choice now, do we?'

He rose to leave and Mike asked him, 'You've seen a copy of Eric Pearson's so-called Deposition?'

Charles nodded. 'That I have,' he said, then frowned. 'How did you get . . .? Never mind, I don't want to know. I've got Price over at Canal Street waiting for SOCO to arrive, then I'm shipping him off to Portland for a chat with Mr Eric Pearson. Should keep him busy.'

He glanced at Mike's plastered wrist and the strapping on his ribs showing beneath his open jacket.

'Seems to me you've got the soft option just now,' he said.

Chapter Thirty-Five

Sunday morning

'It's lovely here,' Maria commented as they walked up the lane towards Embury's cottage.

John nodded. 'Last of old England,' he said. 'Tall trees and shaded lanes and not a sound except for the birds.'

Maria laughed at him. 'Bet it's hell in winter.'

John shook his head in mock disapproval. 'No stamina, these exotic birds,' he said. 'First sign of a little cold and off they fly.'

Laughing again, Maria gave him a shove.

'Hit an old man, would you?'

'Might do! And anyway, John Tynan, I'll have you know I was born and bred in this merrie England, so I'm entitled to hate the winters.' She paused, looked at Johanna, pacing out strongly up ahead of them.

'I think we should get a move on,' she said. 'She looks about ready to storm the cottage walls.'

John nodded and they quickened their pace.

'What's bothering her, do you think?' Maria asked him.

'Blessed if I know, love. She doesn't exactly give a lot away, does she? Ah. There's Embury. But not a sign of Sam. I hope he's here. Embury said he would be by now.'

Johanna stood a few feet from Embury, studiously ignoring his polite greetings.

'I want to speak to Sam,' she demanded. 'I need to speak to him right now.'

'I'm sorry, my dear,' Embury told her, not seeming in the least put out by her manner, 'but Sam isn't here yet. I expected him back about an hour ago, but you never can tell what's going to hold him up.'

'Then I'll wait,' Johanna stated flatly. 'Out here.'

'Just as you like, Mrs Pearson,' Embury told her calmly. 'I'll have some tea sent out to you, shall I? And John, my friend, good to see you. Come in, come in. And, let me guess. This is Maria.' He reached out to clasp Maria's hand, pumping it enthusiastically. 'How is Mike? I read about the accident. Terrible business, of course, terrible.'

Maria exchanged a grin with John as Embury shepherded them into the house.

Johanna remained outside, stiff and immovable as any sentry. Eyes fixed on the distant ribbon of main road, watching and waiting for Sam to arrive.

The arrests were timed to be simultaneous. The solicitor, roused from his late Sunday lie-in. The young father of two on the tenth floor of the tower block. The middle-aged accounts clerk in his quiet suburban cul-de-sac. There seemed on the face of it to be no link. A chance meeting. Reply to the same ad in a contact magazine. Same place of work or mutual friends.

All had their rights read and their houses searched. Their neighbours watched and their families protested their innocence, left behind, bewildered and devastated.

Sitting in his car, Charles listened as he was informed of the arrests. He sighed, hoping the searches would turn up the evidence they needed to bring charges.

Experience told him that nothing would be easy to prove.

He could just see the media reports. A police superintendent. A well-known CPS solicitor and evidence that this had been going on for years. He could just see the headlines. No one was going to come out of this smelling sweet.

By eleven o'clock on Portland Close the need to talk had brought people out on to the street. Eric Pearson watched them – small knots of people gathering on doorsteps; standing around at the corner of the Close; casting knowing, vicious glances in his direction.

Let them do what they liked, he thought. Think what they liked. He'd be ready for them, whatever they might choose to do.

'We've got the hosepipe ready, Dad.'

Eric turned to nod and smile at his son. 'Good,' he said. 'Very good.'

The boy stood uncertainly in the doorway, watching as Eric filled another bottle one third full of petrol, topped it with a layer of oil and stuffed the neck carefully with tightly wadded rag.

'When's Mum coming home?'

'Hmm? Oh, I don't know, son. Soon, I expect. Soon.'

The boy turned away. Eric could feel his unease, his instinct that today was different from those other days. He called after him.

'Don't you worry, now, my boy. It will all be fine. You'll see.'

Eric turned his attention back towards the window. 'After today,' he told himself quietly. 'After today, it will all be over.'

At length Eric decided it was time to call the police. From his home-made weaponry in the top room of the house he called the local station.

There was a street full of them now. All waiting, all watching. All hating him and hated in their turn.

He picked up the receiver and dialled in on the nines. 'I'd like to report a disturbance,' he said. 'On Portland Close. My name? Oh yes, of course I'll give my name.'

Johanna had grown more and more restless. It was almost an hour after they had arrived that she saw a battered old army jeep turn off the main road and rock and clatter its way up towards the house.

Sam got out and eyed her warily.

'Aunt Johanna,' he said. 'Why don't you come inside?'

Johanna had no time for niceties. She dove straight into the questions she needed answering.

'Those negatives, Sam. Did you put them inside the owl? Is it you responsible for planting such filth?'

Sam's bewilderment was obvious even to Johanna.

'Owl?' he said. 'What owl, Johanna? I just brought you the stuff my dad wanted you to have.'

Johanna glared at him. 'Don't play the innocent with me, Sam Pearson. You must have packed the stuff and it was you brought it over.'

Sam was shaking his head. 'I don't know what you're on about, Aunt Jo. My dad packed it up a week or so before he passed on. Knew he didn't have much longer, he did. Wanted to settle things, like. He couldn't make it from his bed by then but he had us bring a load of boxes to him and Elder Thomas packed what he told him in each one. Then the whole lot was put in store till Mr Tynan went with me to pick the stuff up and bring it over.'

He advanced on her, his hands wide. Genuine bewilderment spread across his face.

Johanna stared at him, belief in Sam's innocence fighting with her reluctance even now to see Eric in anything but a good light.

She turned abruptly on her heel and strode towards the door, thrusting it open.

'I want to go now,' she said. 'I've important things to do, so if you could please hurry.'

Then she began to walk back towards the car, body tense and straight, fists clenched tightly, ready to take on anyone or anything that stood in her way.

*

The patrol car pulled to a stop in the middle of Portland Close and the two officers got out and looked around. One lifted his radio close to his mouth and spoke into it.

'Four eight to control, receiving.'

'Go ahead, four eight.'

'We've arrived on Portland. There's quite a crowd gathered, but they're just standing around talking at the moment.'

The controller sighed. 'Well, it came in on the nines, four eight, and we've got a priority one running on Portland. Just see if you can have a word, will you, Alec? Find out what's going on down there?'

The constable grinned into his radio. 'All nuts down here if you ask me, pet. Four eight out.'

It didn't take very much asking to find the cause of the problem. The residents of Portland were only too happy to oblige.

'Just take a look at this thing,' Dora cried, thrusting Eric's letter towards them. 'And you lot are going to let him get away with it.'

'There's not a great deal we can do, love,' the constable told her. 'We could maybe do him for illegal fly posting, or you could get together and get a civil case going against him for defamation. But then you've got to prove it.' He shrugged sympathetically. 'Best advice I can give you all is let it lie. A few days an' it'll all have blown over.'

'A few days . . .' Dora stormed. 'You think we're going to stand by and let this . . . this . . .'

Dora was clearly lost for words. The PC stepped in

swiftly. 'We'll have a word, love. See if we can sort it out, eh?'

He smiled encouragingly at the now furious Dora. Both officers crossed the street to Eric Pearson's house.

'They don't give a damn how we feel!' Dora exploded. Her first anger had abated a little, given way to frustration. She was close to tears.

'There, there, Dora love,' Lizzie told her, putting an arm around the older woman's shoulders.

'Can't rely on them lot,' someone else said. ' "Take out a civil action," ' he mimicked. ' "Do him for fly posting." '

'You come back inside and have a cuppa with me,' Lizzie said, shaking Dora gently. 'That's it, you come with me.'

Dora nodded. 'All right, Lizzie dear, I will, thank you. But he's not going to get away with it. Not this time.'

'Damn right he's not,' someone muttered behind the two women as they walked away. There was a general murmur of agreement.

No one seemed quite sure what action should be taken, but one thing they were all decided on. This time, Eric Pearson was going to have to go.

Across the Close the two policemen were attempting to talk to Eric. He wouldn't let them in, but leaned out of the living room window and shouted down.

'Well? And what are you going to do about that lot?'

The two officers exchanged an exasperated glance.

'Well, sir, there's not a lot we can do. There's nothing

to say that residents can't gather in their own street, now, is there?'

Eric gritted his teeth. 'There'll be trouble, officer. I'm warning you now. There'll be trouble.'

He slammed the window closed.

Sighing irritably, Alec lifted the radio close to his mouth once more. 'Four eight to control, receiving.'

'Go ahead, four eight.'

'No joy here, control. There's a lot of noise from Pearson but that's about it. No offences disclosed and not a hell of a lot of sense out of anyone either.' He paused and glanced about him for the last time. 'Resume now, can we, pet?'

'Four eight from control. Yes, go ahead. I've something else for you over on Bringsmere Drive. A possible ten twenty-three. Neighbours report the occupants are away.'

'Four eight to control. On way.'

That was more like it. Possible robbery in progress. Anything was better than dealing with the public relations mess on Portland.

Eric Pearson watched as they headed towards their car.

'They'll be back,' he said to himself. 'Oh yes, they'll soon be back.'

On the way back from Embury's Johanna had begun to talk. For the first ten minutes or so she had maintained the same stolid silence that had marked the outward journey. Then she had begun to speak.

'I believed him,' she said softly. 'Believed him. Always. Saw only what I wanted to see.

'I loved him, you know. I suppose I must still love him or it wouldn't matter to me as much as it does. It wouldn't hurt to know how much he's lied to me. How long he's lied to me and how long I've listened. Believing what I wanted to believe.'

'Lied about what, Johanna?' Maria asked gently, half afraid to speak in case it broke the spell that Johanna had woven around herself. Equally afraid of the silence that might come without her prompting.

Johanna seemed barely to have heard her. She continued as though there had been no interruption.

'We were happy there, you know. Sheltered from the outside and from all the corruption. Then Eric went away to study. Be a teacher. Teach our own without worries about the law.

'I told them all along that no one cared really. That there were plenty of people teaching their own children without a qualification to their name. But, no. They would have it right. The Elders, with all their worry about the law. About doing the right thing. And Eric went. Out into the world with all its doubts and its corruption, and he enjoyed it. Liked being out there. Thought by teaching away from our house he could make a difference. And I believed in him. Believed everything he told me.'

'You loved him,' Maria said gently, only half understanding where Johanna was heading. Wanting to help. 'You loved him, Johanna. We try our hardest to believe in those we love.'

'Then we're fools,' Johanna stated, angrily. Her voice flat and harsh with pain.

They had turned down the main road towards Portland Close.

'Drop me here,' Johanna demanded. 'I don't want you coming down.'

Obediently, John stopped the car opposite the shops. Johanna got out hurriedly.

'Are you sure you'll be all right?' John asked her.

Johanna nodded impatiently. 'Of course, of course. Best you don't come, though. I've things to do now and you'd only be in the way.'

They watched her as she strode off, heading towards a little gravel path that led out of sight down the hill.

'You think we should go after her?' Maria asked. 'John, I really don't think . . .'

'Neither do I,' he said. 'We'll go down by the road. It's a bit of a maze around here.' He grimaced, remembering the problems he'd had when he'd come out here with Sam. 'Just hope I can remember the way.'

Eric had been patient. He'd waited and watched as the crowd in the street ebbed and flowed, sometimes dispersing altogether, only to return a little later, grown in strength.

He could feel its anger. The slow change in mood as

people discovered that the notice Dora had found taped to the lamp post was not the only one.

It must seem to them, Eric thought, that the whole world knew by now how shabbily the residents of Portland Close had treated Eric Pearson and his family.

Guilt would make them act. Guilt and anger would force them to turn on him again and he'd be ready this time. More than ready.

He'd phoned the *Chronicle* after he'd rung the police, not expecting anyone to be there, but he'd left a message anyway on Andrews' machine.

Done the same on his home number.

He had little faith in Andrews, but he was local and had, Eric knew, too many journalistic instincts to ignore a good story.

A loud pounding on the door made Eric look down. A man he recognized vaguely as living at the other end of the Close was hammering on his door, a piece of paper clasped in his hand.

'What do you want?' Eric shouted down.

'You. Down here. Now.'

Eric glanced behind him and gave the signal to one of his boys to get the hose turned on. Moments later the man at the door was dancing back, enraged as water from the upstairs window poured down upon his head.

Eric roared with laughter at the man, who was swearing and cursing and dodging back to escape the spray.

He could almost see the mood in the street begin to change.

The man, shaking water from his hair, picked up a

stone from Ellie Masouk's little garden and hurled it at the window.

'Well done, boys!' Eric shouted gleefully. 'There'll be more along in a minute. Just you wait.'

He smiled in great satisfaction at the sound of his children's laughter coming from the bathroom overhead.

Eric turned from the window and reached for the telephone. Once again he called in on the nines, giving his name to the controller.

'I should hurry this time,' he told her, 'before you have a riot on your hands.'

As he put the telephone back on its rest he heard with satisfaction something hard and heavy thumping, picking up a steady rhythm, against his front door.

Smiling now, Eric called up once again to his children to get to work with the hose. Then he dragged the crate of home-made firebombs out from behind the sofa, took one out, lit the cloth fuse and hurled the bottle out of the open window.

It exploded on impact, right in front of the main body of the crowd. A sheet of flame spread out across the ground, quickly followed by screams of fear and rage.

Eric Pearson was grinning broadly as he selected a second bottle from his little store, made sure the rag fuse was wedged in tight and lit the cotton wick.

This time his aim was more precise, though it meant throwing sideways to get at those still pounding at his door; three men, swinging what looked like a broken fence post between them. Battering against the lock.

The door gave way just as the bottle hit the ground.

Eric heard someone scream. Saw a man jumping back, the leg of his trousers in flames.

'Put him out, boys!' Eric yelled, noting with satisfaction the accuracy with which the children aimed the hose at the burning man, and those who tried to beat out the flames with their bare hands, rolling him on the floor in an effort to stop the burning.

Eric was enjoying himself now. Gone beyond thought. He had forgotten, almost, what this was all about. His mind pushed too far, he knew only that he had to win.

Carefully taking another petrol bomb, he lit the fuse. He launched it from the window, just as the first of the police cars, sirens blaring, careered into the Close.

By the time Johanna entered the Close the crowd was silent and the police had restored some semblance of order. Johanna gave them barely a glance.

Dimly, she recognized John Tynan's car. And a second, pulling up just behind it. That journalist, of course, here after a story.

Well, he would have one now. Johanna would make sure of that.

There was a policeman standing by the front door.

'I live here,' Johanna told him, her voice icily calm. 'And I want to go to my children.'

He let her through. The children were crowded in the kitchen doorway, calling to her. Johanna gathered them to her, crooning softly to them, telling them that it would be all right, to just sit down and keep calm.

She got them around the kitchen table. Told the eldest to make tea. Fished a couple of packs of biscuits out of the tin. Allowed them chocolate ones as a special treat. Easing them back into some state of normality.

All the time, above them, she could hear Eric shouting.

Glancing out through the window she could see the crowd standing silently in the street. That woman John had with him, kneeling in the mud beside the hurt man as though she knew what she was doing.

Johanna could see, through the kitchen door, that the policeman at the front was much more interested in looking at the beautiful black woman than he was in watching her.

Taking a last look to make sure the children were settled, and slipping something into the pocket of her coat, Johanna seized the moment.

She was up the stairs in seconds. The policeman in the doorway had not even noticed her as she'd passed by.

Inside the room Eric was standing by the window. His hands were cuffed together and two police officers stood close beside him. One she recognized as the sergeant who'd come here before.

They were clearly getting ready to leave. One officer bent, as Johanna watched, to pick up the milk crate packed with half-filled bottles. Eric's baseball bat was tucked beneath the officer's arm and that long knife Eric had been so insistent on keeping handy was balanced across the top of the crate.

Drawers and cupboards hung wide open. Evidently they must have delayed leaving until Eric told them of any other weapons he had hidden. Well, Johanna thought, now is the only time I'm going to get.

'Eric,' she said, stepping forward, her face expressing deepest concern.

Eric was smiling at her. 'They'll take notice now, Johanna. I'll get my day in court now.'

'You'll get a bloody sight more than that,' Price told him in an undertone. 'If you'll just stand aside, Mrs Pearson.'

Obediently, Johanna stepped away from the head of the stairs. The officer carrying the crate went first, then Price, guiding Eric by the arm.

Johanna chose her moment well. The hand holding the mille fleur paperweight crashed down on Eric Pearson's head. The first blow brought him to his knees. The second Price almost intercepted. Almost but not quite. Desperation gave Johanna speed and strength she had not thought she could possess. Eric Pearson lay, face down, sprawling across the top steps, a gaping hole in the back of his skull.

'Why, for God's sake?' Price had Joanna's arm pinned behind her back and was cuffing her hands together.

'He lied to me,' Johanna said simply. 'About those

photographs, about those little boys.' She twisted her head around to look at Price.

'I couldn't let him get away with it, you see.'

Price stared at her. 'Then why not let the courts decide?'

Johanna Pearson shook her head. 'Oh no,' she said, her voice gentle with regret. 'I couldn't do that. They'd have locked him away, you see, and Eric would not have been able to cope with that.' She looked down at the body of her dead husband. The stairs were crowded now. Other officers and paramedics were arriving on the scene. 'It's better this way,' she told Price. 'Better for everyone.'

Outside, John and Maria stood with Andrews. The journalist had arrived, not at Eric's summons but at Dora's, drawn by the evident distress of the woman and her equally evident sense of hopelessness that the problem could be solved.

This wasn't the story he had come to write.

Johanna Pearson saw them as Price brought her from the house.

The children stared out from the window, bewildered faces pressed against the plastic.

'You there,' Johanna called to John. Price paused and John came over to them.

'You'll call Sam,' she said. 'Get him to tell Elder Thomas. The children must go back to the House.' She nodded as though to confirm what she had just said. 'You'll see to it.'

Price raised an eyebrow at John, then led Johanna away to the waiting car.

'You think social services will let them?' Maria asked.

'I don't know, my dear. You know how the system works better than I do. But I can't think of anyone else willingly wanting six very disturbed children. Can you?'

Maria sighed, her gaze held by six pairs of eyes, watching intently as their world fell apart around them.

Chapter Thirty-Six

Sunday evening

'Eric's dead,' Maria said quietly, seating herself on the edge of Mike's bed. It was almost nine o'clock. Mike had spent a day of intense frustration imagining what might be happening and willing Maria, John, Price or anyone to come and put him out of his misery.

He'd tried to reach Charles by phone, only to be told that he was conducting an interview. Now, as though such largesse was a reward, he had Maria *and* Price here at his bedside.

'Eric's dead?' he echoed, his tone disbelieving. 'How?'

'Johanna,' Maria told him.

'Whacked the fucker with a bloody paperweight,' Price added, his expression disgusted. 'And yours truly not two feet away.'

Mike listened as they filled him in on the day's events. 'There've been more arrests,' Maria told him.

'Yeah, and the bloody press is having a field day.' Price grimaced. 'You can just see the headlines, can't you? "Man Murdered by Wife While Being Handcuffed." ' He snorted angrily. 'I'm officially on holiday as of now.'

'They've suspended you?' Mike asked, deeply concerned. Price was a good man.

'Not so you'd notice,' he said. 'Compassionate

bloody leave till they figure out whether or not to bust me to playground duty.'

He flopped angrily in the plastic chair and reached over to steal more of Mike's fruit. Munched in a clouded silence that spoke volumes about his feelings for Eric Pearson and his crazy wife.

Maria smiled. 'I had a word with the doctor,' she said. 'They say I can take you home tomorrow.'

'Home?' The thought of his drab flat was not encouraging.

'To John's. I'm on holiday too as of tomorrow.'

Mike smiled properly for the first time in what felt like days.

'Marry me?' he asked, ignoring Price.

Maria squeezed his hand. 'Maybe,' she said. 'I'll give it some thought.'

Chapter Thirty-Seven

For three days a police cordon was maintained at the end of Portland Close. The Pearson house sealed off and a duty officer was left guarding the front door.

It was a boring job. Those on duty were glad of the distraction when the locals talked to them and brought them too many cups of tea.

It was a quiet place, Portland Close. That was the general consensus, anyway. Ordinary. Kids playing in the streets, people chatting on the corner, tending to their bits of garden.

At the end of the third day, the cordon was lifted. The policeman went away and the local council boarded up the broken door.

Later the same night, when the late summer dusk had turned to full dark, the door was prised open.

There were three or four of them involved – stories varied depending on who told them, but whatever their number, they carried sledge hammers and steel bars and smashed everything left behind in the big house at Portland Close.

Even the stairs, where Eric Pearson's blood had

soaked the carpet and seeped through into the wood, was smashed into splinters.

No one in the Close had heard a thing.

A few days later, Ellie and Rezah Masouk came home. Rezah let go of Farouzi's hand just long enough to lift the new baby in its carry chair from the car, then clasped her hand tightly once again.

Fara chattered like a bird, tugging on her father's fingers to make certain he was listening. Then running to Dora, as their front door opened and comfortable, familiar Dora reached out her arms towards the little girl.

Ellie stood beside the car, staring at the big house, at the steel grilles covering the windows and door, preserving what little was left of the inside.

'They're gone, then?' she asked quietly, as Dora came over to her.

The woman nodded. 'Oh yes, my dear, they're gone,' she said, satisfaction giving richness to her voice.

She reached out and hugged the younger woman to her.

'And it's so good to have you back,' she said.